THE HARDY BOYS®

UNDERCOVER BROTHERS™

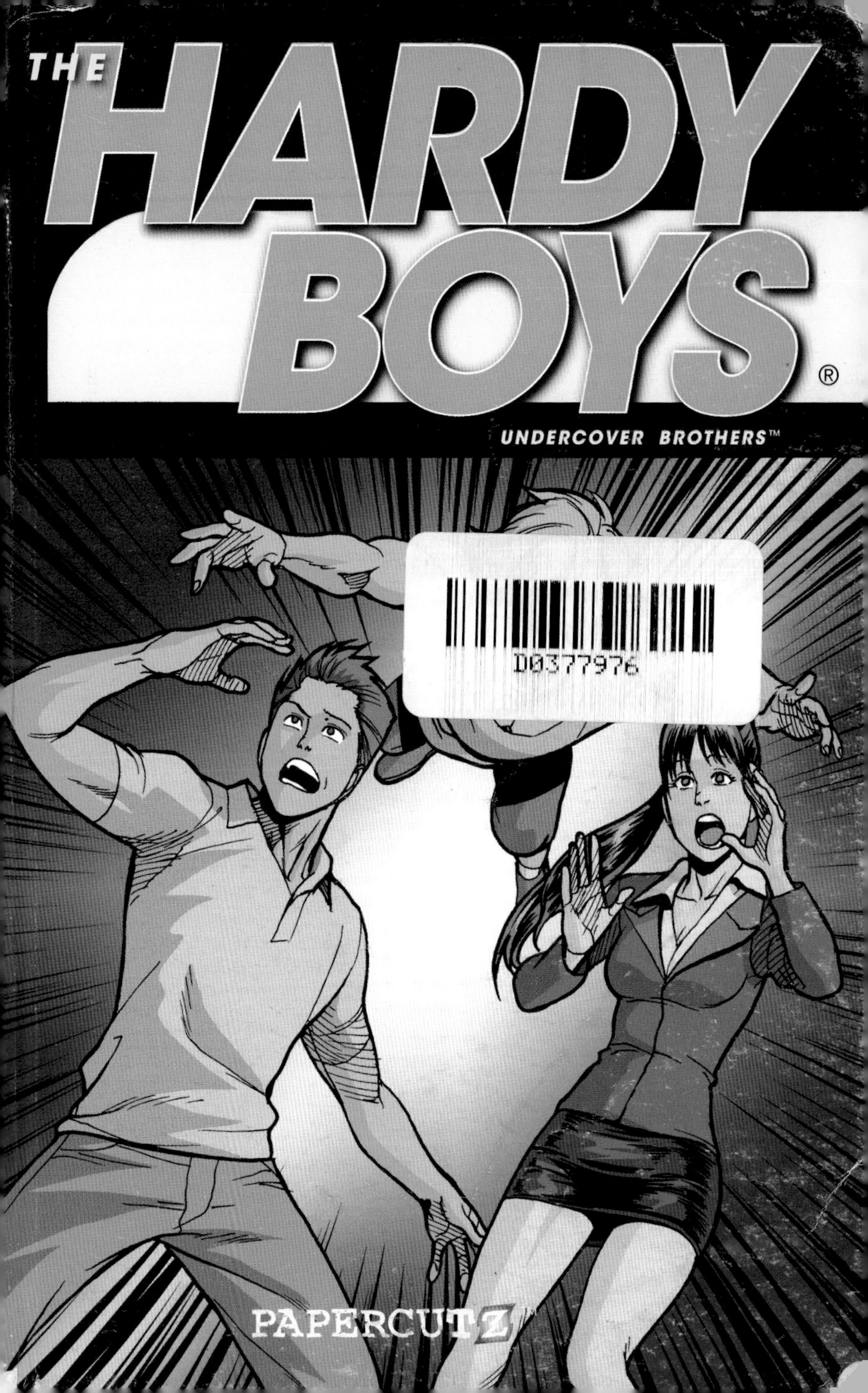

PAPERCUTZ™

THE HARDY BOYS GRAPHIC NOVELS FROM PAPERCUTZ

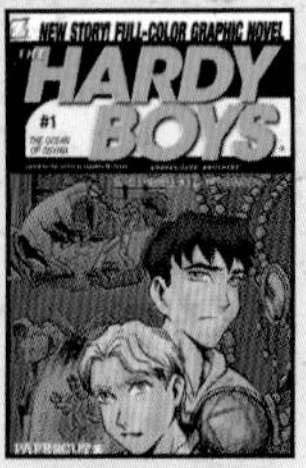
NEW STORY! FULL-COLOR GRAPHIC NOVEL
HARDY BOYS
#1
PAPERCUTZ
#1 "The Ocean of Osyria"

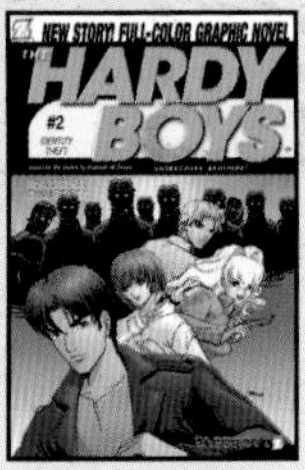
NEW STORY! FULL-COLOR GRAPHIC NOVEL
HARDY BOYS
#2
#2 "Identity Theft"

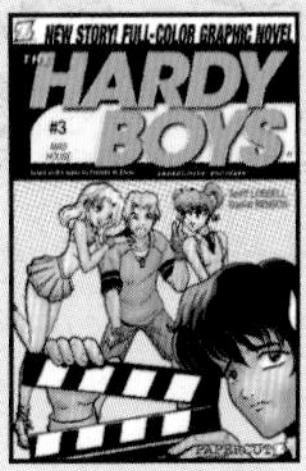
NEW STORY! FULL-COLOR GRAPHIC NOVEL
HARDY BOYS
#3
PAPERCUTZ
#3 "Mad House"

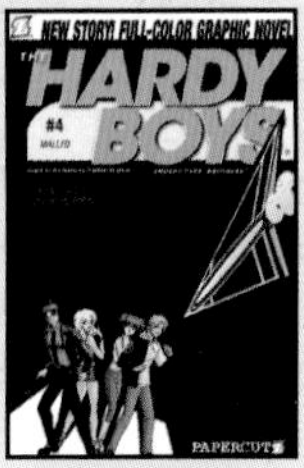
NEW STORY! FULL-COLOR GRAPHIC NOVEL
HARDY BOYS
#4
PAPERCUTZ
#4 "Malled"

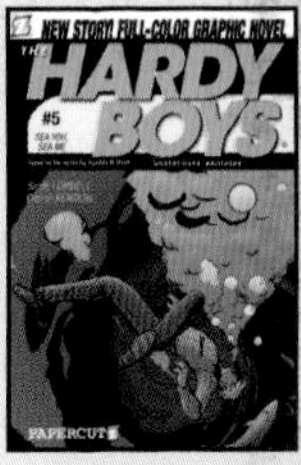
NEW STORY! FULL-COLOR GRAPHIC NOVEL
HARDY BOYS
#5
PAPERCUTZ
#5 "Sea You, Sea Me!"

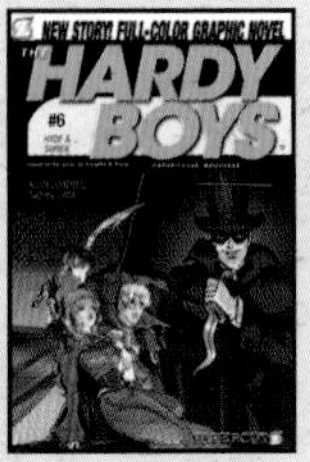
NEW STORY! FULL-COLOR GRAPHIC NOVEL
HARDY BOYS
#6
PAPERCUTZ
#6 "Hyde & Shriek"

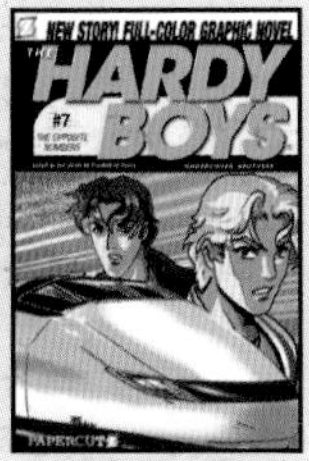
NEW STORY! FULL-COLOR GRAPHIC NOVEL
HARDY BOYS
#7
PAPERCUTZ
#7 "The Opposite Numbers"

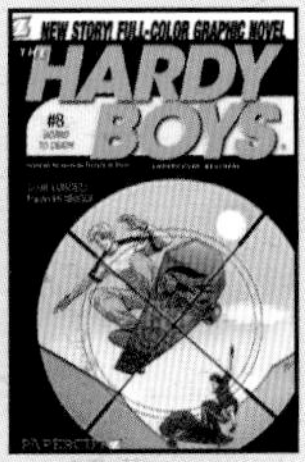
NEW STORY! FULL-COLOR GRAPHIC NOVEL
HARDY BOYS
#8
PAPERCUTZ
#8 "Board To Death"

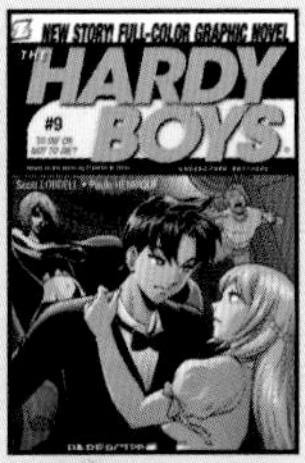
NEW STORY! FULL-COLOR GRAPHIC NOVEL
HARDY BOYS
#9
#9 "To Die Or Not To Die?"

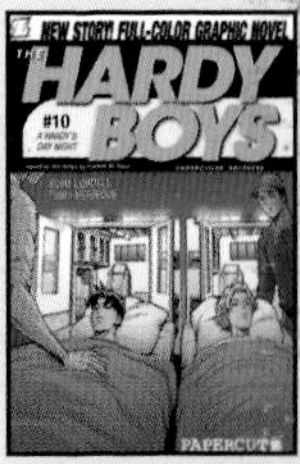
NEW STORY! FULL-COLOR GRAPHIC NOVEL
HARDY BOYS
#10
PAPERCUTZ
#10 "A Hardy Day's Night"

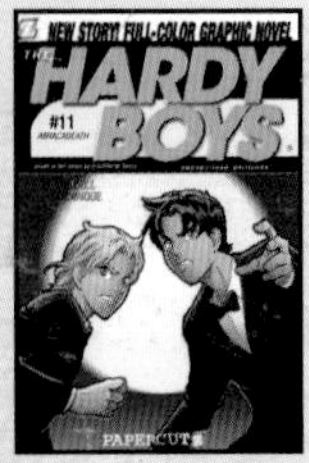
NEW STORY! FULL-COLOR GRAPHIC NOVEL
HARDY BOYS
#11
PAPERCUTZ
#11 "Abracadeath"

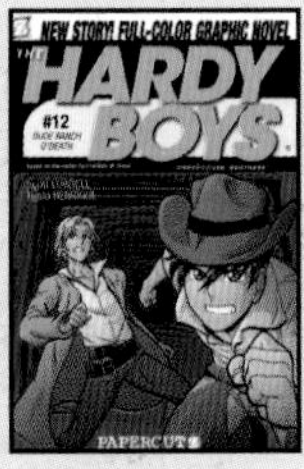
NEW STORY! FULL-COLOR GRAPHIC NOVEL
HARDY BOYS
#12
PAPERCUTZ
#12 "Dude Ranch O' Death!"

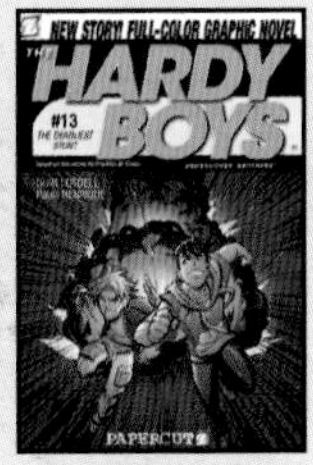
NEW STORY! FULL-COLOR GRAPHIC NOVEL
HARDY BOYS
#13
PAPERCUTZ
#13 "The Deadliest Stunt"

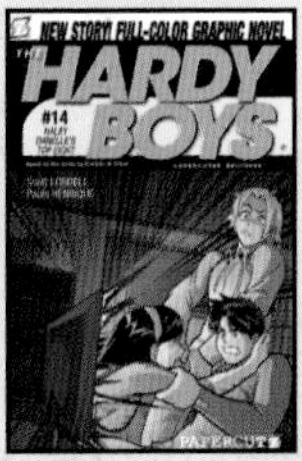
NEW STORY! FULL-COLOR GRAPHIC NOVEL
HARDY BOYS
#14
PAPERCUTZ
#14 "Haley Danelle's Top Eight!"

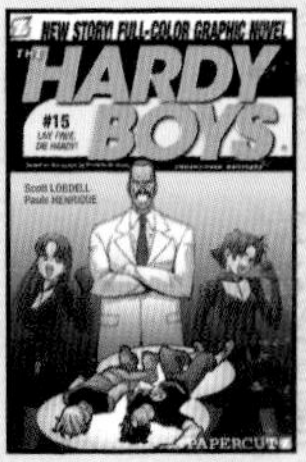
NEW STORY! FULL-COLOR GRAPHIC NOVEL
HARDY BOYS
#15
PAPERCUTZ
#15 "Live Free, Die Hardy!"

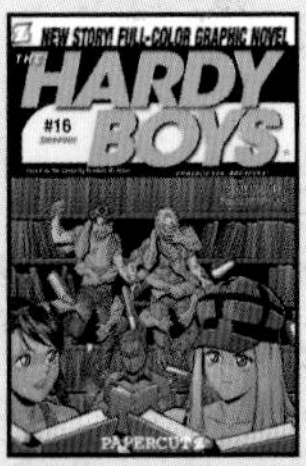
NEW STORY! FULL-COLOR GRAPHIC NOVEL
HARDY BOYS
#16
PAPERCUTZ
#16 "Shhhhhh!"

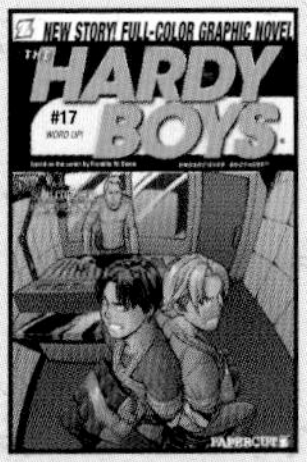
NEW STORY! FULL-COLOR GRAPHIC NOVEL
HARDY BOYS
#17
PAPERCUTZ
#17 "Word Up!"

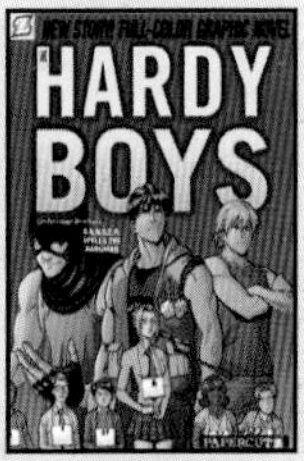
HARDY BOYS
PAPERCUTZ
Coming Soon! #18 "D.A.N.G.E.R Spells the Hangman"

$7.95 each in paperback, $12.95 each in hardcover.

Please add $4.00 for postage and handling for the first book, add $1.00 for each additional book. Please make check payable to NBM Publishing. Send to: **Papercutz, 40 Exchange Place, Suite 1308, New York, NY 10005 • 1-800-886-1223 • www.papercutz.com**

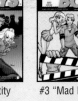

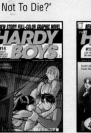

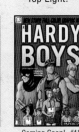

Word Up!
SCOTT LOBDELL — Writer
PAULO HENRIQUE MARCONDES — Artist
MARK LERER — Letterer
LAURIE E. SMITH — Colorist
MIKHAELA REID & MASHEKA WOOD— Production
MICHAEL PETRANEK — Editorial Assistant
JIM SALICRUP
Editor-in-Chief

ISBN 13: 978-1-59707-147-5 paperback edition
ISBN 10: 1-59707-147-1 paperback edition
ISBN 13: 978-1-59707-148-2 hardcover edition
ISBN 10: 1-59707-148-X hardcover edition

Printed in China March 2009
by New Era Printing Limited
Room 1101-1103, Trende Centre
29-31 Cheung Lee St
Chai Wan, Hong Kong

Distributed by Macmillan.

10 9 8 7 6 5 4 3 2 1

THE HARDY BOYS

#17

UNDERCOVER BROTHERS™

Word Up!

SCOTT LOBDELL • Writer

PAULO HENRIQUE MARCONDES • Artist

Based on the series by
FRANKLIN W. DIXON

PAPERCUTZ™

New York

CHAPTER ONE:
"OH MY STARS AND GARTERS!"

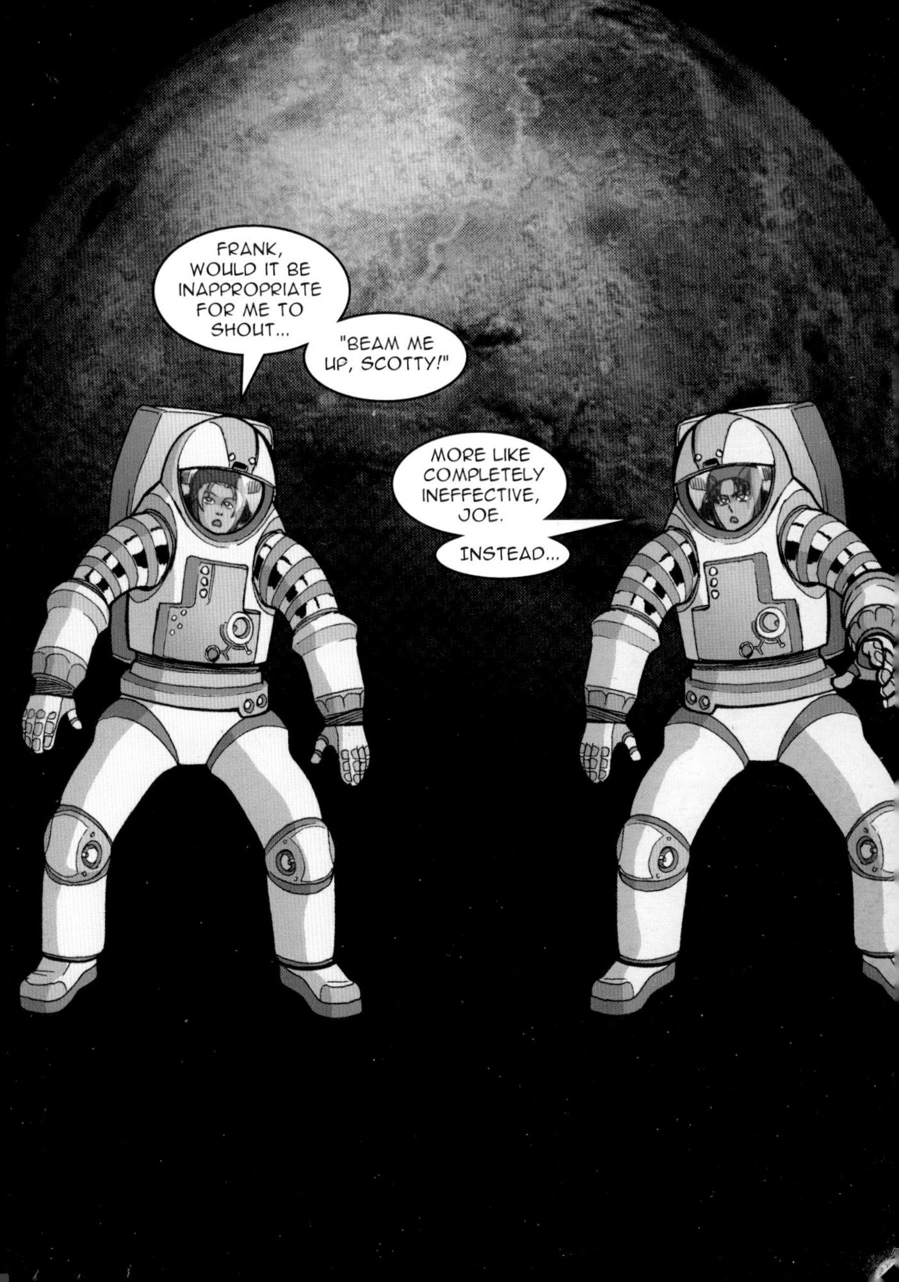
FRANK, WOULD IT BE INAPPROPRIATE FOR ME TO SHOUT...
"BEAM ME UP, SCOTTY!"
MORE LIKE COMPLETELY INEFFECTIVE, JOE.
INSTEAD...

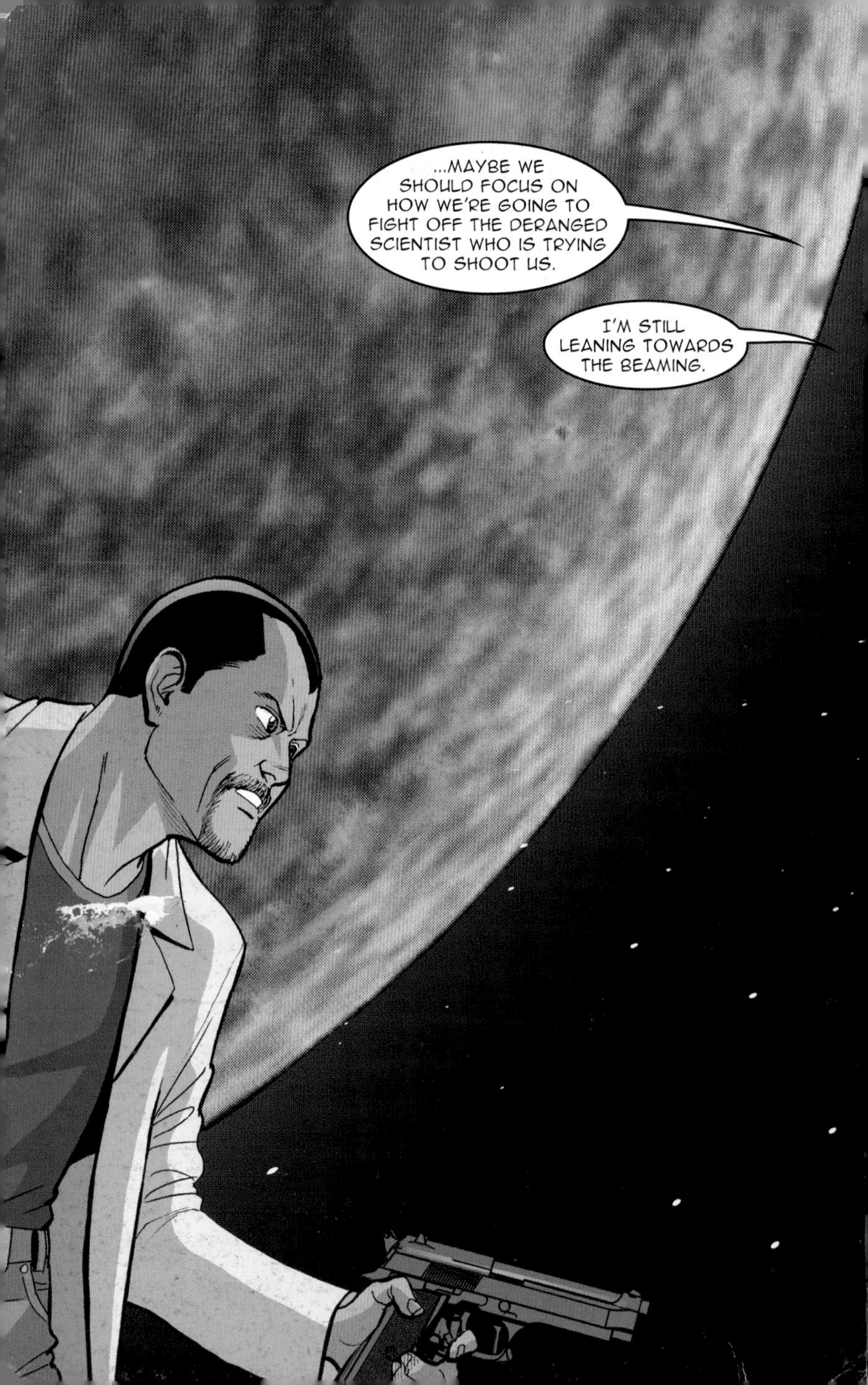
...MAYBE WE SHOULD FOCUS ON HOW WE'RE GOING TO FIGHT OFF THE DERANGED SCIENTIST WHO IS TRYING TO SHOOT US.
I'M STILL LEANING TOWARDS THE BEAMING.

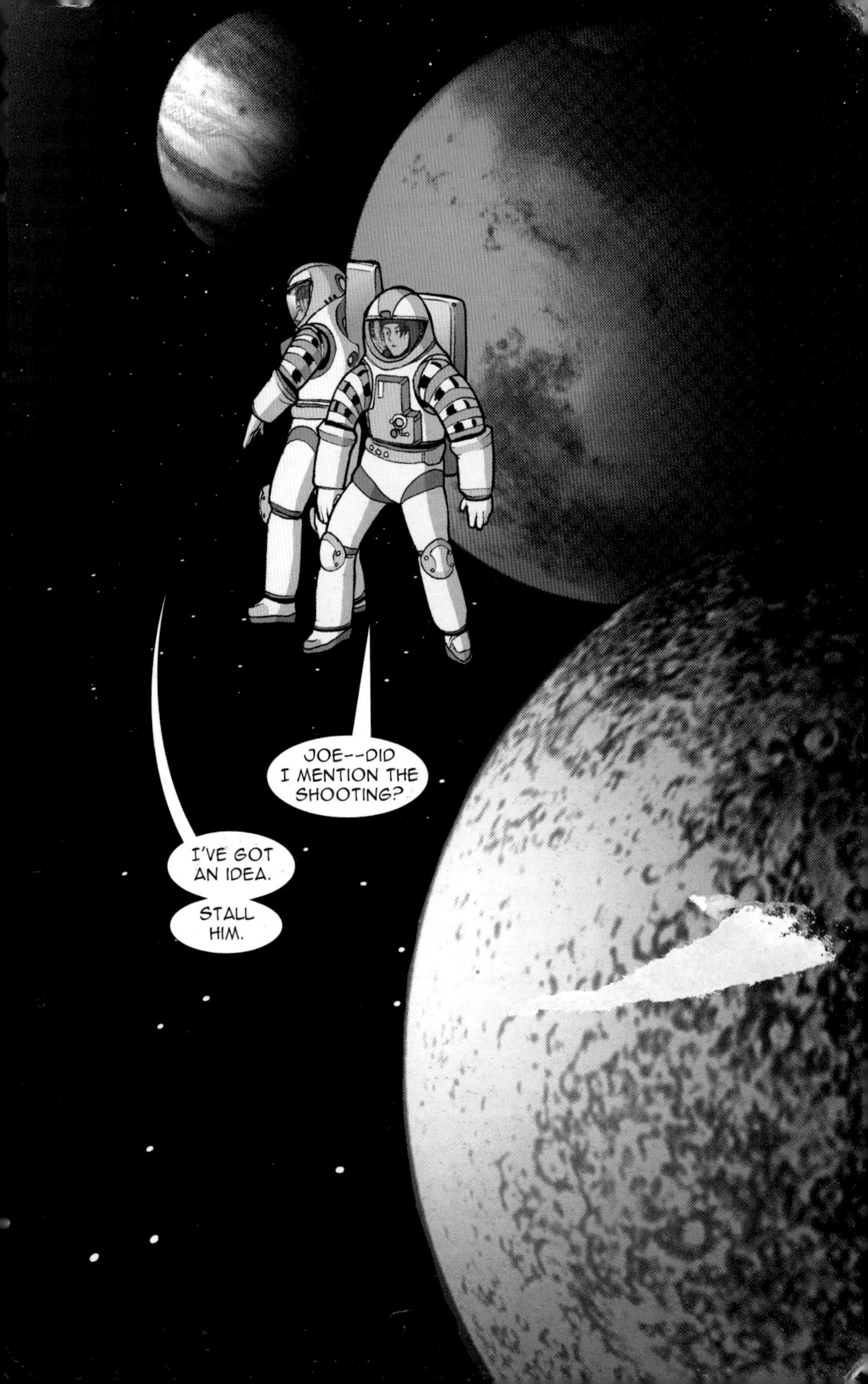
JOE--DID I MENTION THE SHOOTING?
I'VE GOT AN IDEA.
STALL HIM.

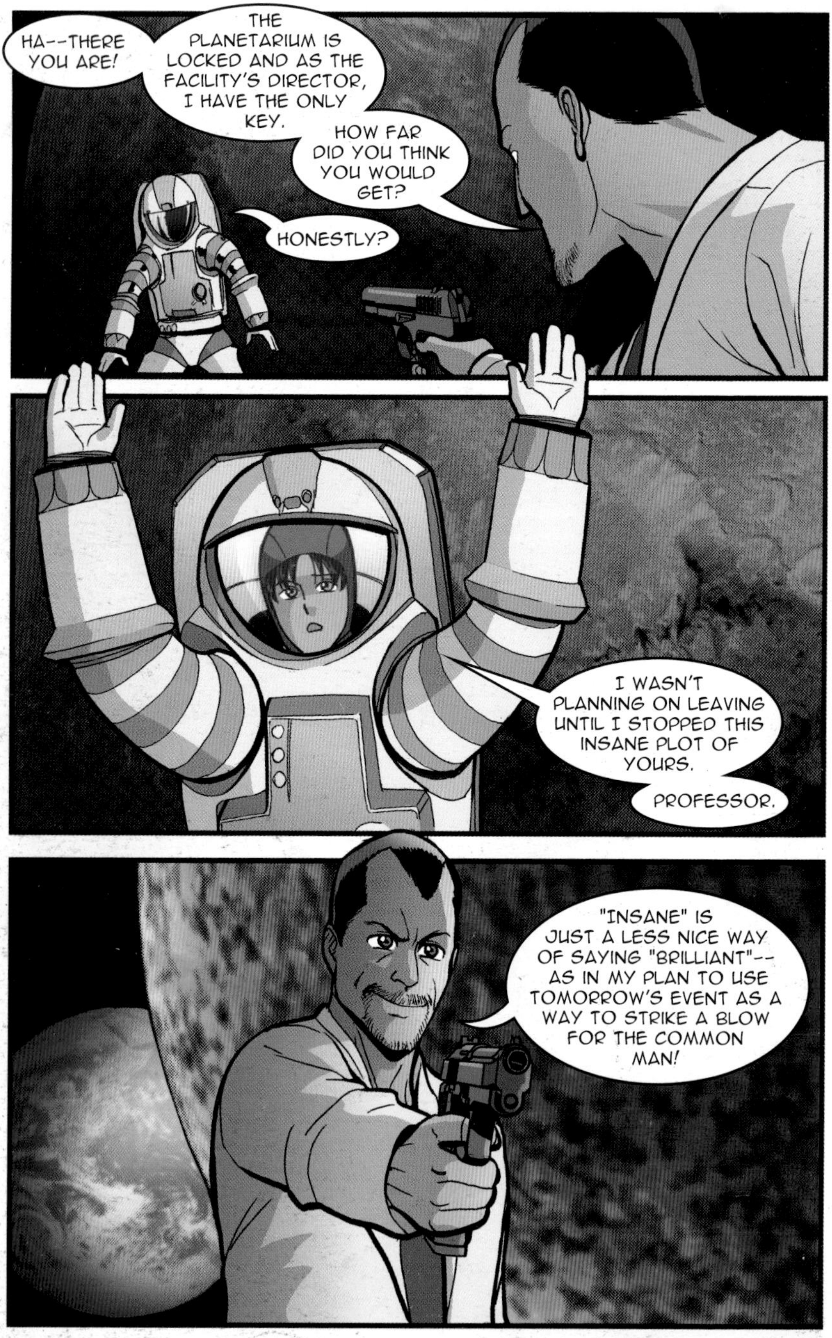
HA--THERE YOU ARE!
THE PLANETARIUM IS LOCKED AND AS THE FACILITY'S DIRECTOR, I HAVE THE ONLY KEY.
HOW FAR DID YOU THINK YOU WOULD GET?
HONESTLY?
I WASN'T PLANNING ON LEAVING UNTIL I STOPPED THIS INSANE PLOT OF YOURS.
PROFESSOR.
"INSANE" IS JUST A LESS NICE WAY OF SAYING "BRILLIANT"--AS IN MY PLAN TO USE TOMORROW'S EVENT AS A WAY TO STRIKE A BLOW FOR THE COMMON MAN!

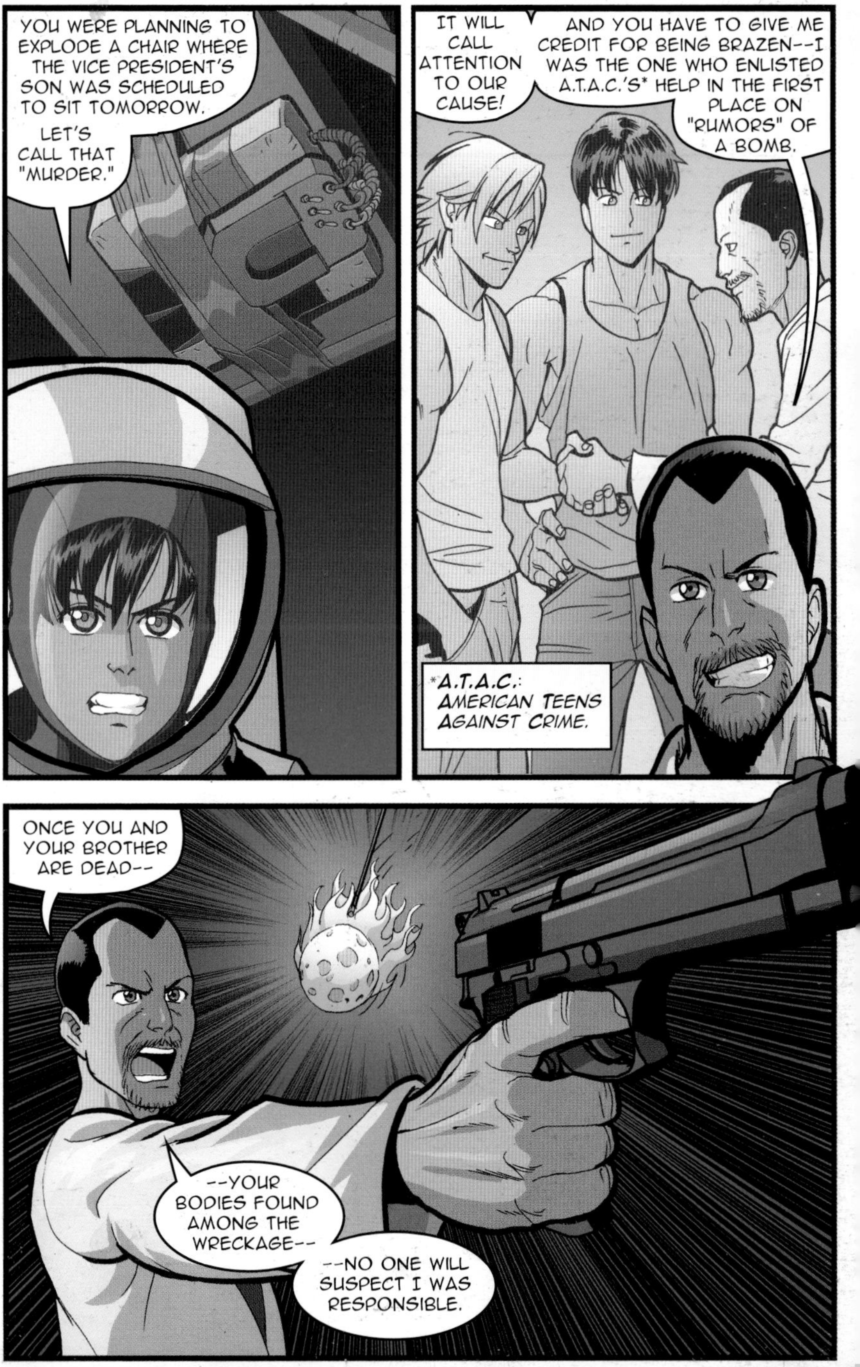
YOU WERE PLANNING TO EXPLODE A CHAIR WHERE THE VICE PRESIDENT'S SON WAS SCHEDULED TO SIT TOMORROW.
LET'S CALL THAT "MURDER."
IT WILL CALL ATTENTION TO OUR CAUSE!
AND YOU HAVE TO GIVE ME CREDIT FOR BEING BRAZEN--I WAS THE ONE WHO ENLISTED A.T.A.C.'S* HELP IN THE FIRST PLACE ON "RUMORS" OF A BOMB.
*A.T.A.C.: AMERICAN TEENS AGAINST CRIME.
ONCE YOU AND YOUR BROTHER ARE DEAD--
--YOUR BODIES FOUND AMONG THE WRECKAGE--
--NO ONE WILL SUSPECT I WAS RESPONSIBLE.

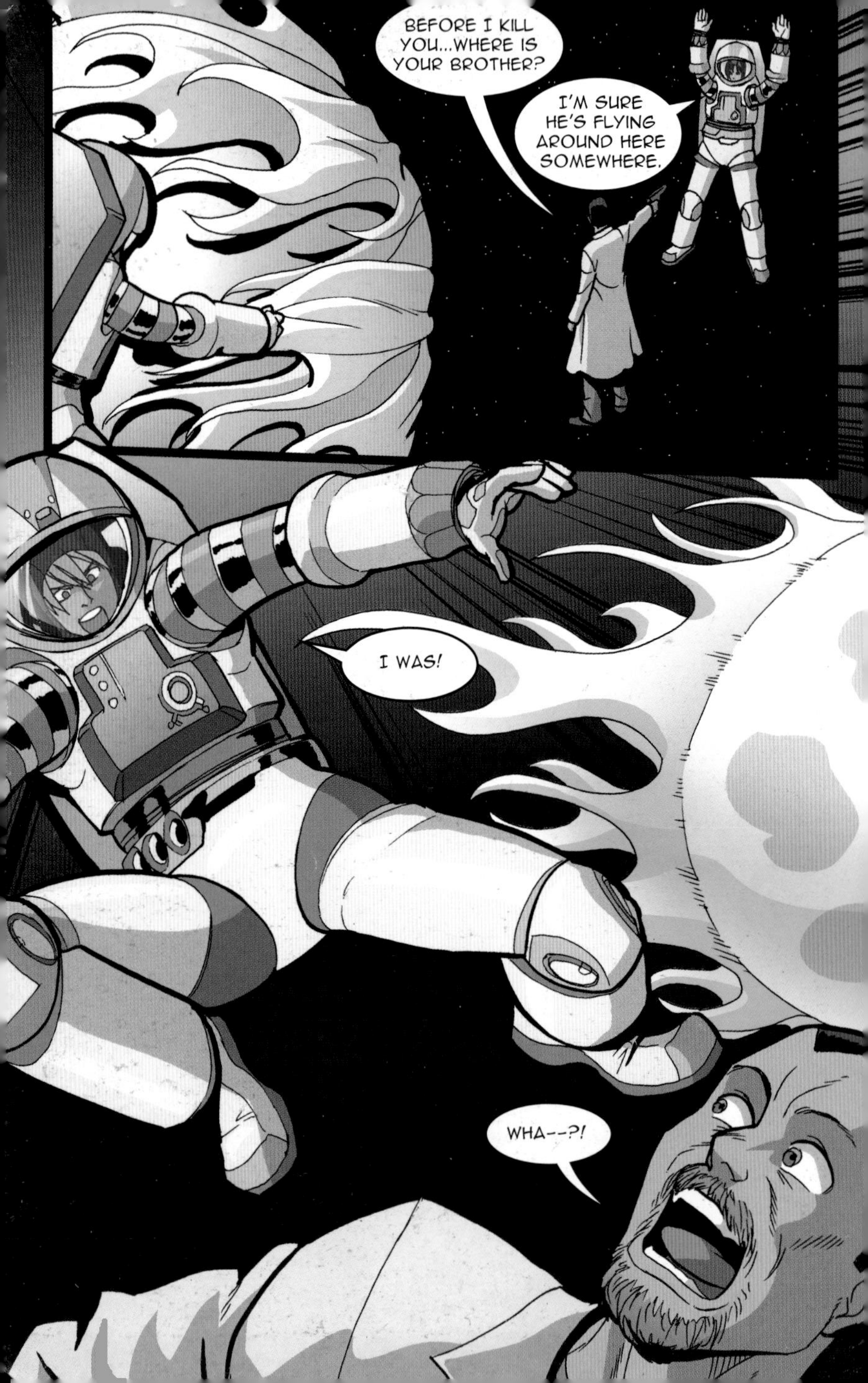
BEFORE I KILL YOU...WHERE IS YOUR BROTHER?
I'M SURE HE'S FLYING AROUND HERE SOMEWHERE.
I WAS!
WHA--?!

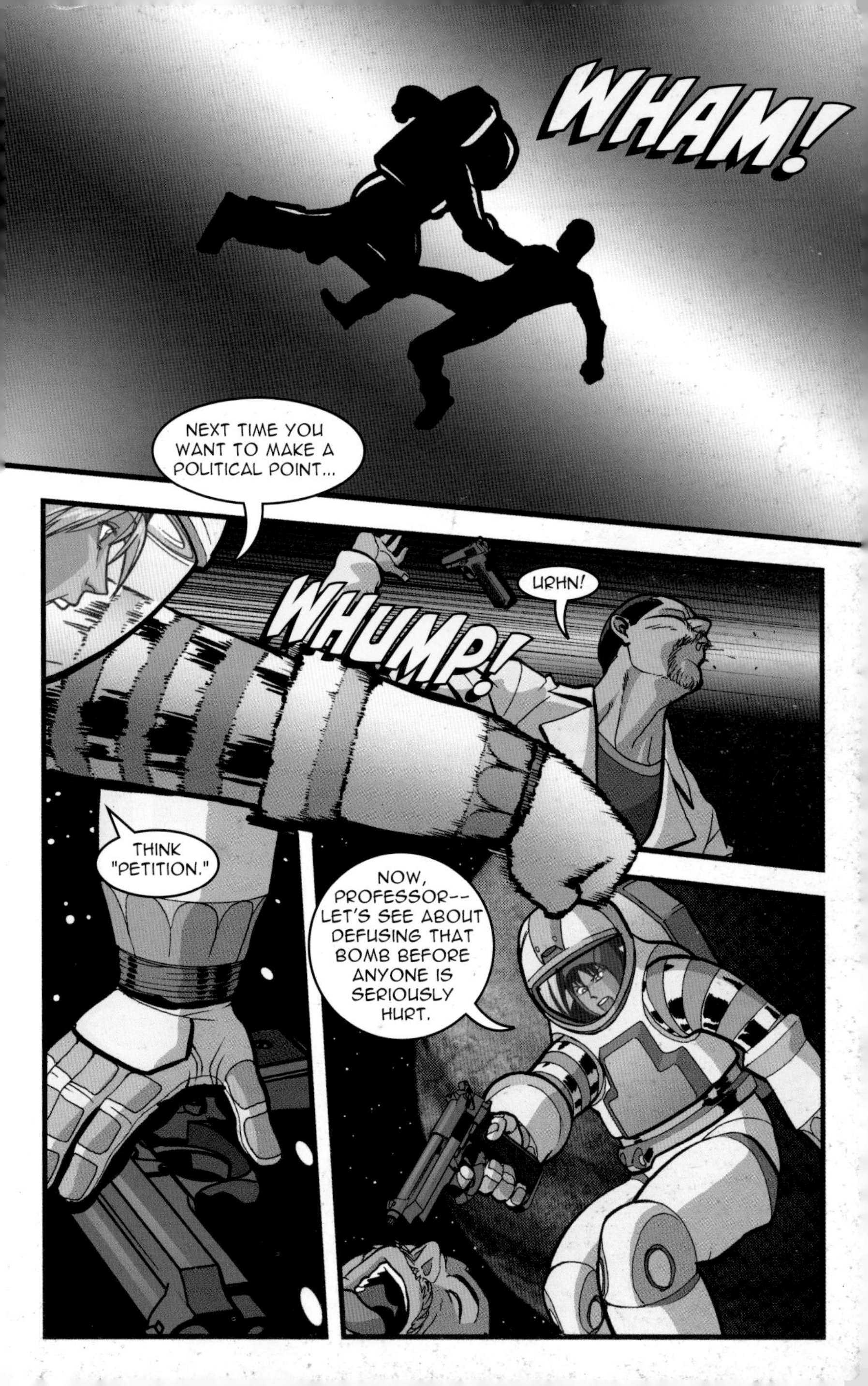
WHAM!
NEXT TIME YOU WANT TO MAKE A POLITICAL POINT...
WHUMP!
URHN!
THINK "PETITION."
NOW, PROFESSOR-- LET'S SEE ABOUT DEFUSING THAT BOMB BEFORE ANYONE IS SERIOUSLY HURT.

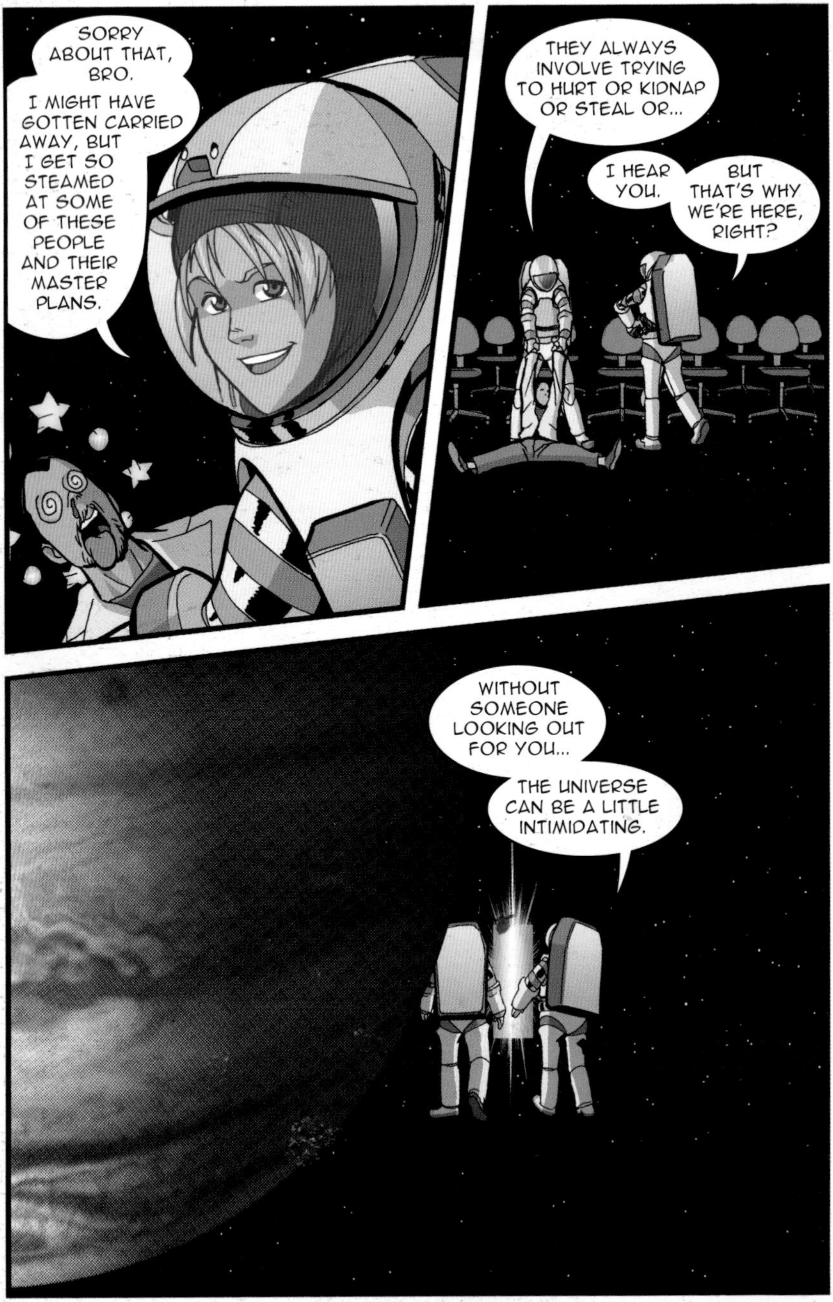
SORRY ABOUT THAT, BRO.
I MIGHT HAVE GOTTEN CARRIED AWAY, BUT I GET SO STEAMED AT SOME OF THESE PEOPLE AND THEIR MASTER PLANS.
THEY ALWAYS INVOLVE TRYING TO HURT OR KIDNAP OR STEAL OR...
I HEAR YOU.
BUT THAT'S WHY WE'RE HERE, RIGHT?
WITHOUT SOMEONE LOOKING OUT FOR YOU...
THE UNIVERSE CAN BE A LITTLE INTIMIDATING.

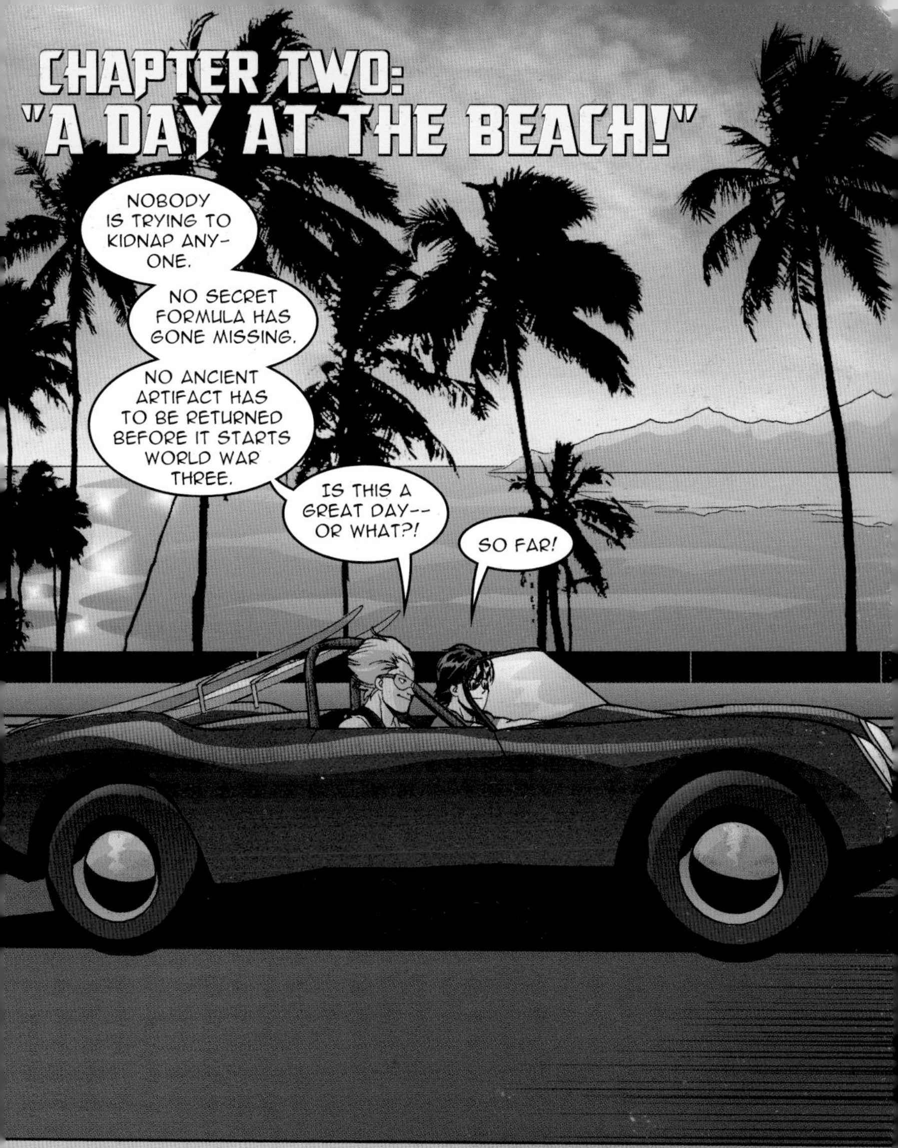
CHAPTER TWO:
"A DAY AT THE BEACH!"
NOBODY IS TRYING TO KIDNAP ANY-ONE.
NO SECRET FORMULA HAS GONE MISSING.
NO ANCIENT ARTIFACT HAS TO BE RETURNED BEFORE IT STARTS WORLD WAR THREE.
IS THIS A GREAT DAY-- OR WHAT?!
SO FAR!

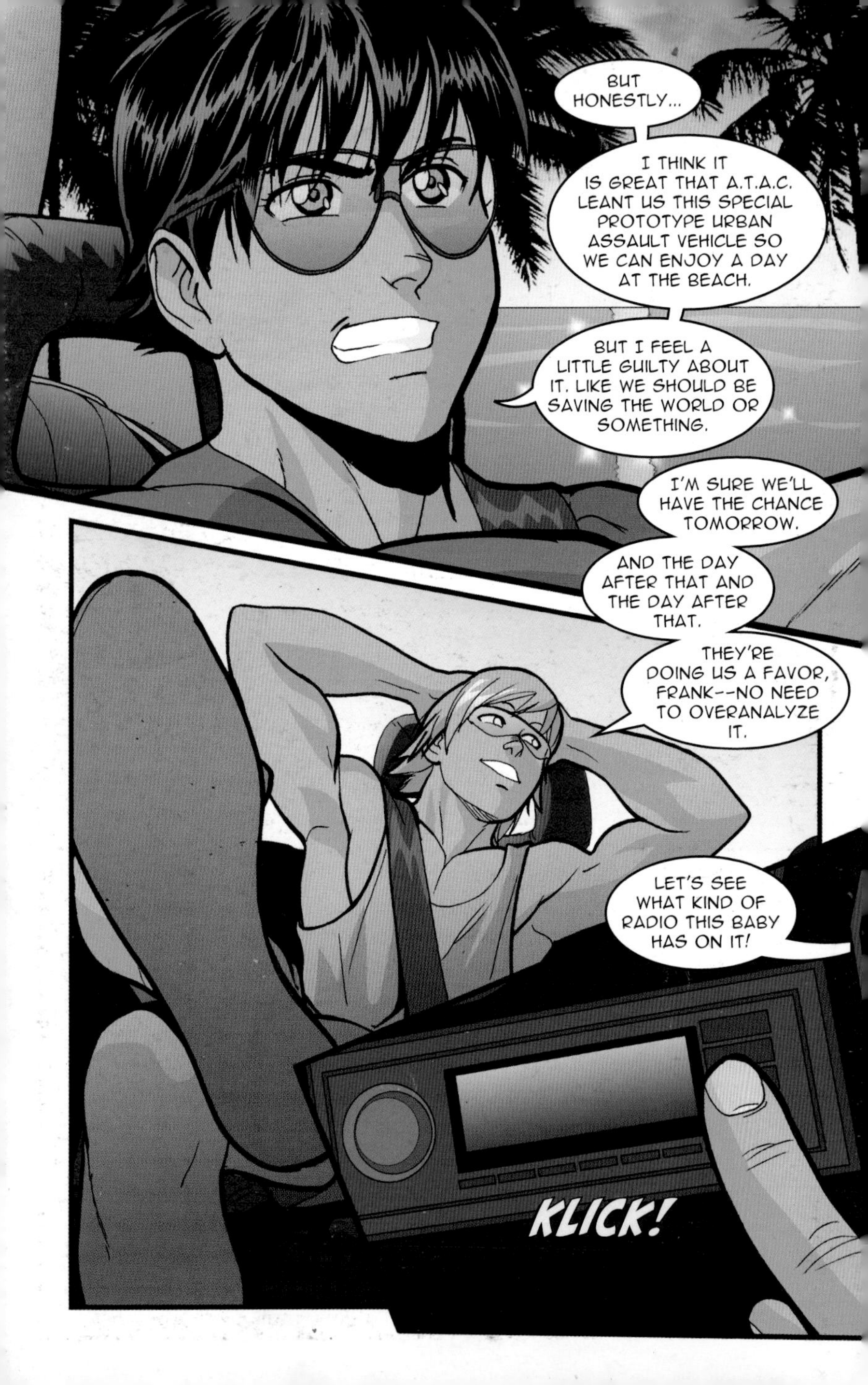
BUT HONESTLY...
I THINK IT IS GREAT THAT A.T.A.C. LEANT US THIS SPECIAL PROTOTYPE URBAN ASSAULT VEHICLE SO WE CAN ENJOY A DAY AT THE BEACH.
BUT I FEEL A LITTLE GUILTY ABOUT IT. LIKE WE SHOULD BE SAVING THE WORLD OR SOMETHING.
I'M SURE WE'LL HAVE THE CHANCE TOMORROW.
AND THE DAY AFTER THAT AND THE DAY AFTER THAT.
THEY'RE DOING US A FAVOR, FRANK--NO NEED TO OVERANALYZE IT.
LET'S SEE WHAT KIND OF RADIO THIS BABY HAS ON IT!
KLICK!

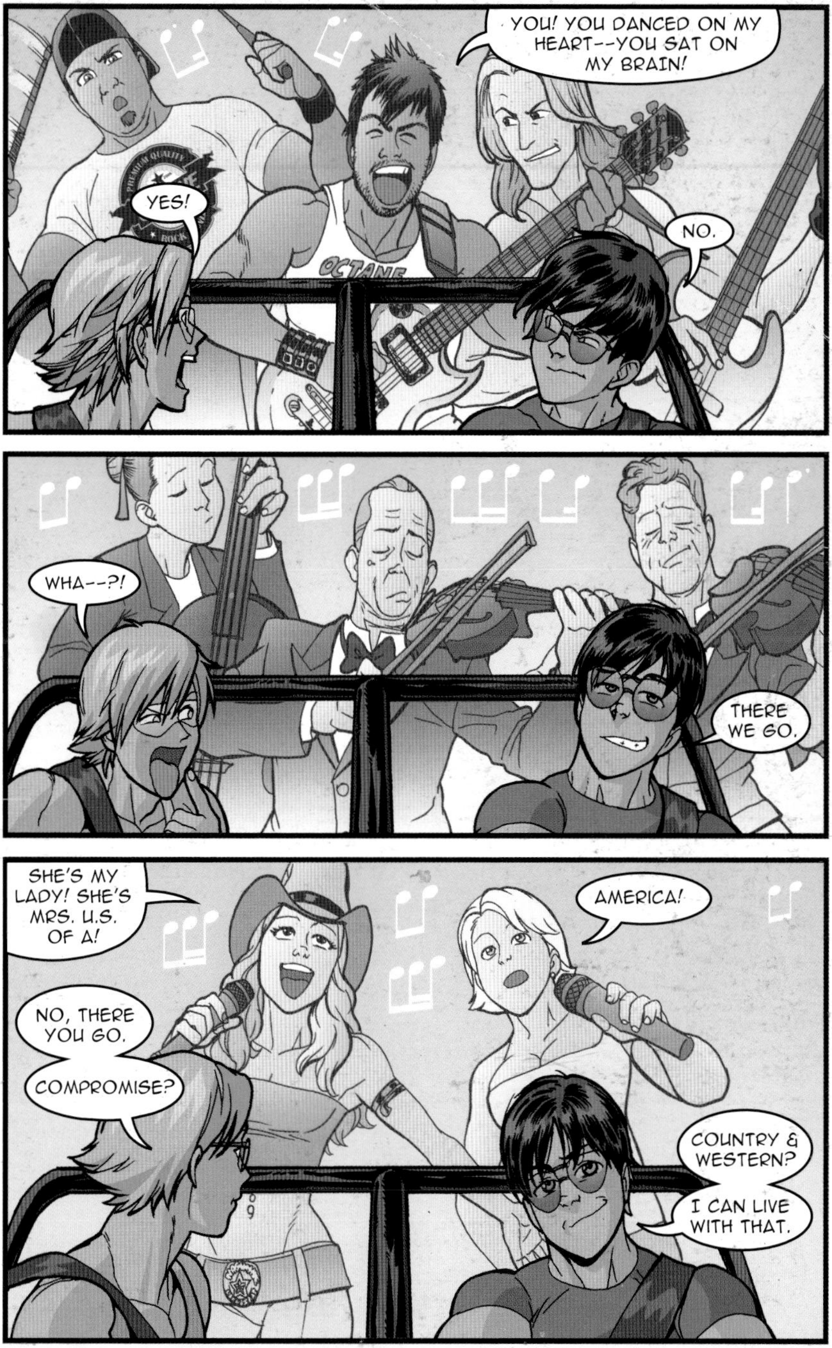
YOU! YOU DANCED ON MY HEART--YOU SAT ON MY BRAIN!
YES!
NO.
WHA--?!
THERE WE GO.
SHE'S MY LADY! SHE'S MRS. U.S. OF A!
AMERICA!
NO, THERE YOU GO.
COMPROMISE?
COUNTRY & WESTERN?
I CAN LIVE WITH THAT.

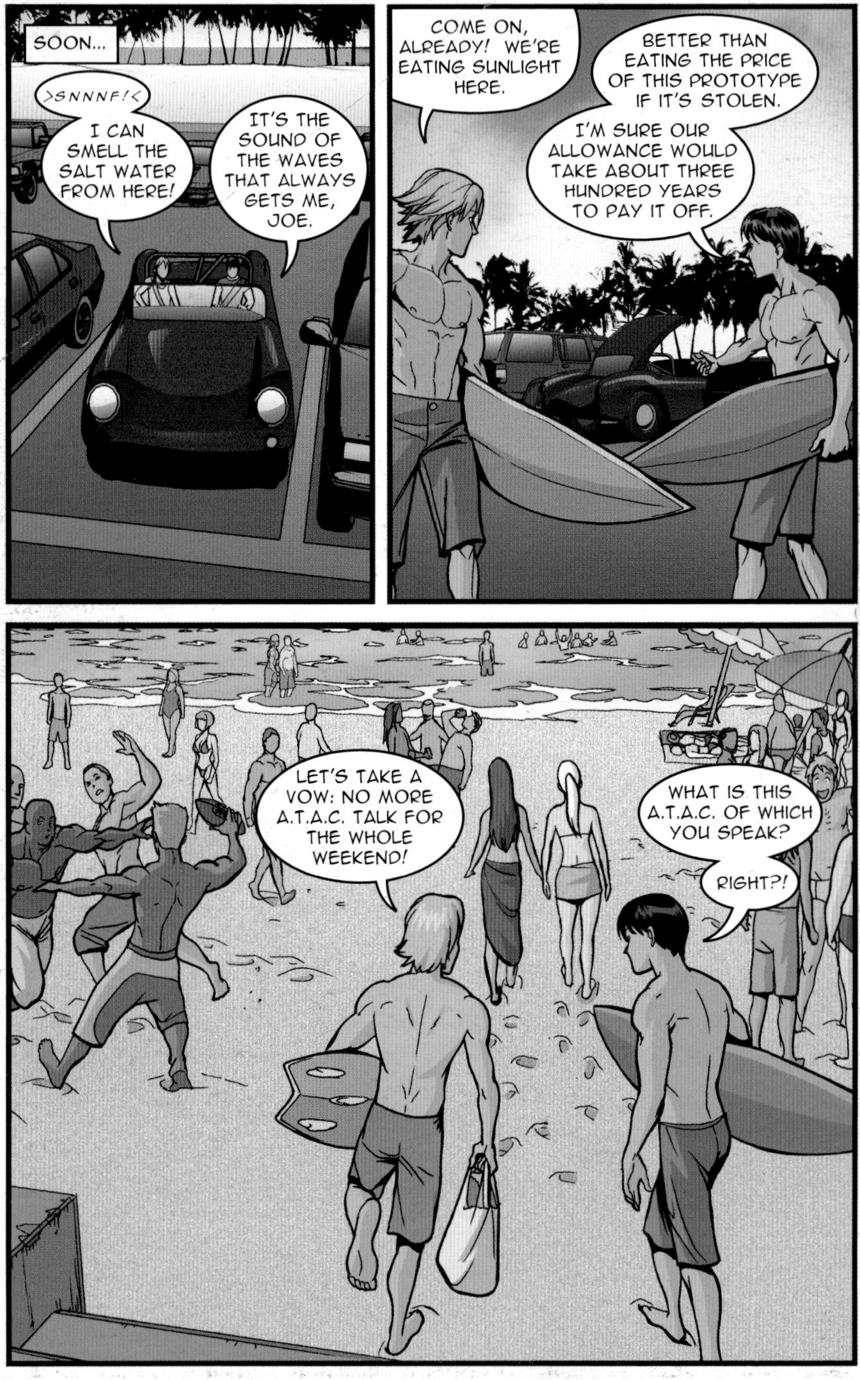
SOON...
>SNNNF!<
I CAN SMELL THE SALT WATER FROM HERE!
IT'S THE SOUND OF THE WAVES THAT ALWAYS GETS ME, JOE.
COME ON, ALREADY! WE'RE EATING SUNLIGHT HERE.
BETTER THAN EATING THE PRICE OF THIS PROTOTYPE IF IT'S STOLEN.
I'M SURE OUR ALLOWANCE WOULD TAKE ABOUT THREE HUNDRED YEARS TO PAY IT OFF.
LET'S TAKE A VOW: NO MORE A.T.A.C. TALK FOR THE WHOLE WEEKEND!
WHAT IS THIS A.T.A.C. OF WHICH YOU SPEAK?
RIGHT?!

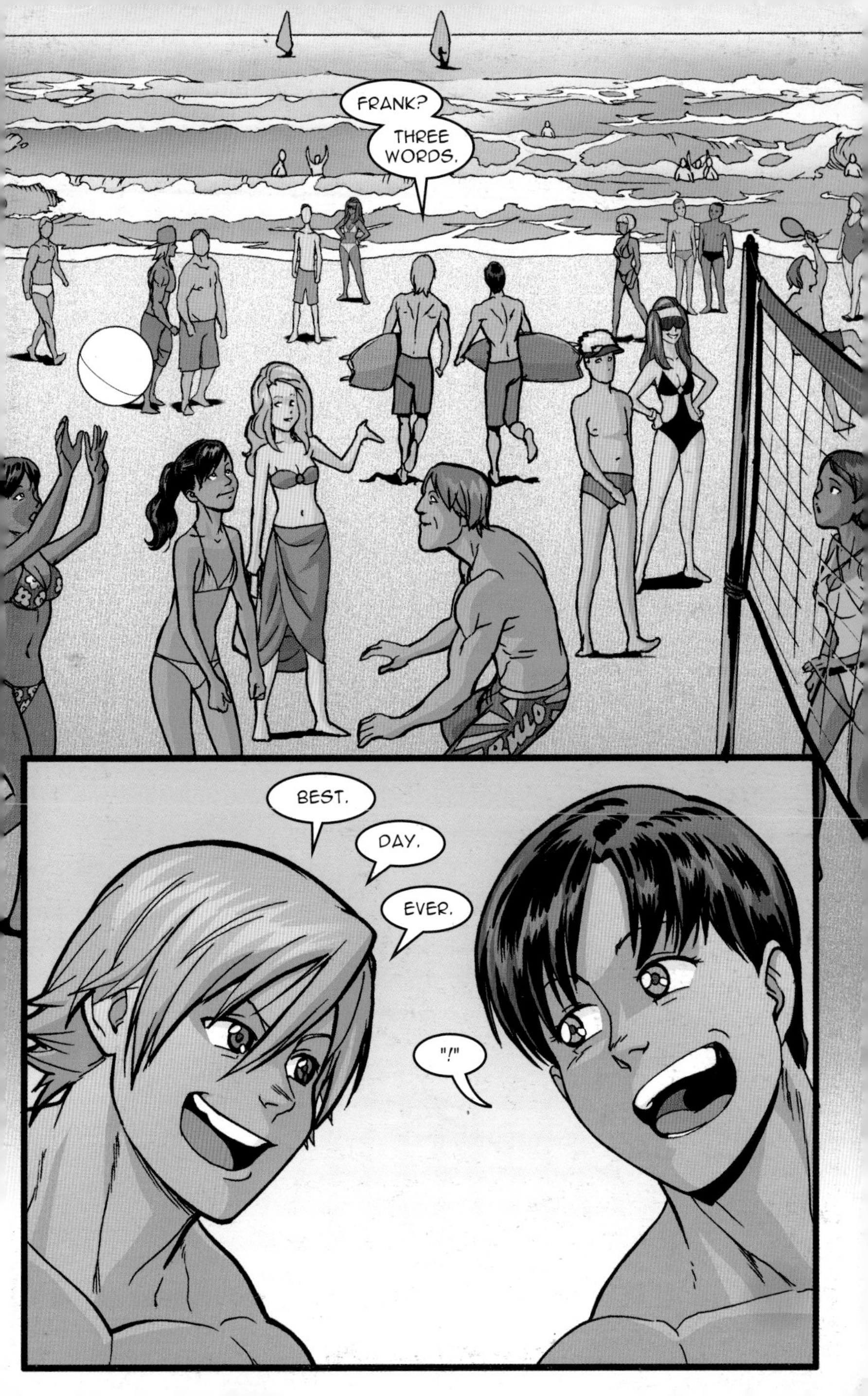
FRANK?
THREE WORDS.
BEST.
DAY.
EVER.
"!"

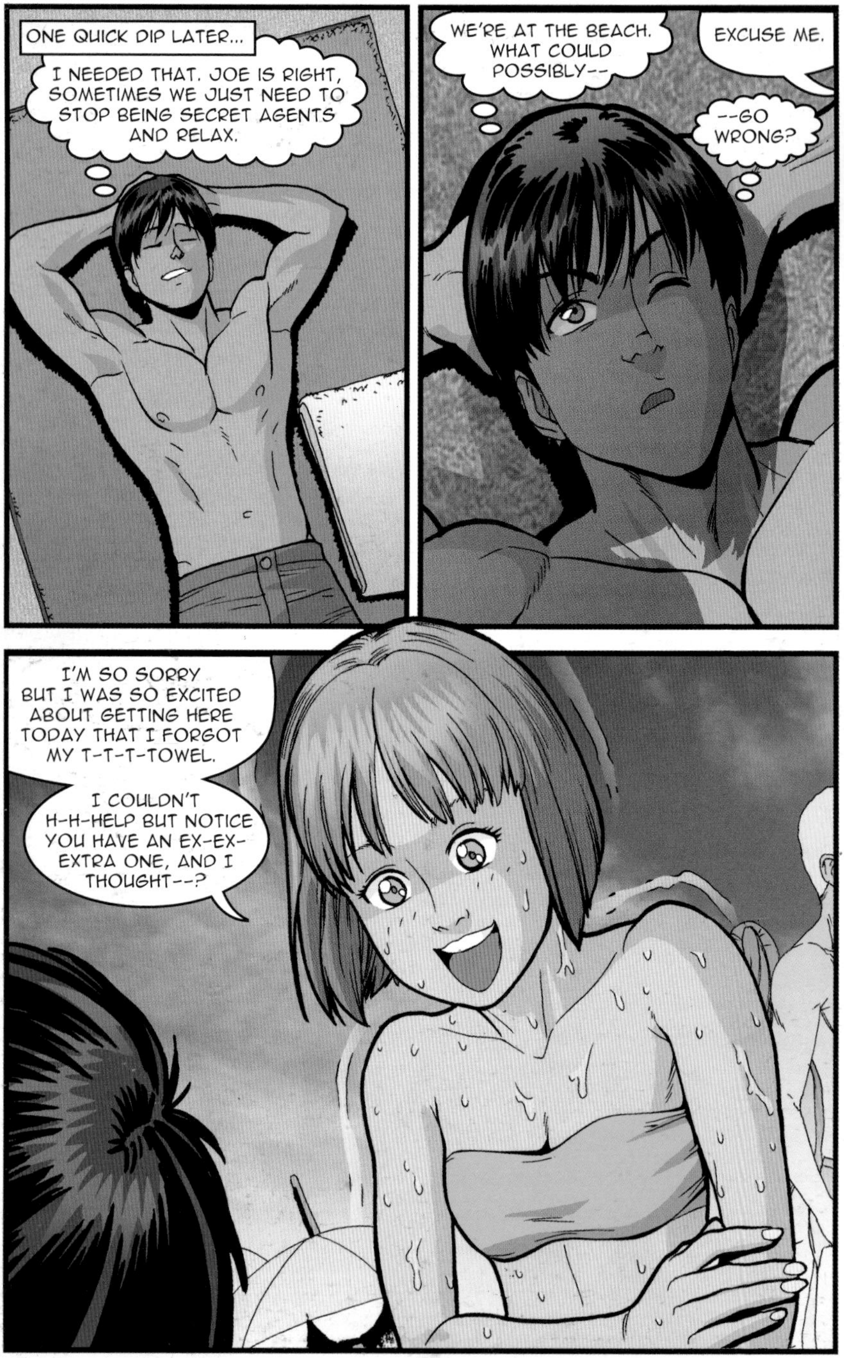
ONE QUICK DIP LATER...
I NEEDED THAT. JOE IS RIGHT, SOMETIMES WE JUST NEED TO STOP BEING SECRET AGENTS AND RELAX.
WE'RE AT THE BEACH. WHAT COULD POSSIBLY--
EXCUSE ME.
--GO WRONG?
I'M SO SORRY BUT I WAS SO EXCITED ABOUT GETTING HERE TODAY THAT I FORGOT MY T-T-T-TOWEL.
I COULDN'T H-H-HELP BUT NOTICE YOU HAVE AN EX-EX-EXTRA ONE, AND I THOUGHT--?

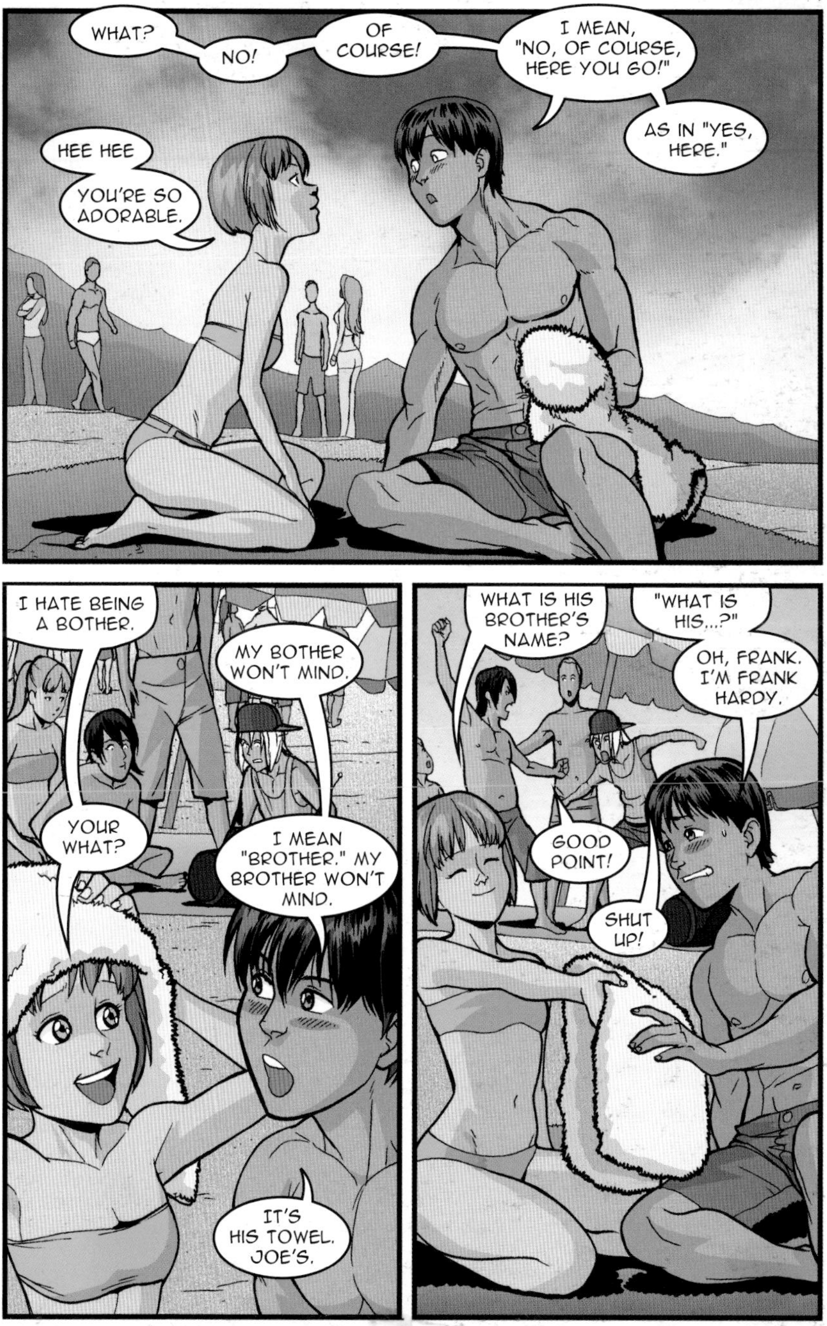
WHAT?
NO!
OF COURSE!
I MEAN, "NO, OF COURSE, HERE YOU GO!"
AS IN "YES, HERE."
HEE HEE
YOU'RE SO ADORABLE.
I HATE BEING A BOTHER.
MY BOTHER WON'T MIND.
YOUR WHAT?
I MEAN "BROTHER." MY BROTHER WON'T MIND.
IT'S HIS TOWEL. JOE'S.
WHAT IS HIS BROTHER'S NAME?
"WHAT IS HIS...?"
OH, FRANK. I'M FRANK HARDY.
GOOD POINT!
SHUT UP!

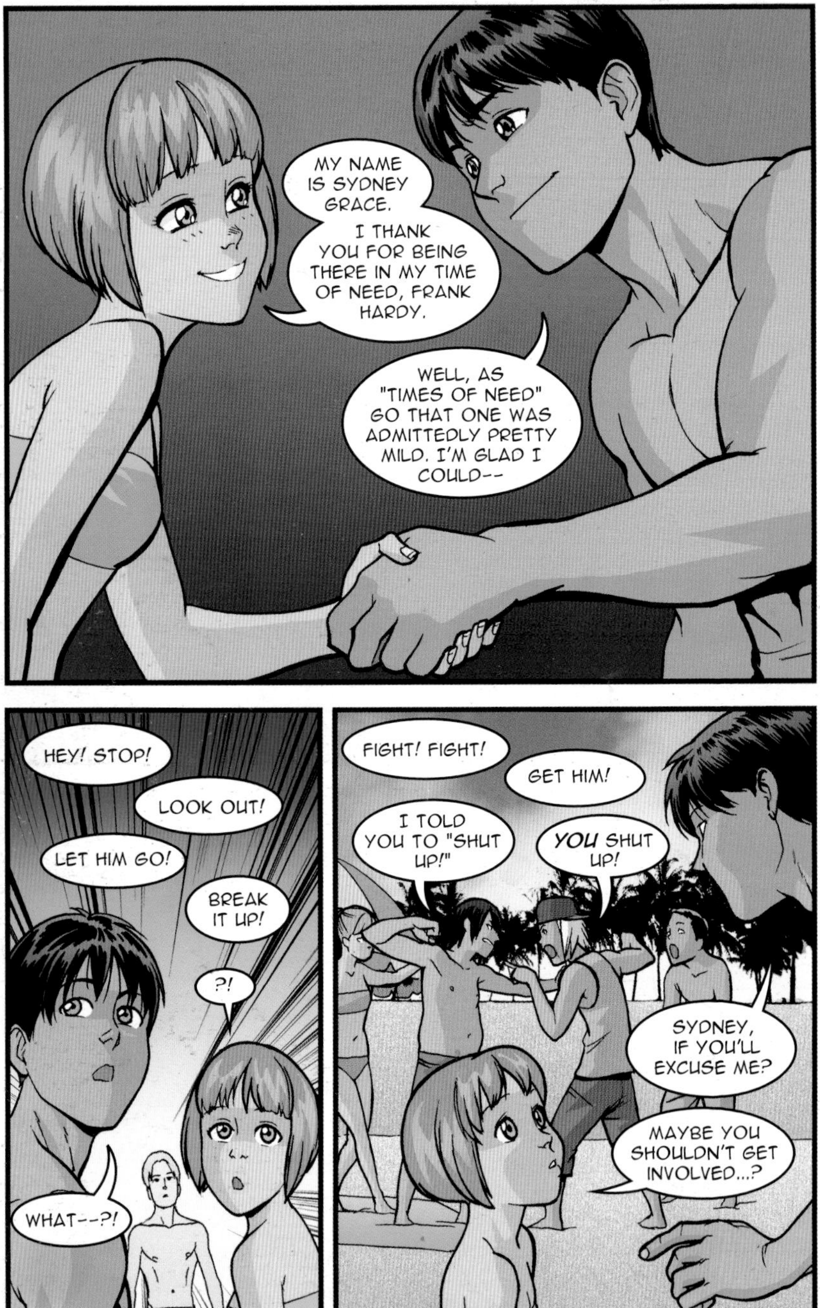
MY NAME IS SYDNEY GRACE.
I THANK YOU FOR BEING THERE IN MY TIME OF NEED, FRANK HARDY.
WELL, AS "TIMES OF NEED" GO THAT ONE WAS ADMITTEDLY PRETTY MILD. I'M GLAD I COULD--
HEY! STOP!
LOOK OUT!
LET HIM GO!
BREAK IT UP!
?!
WHAT--?!
FIGHT! FIGHT!
GET HIM!
I TOLD YOU TO "SHUT UP!"
YOU SHUT UP!
SYDNEY, IF YOU'LL EXCUSE ME?
MAYBE YOU SHOULDN'T GET INVOLVED...?

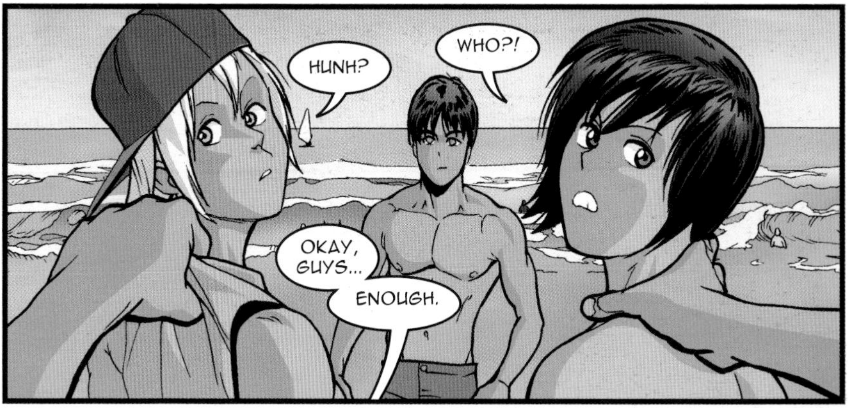
HUNH?
WHO?!
OKAY, GUYS...
ENOUGH.

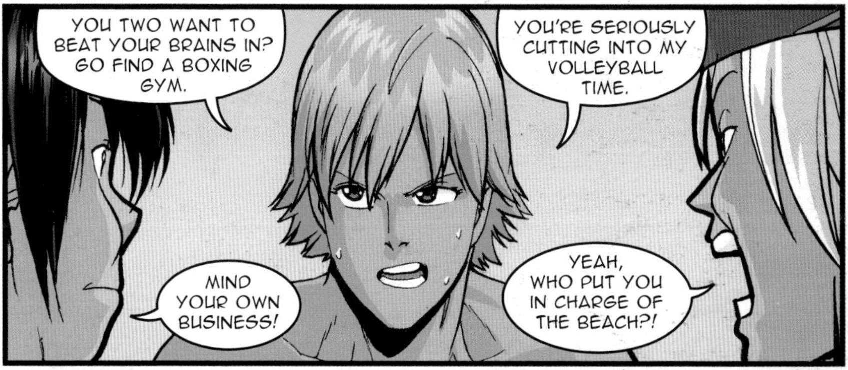
YOU TWO WANT TO BEAT YOUR BRAINS IN? GO FIND A BOXING GYM.
YOU'RE SERIOUSLY CUTTING INTO MY VOLLEYBALL TIME.
MIND YOUR OWN BUSINESS!
YEAH, WHO PUT YOU IN CHARGE OF THE BEACH?!

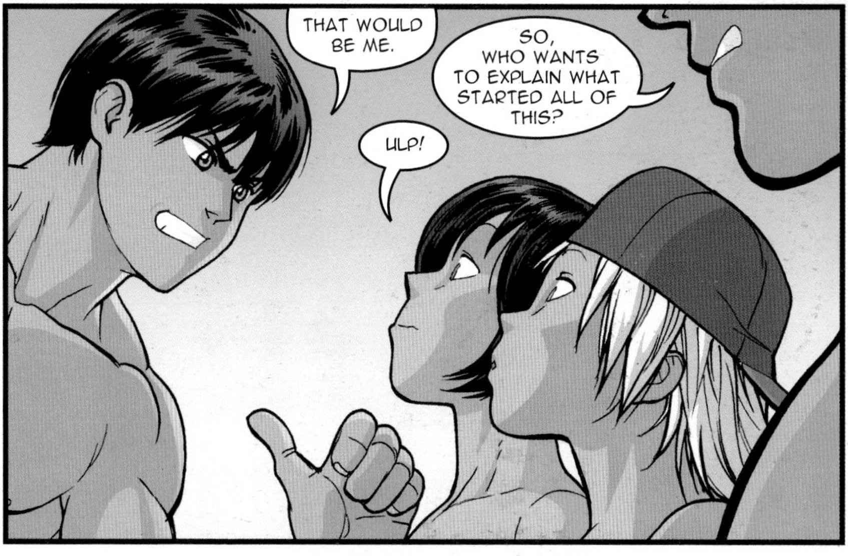
THAT WOULD BE ME.
SO, WHO WANTS TO EXPLAIN WHAT STARTED ALL OF THIS?
ULP!

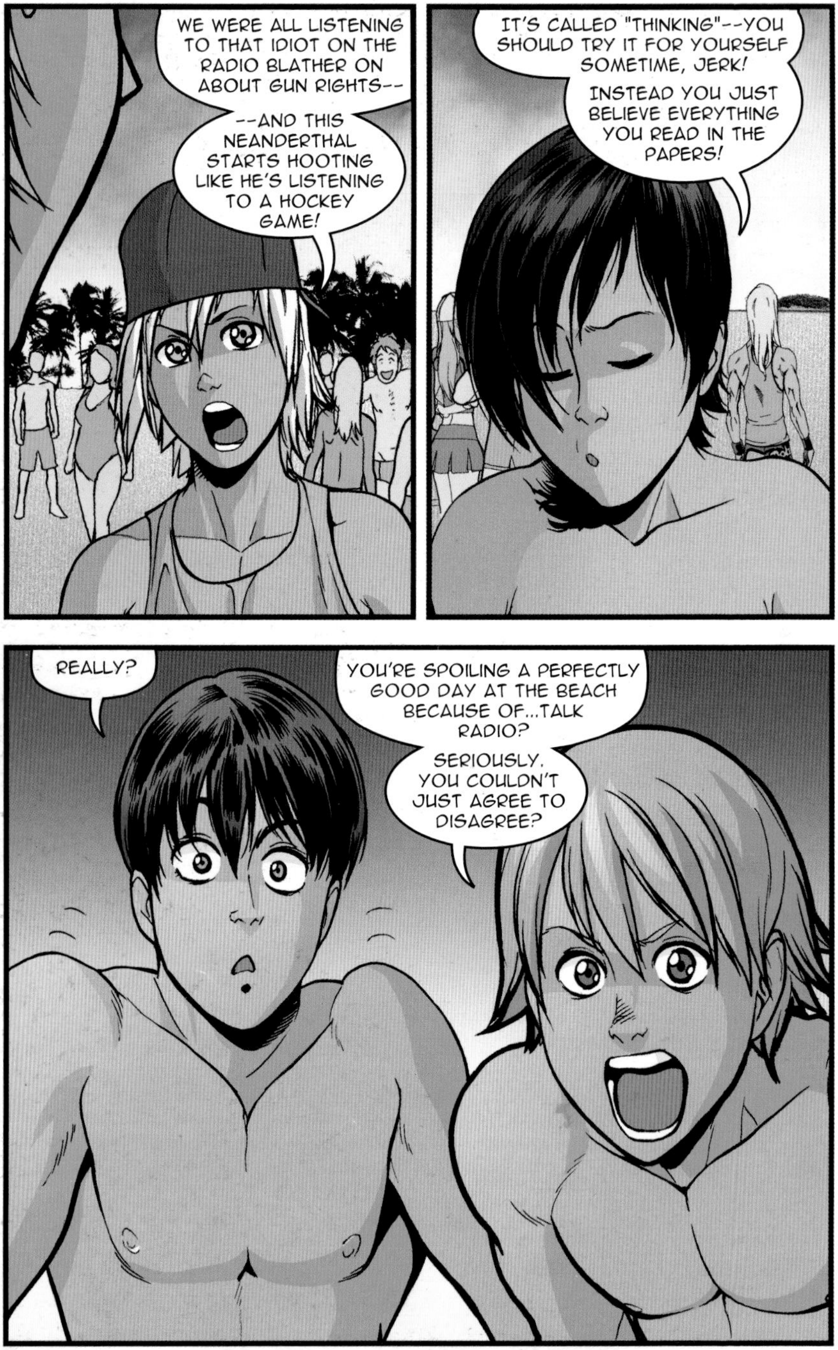
WE WERE ALL LISTENING TO THAT IDIOT ON THE RADIO BLATHER ON ABOUT GUN RIGHTS--
--AND THIS NEANDERTHAL STARTS HOOTING LIKE HE'S LISTENING TO A HOCKEY GAME!
IT'S CALLED "THINKING"--YOU SHOULD TRY IT FOR YOURSELF SOMETIME, JERK!
INSTEAD YOU JUST BELIEVE EVERYTHING YOU READ IN THE PAPERS!
REALLY?
YOU'RE SPOILING A PERFECTLY GOOD DAY AT THE BEACH BECAUSE OF...TALK RADIO?
SERIOUSLY. YOU COULDN'T JUST AGREE TO DISAGREE?

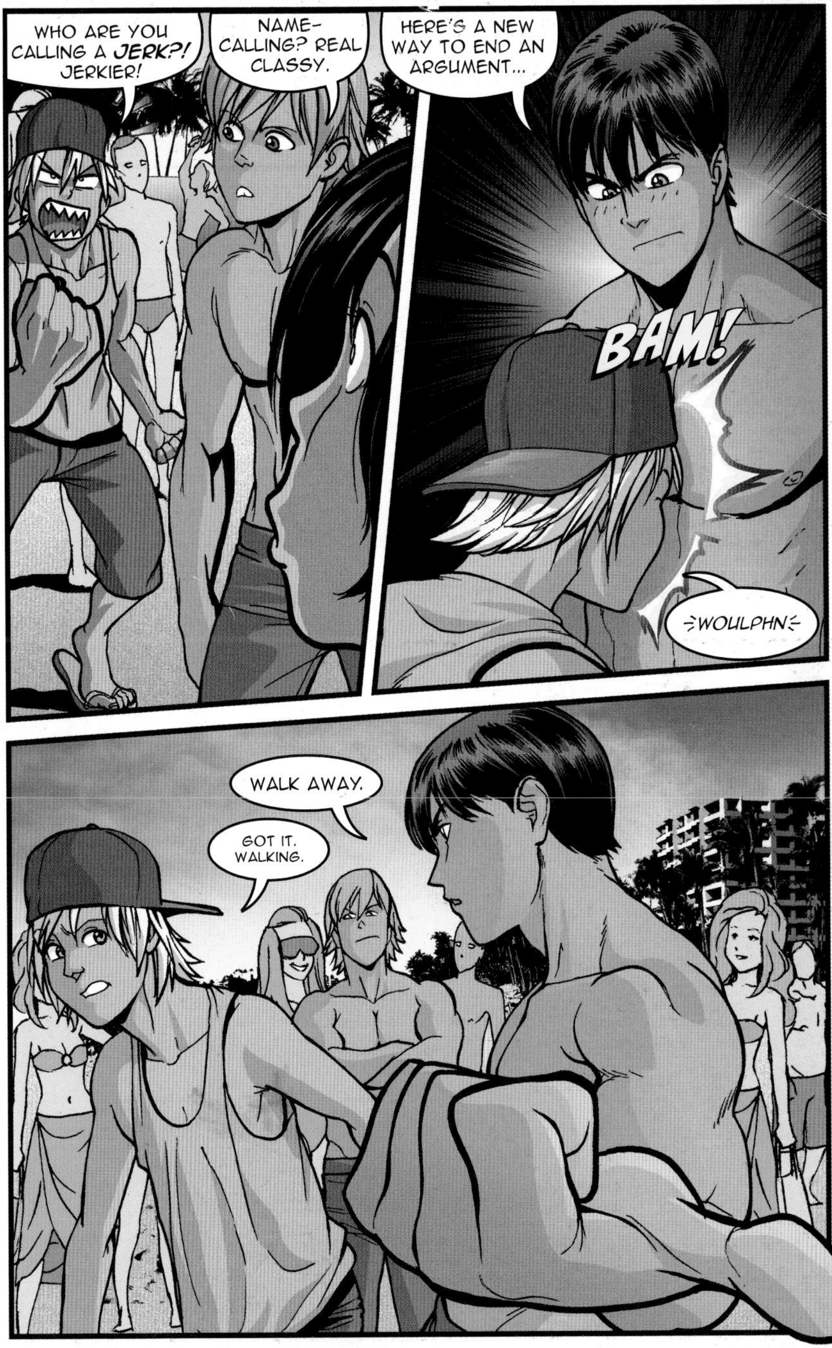
WHO ARE YOU CALLING A JERK?! JERKIER!
NAME-CALLING? REAL CLASSY.
HERE'S A NEW WAY TO END AN ARGUMENT...
BAM!
WOULPHN
WALK AWAY.
GOT IT. WALKING.

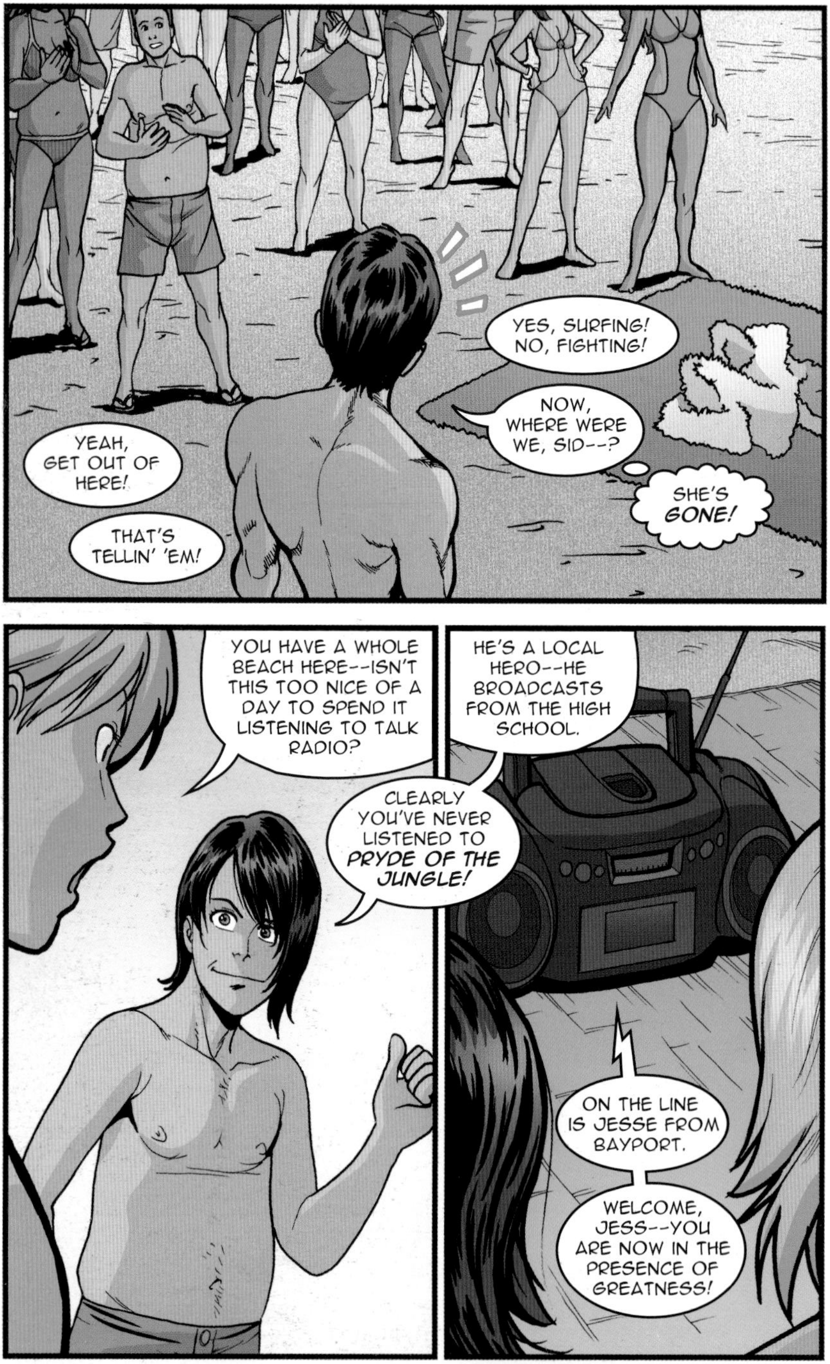
YES, SURFING! NO, FIGHTING!
NOW, WHERE WERE WE, SID--?
SHE'S *GONE!*
YEAH, GET OUT OF HERE!
THAT'S TELLIN' 'EM!
YOU HAVE A WHOLE BEACH HERE--ISN'T THIS TOO NICE OF A DAY TO SPEND IT LISTENING TO TALK RADIO?
CLEARLY YOU'VE NEVER LISTENED TO *PRYDE OF THE JUNGLE!*
HE'S A LOCAL HERO--HE BROADCASTS FROM THE HIGH SCHOOL.
ON THE LINE IS JESSE FROM BAYPORT.
WELCOME, JESS--YOU ARE NOW IN THE PRESENCE OF GREATNESS!

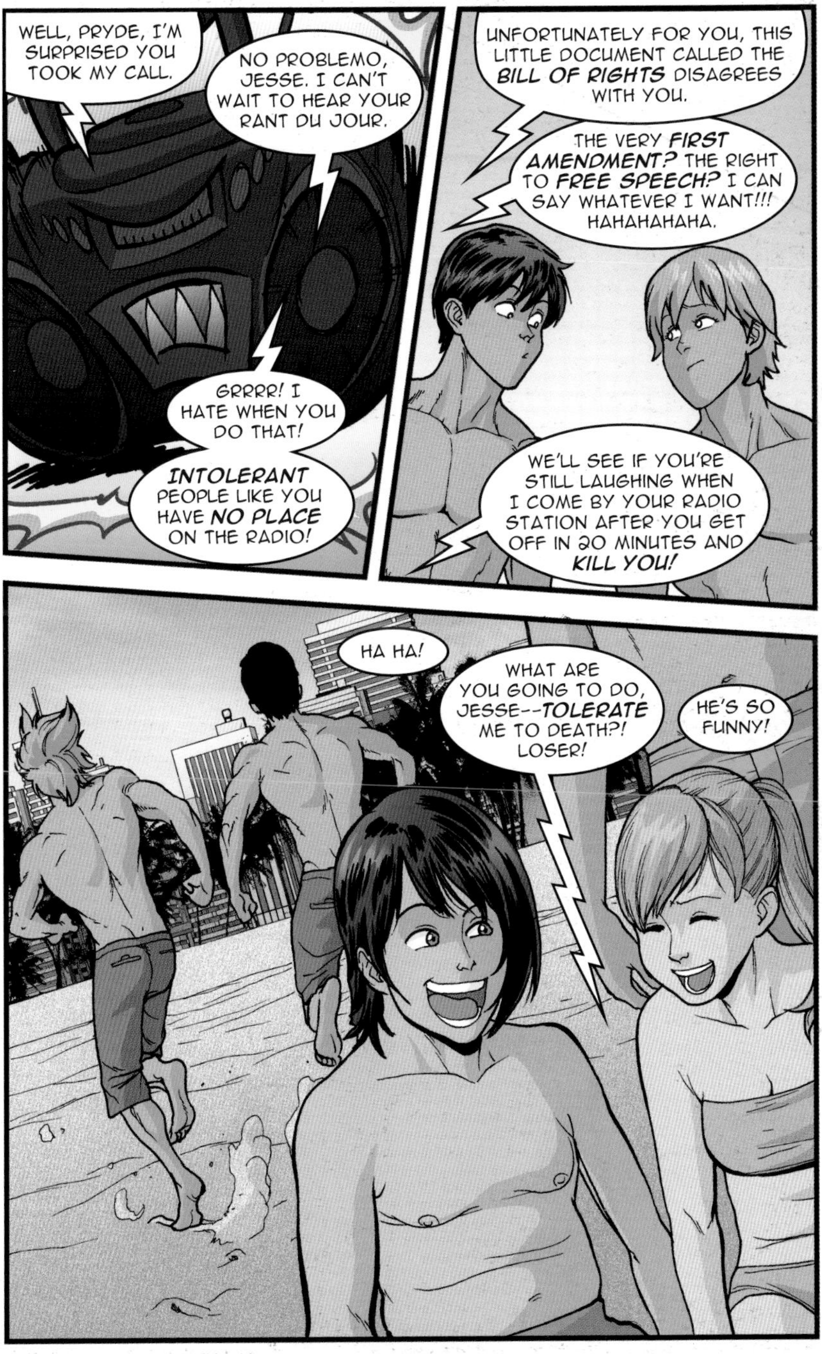
WELL, PRYDE, I'M SURPRISED YOU TOOK MY CALL.
NO PROBLEMO, JESSE. I CAN'T WAIT TO HEAR YOUR RANT DU JOUR.
GRRRR! I HATE WHEN YOU DO THAT!
INTOLERANT PEOPLE LIKE YOU HAVE NO PLACE ON THE RADIO!
UNFORTUNATELY FOR YOU, THIS LITTLE DOCUMENT CALLED THE BILL OF RIGHTS DISAGREES WITH YOU.
THE VERY FIRST AMENDMENT? THE RIGHT TO FREE SPEECH? I CAN SAY WHATEVER I WANT!!! HAHAHAHAHA.
WE'LL SEE IF YOU'RE STILL LAUGHING WHEN I COME BY YOUR RADIO STATION AFTER YOU GET OFF IN 20 MINUTES AND KILL YOU!
HA HA!
WHAT ARE YOU GOING TO DO, JESSE--TOLERATE ME TO DEATH?! LOSER!
HE'S SO FUNNY!

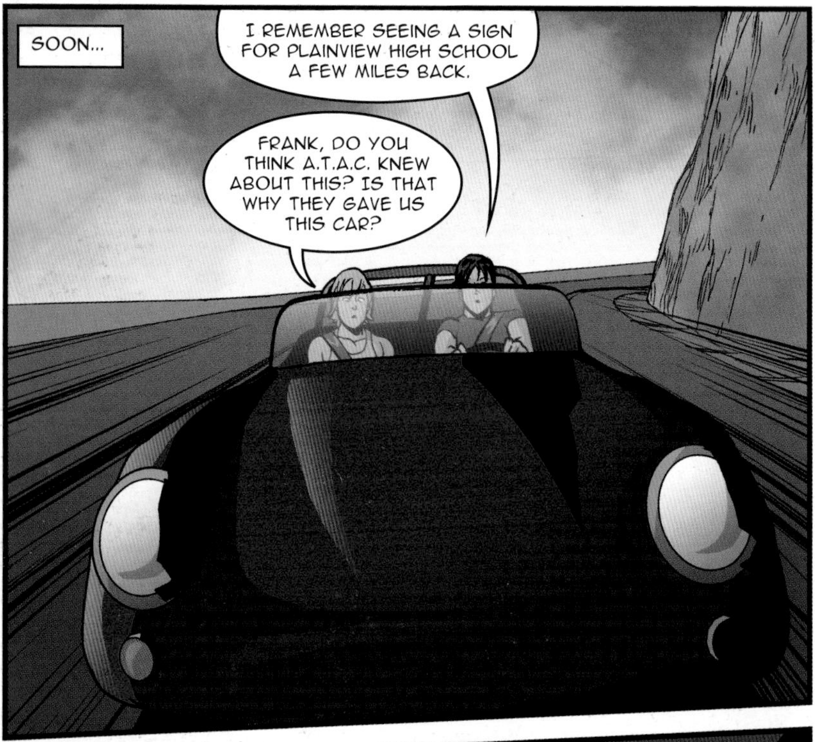
SOON...
I REMEMBER SEEING A SIGN FOR PLAINVIEW HIGH SCHOOL A FEW MILES BACK.
FRANK, DO YOU THINK A.T.A.C. KNEW ABOUT THIS? IS THAT WHY THEY GAVE US THIS CAR?

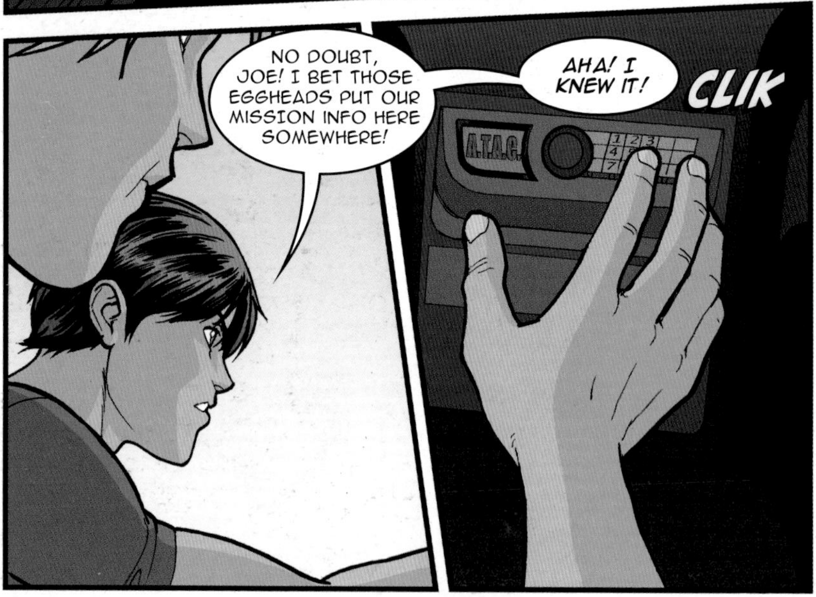
NO DOUBT, JOE! I BET THOSE EGGHEADS PUT OUR MISSION INFO HERE SOMEWHERE!
AHA! I KNEW IT!
CLIK
A.T.A.C.

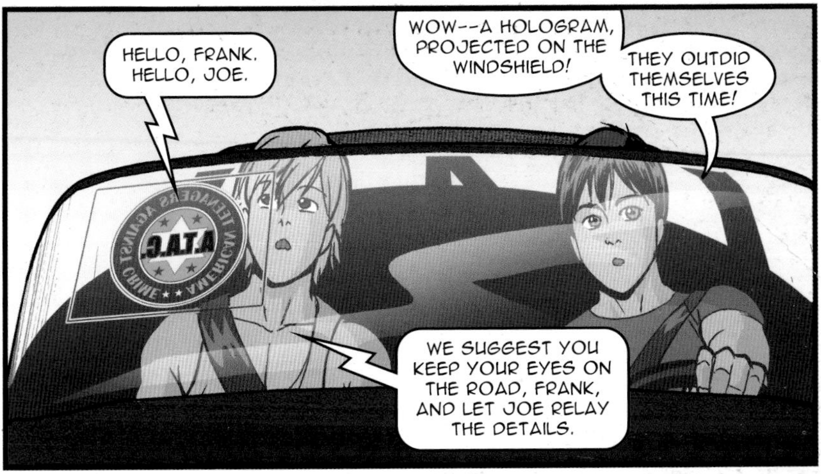
HELLO, FRANK. HELLO, JOE.
WOW--A HOLOGRAM, PROJECTED ON THE WINDSHIELD!
THEY OUTDID THEMSELVES THIS TIME!
A.T.A.C. AMERICAN TEENAGERS AGAINST CRIME
WE SUGGEST YOU KEEP YOUR EYES ON THE ROAD, FRANK, AND LET JOE RELAY THE DETAILS.

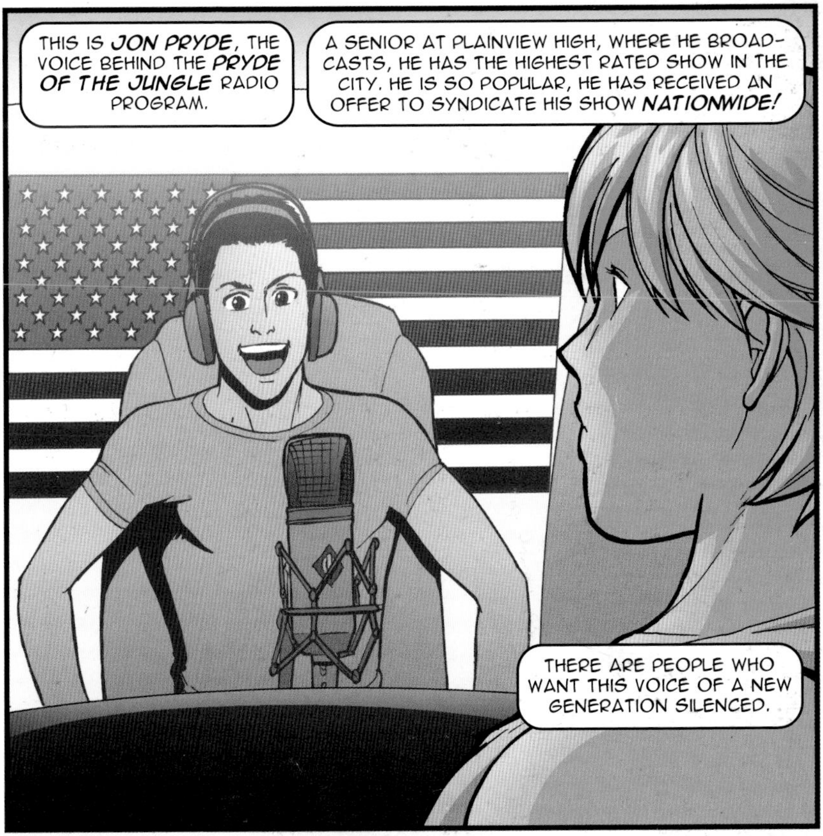
THIS IS JON PRYDE, THE VOICE BEHIND THE PRYDE OF THE JUNGLE RADIO PROGRAM.
A SENIOR AT PLAINVIEW HIGH, WHERE HE BROADCASTS, HE HAS THE HIGHEST RATED SHOW IN THE CITY. HE IS SO POPULAR, HE HAS RECEIVED AN OFFER TO SYNDICATE HIS SHOW NATIONWIDE!
THERE ARE PEOPLE WHO WANT THIS VOICE OF A NEW GENERATION SILENCED.

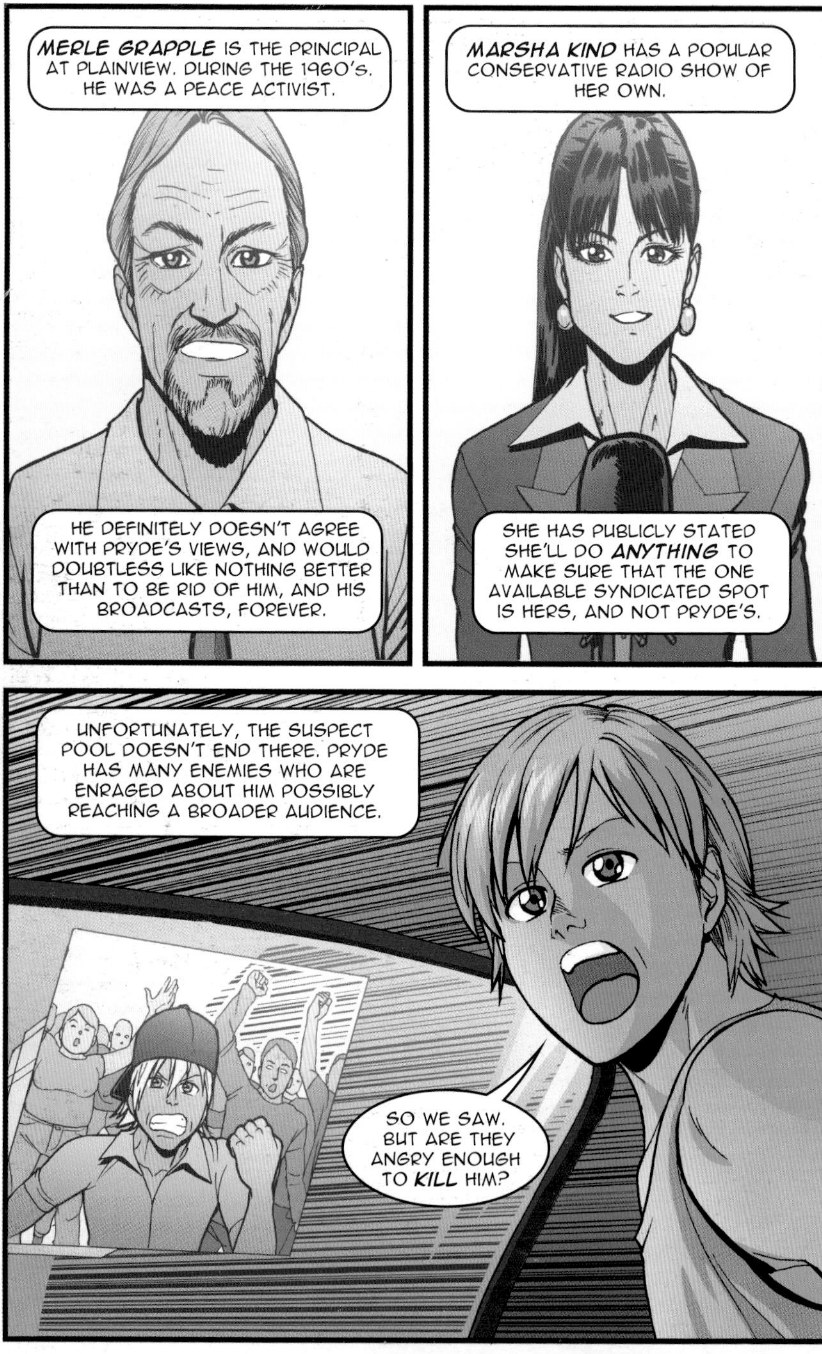
MERLE GRAPPLE IS THE PRINCIPAL AT PLAINVIEW. DURING THE 1960'S. HE WAS A PEACE ACTIVIST.
HE DEFINITELY DOESN'T AGREE WITH PRYDE'S VIEWS, AND WOULD DOUBTLESS LIKE NOTHING BETTER THAN TO BE RID OF HIM, AND HIS BROADCASTS, FOREVER.
MARSHA KIND HAS A POPULAR CONSERVATIVE RADIO SHOW OF HER OWN.
SHE HAS PUBLICLY STATED SHE'LL DO ANYTHING TO MAKE SURE THAT THE ONE AVAILABLE SYNDICATED SPOT IS HERS, AND NOT PRYDE'S.
UNFORTUNATELY, THE SUSPECT POOL DOESN'T END THERE. PRYDE HAS MANY ENEMIES WHO ARE ENRAGED ABOUT HIM POSSIBLY REACHING A BROADER AUDIENCE.
SO WE SAW. BUT ARE THEY ANGRY ENOUGH TO KILL HIM?

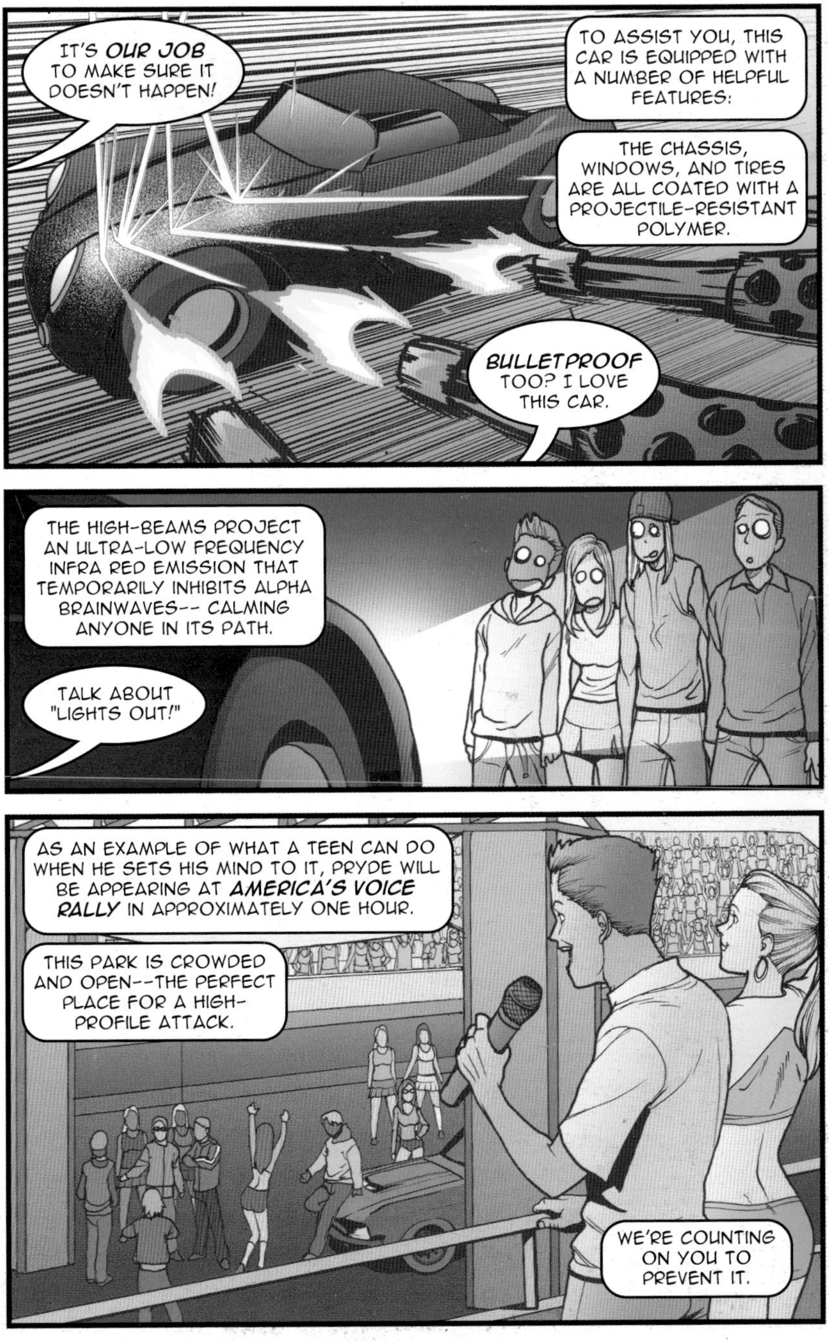
IT'S OUR JOB TO MAKE SURE IT DOESN'T HAPPEN!
TO ASSIST YOU, THIS CAR IS EQUIPPED WITH A NUMBER OF HELPFUL FEATURES:
THE CHASSIS, WINDOWS, AND TIRES ARE ALL COATED WITH A PROJECTILE-RESISTANT POLYMER.
BULLETPROOF TOO? I LOVE THIS CAR.
THE HIGH-BEAMS PROJECT AN ULTRA-LOW FREQUENCY INFRA RED EMISSION THAT TEMPORARILY INHIBITS ALPHA BRAINWAVES-- CALMING ANYONE IN ITS PATH.
TALK ABOUT "LIGHTS OUT!"
AS AN EXAMPLE OF WHAT A TEEN CAN DO WHEN HE SETS HIS MIND TO IT, PRYDE WILL BE APPEARING AT AMERICA'S VOICE RALLY IN APPROXIMATELY ONE HOUR.
THIS PARK IS CROWDED AND OPEN--THE PERFECT PLACE FOR A HIGH-PROFILE ATTACK.
WE'RE COUNTING ON YOU TO PREVENT IT.

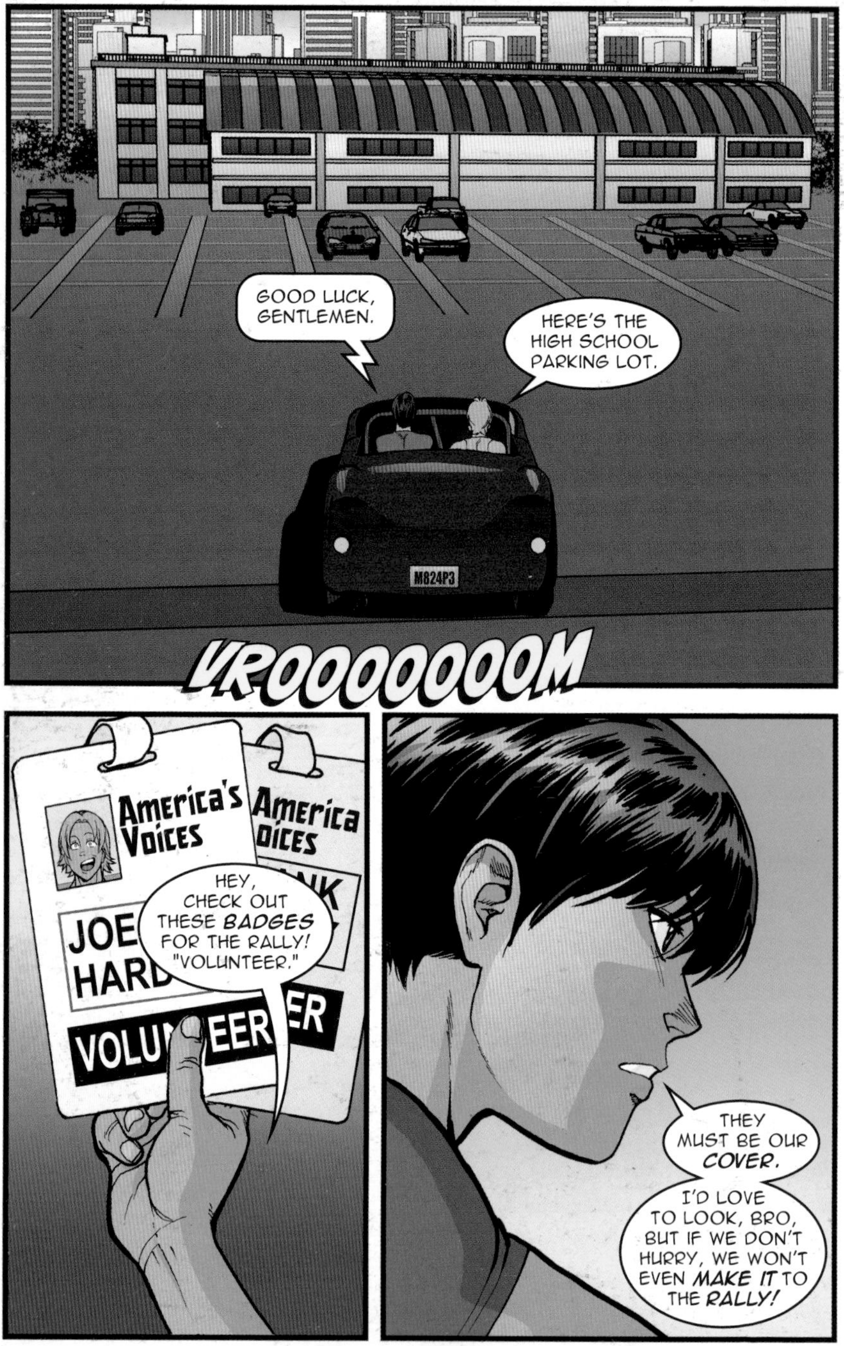
GOOD LUCK, GENTLEMEN.
HERE'S THE HIGH SCHOOL PARKING LOT.
M824P3
VROOOOOOOM
America's Voices
JOE HARD
VOLUNTEER
America Voices
ER
HEY, CHECK OUT THESE BADGES FOR THE RALLY! "VOLUNTEER."
THEY MUST BE OUR COVER.
I'D LOVE TO LOOK, BRO, BUT IF WE DON'T HURRY, WE WON'T EVEN MAKE IT TO THE RALLY!

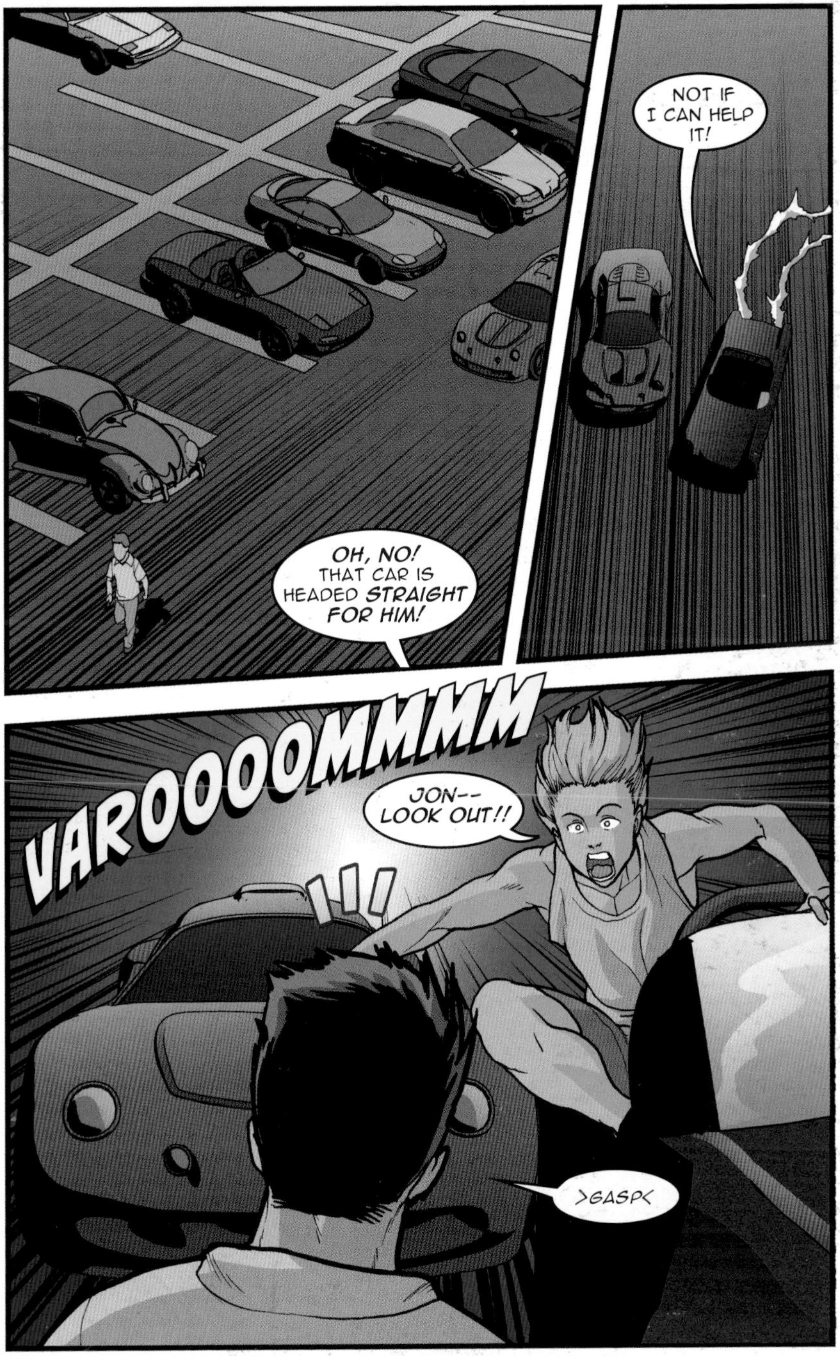
OH, NO! THAT CAR IS HEADED STRAIGHT FOR HIM!
NOT IF I CAN HELP IT!
VAROOOOMMMMM
JON-- LOOK OUT!!
>GASP<

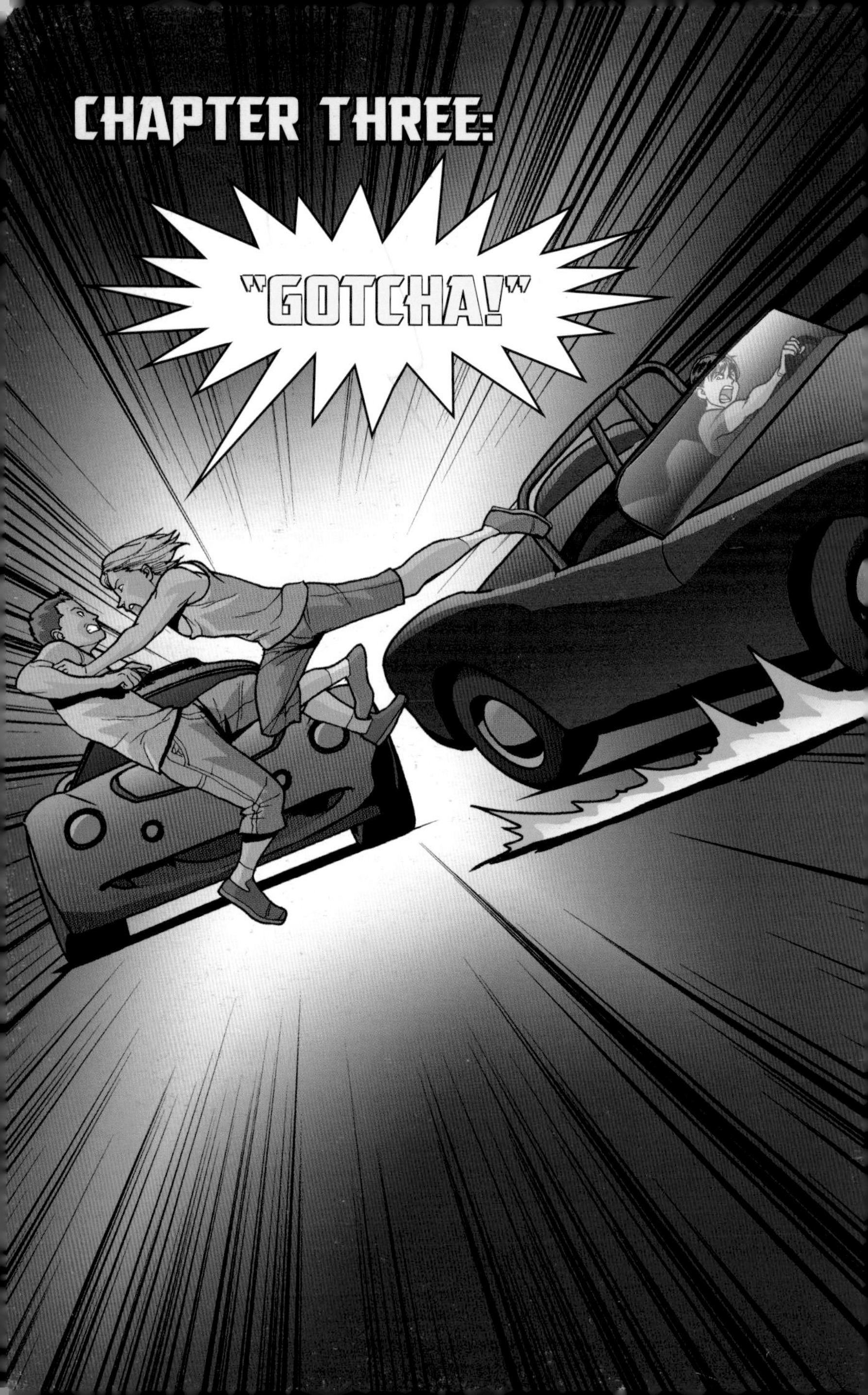
CHAPTER THREE:
"GOTCHA!"

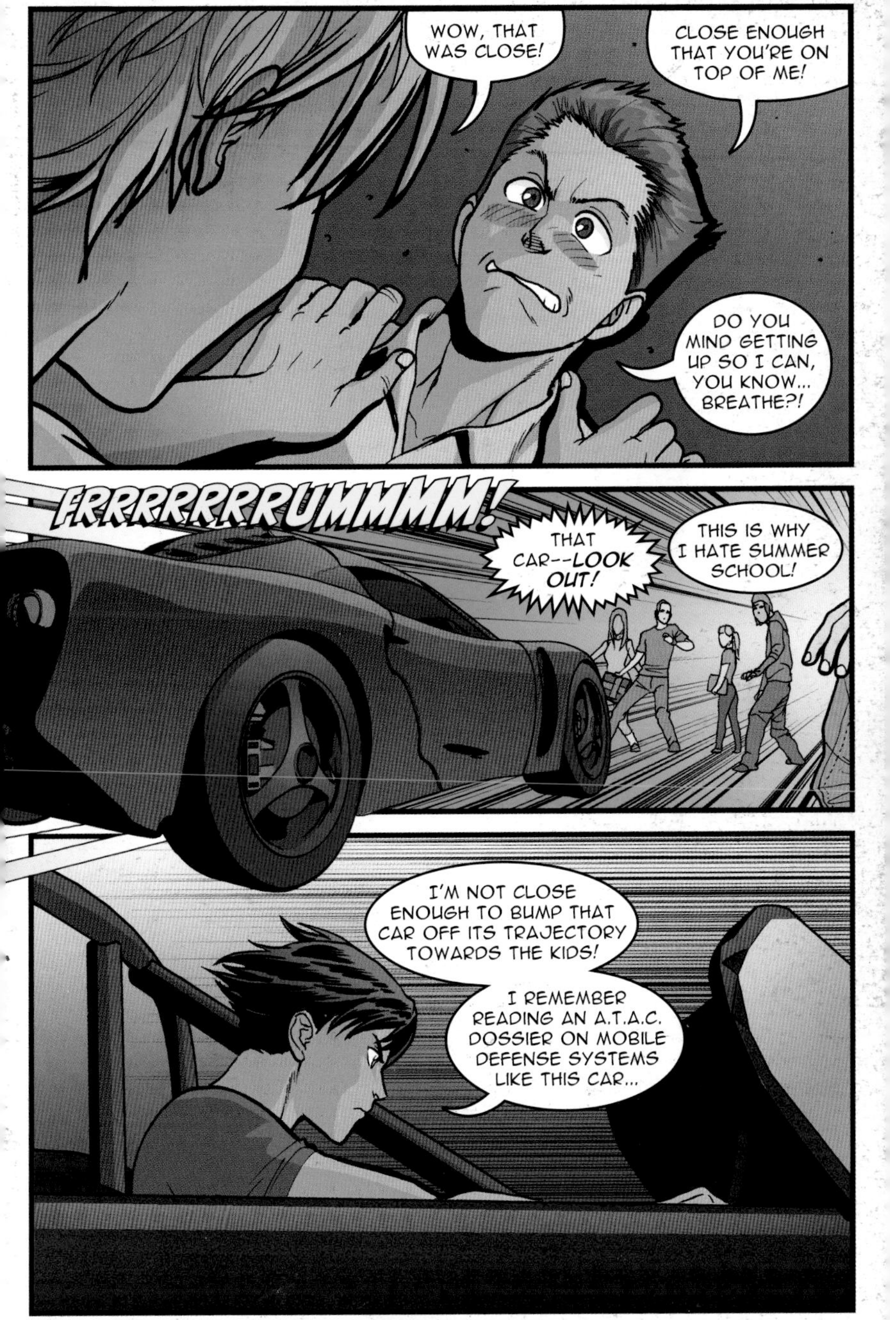
WOW, THAT WAS CLOSE!
CLOSE ENOUGH THAT YOU'RE ON TOP OF ME!
DO YOU MIND GETTING UP SO I CAN, YOU KNOW... BREATHE?!
FRRRRRRRUMMMMM!
THAT CAR--LOOK OUT!
THIS IS WHY I HATE SUMMER SCHOOL!
I'M NOT CLOSE ENOUGH TO BUMP THAT CAR OFF ITS TRAJECTORY TOWARDS THE KIDS!
I REMEMBER READING AN A.T.A.C. DOSSIER ON MOBILE DEFENSE SYSTEMS LIKE THIS CAR...

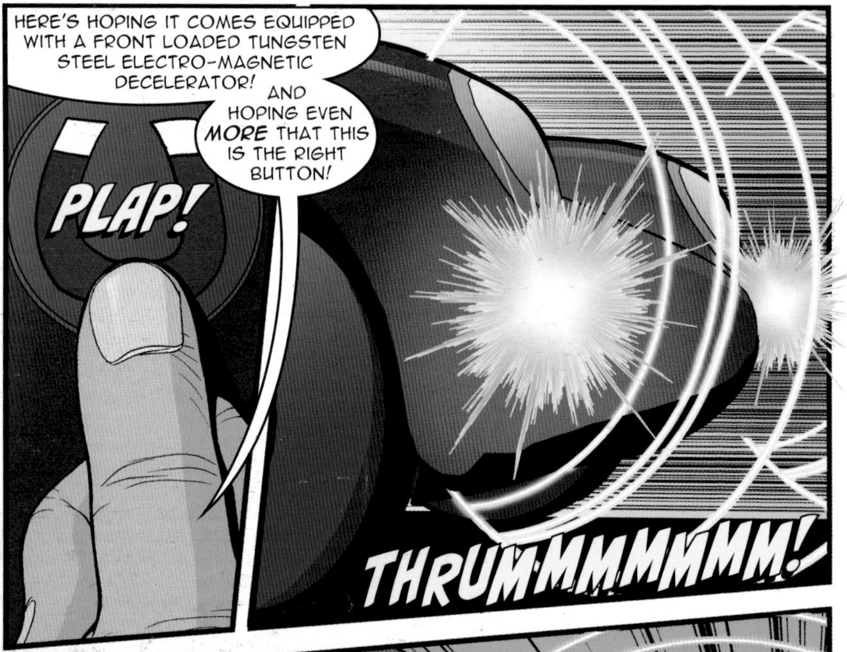
HERE'S HOPING IT COMES EQUIPPED WITH A FRONT LOADED TUNGSTEN STEEL ELECTRO-MAGNETIC DECELERATOR!
AND HOPING EVEN MORE THAT THIS IS THE RIGHT BUTTON!
PLAP!
THRUMMMMMMMM!
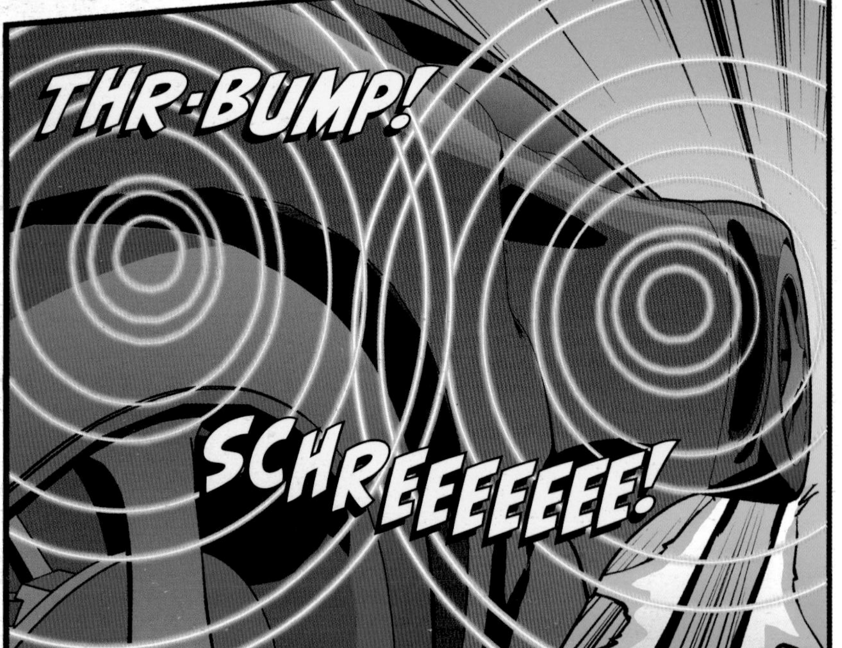
THR-BUMP!
SCHREEEEEEEE!

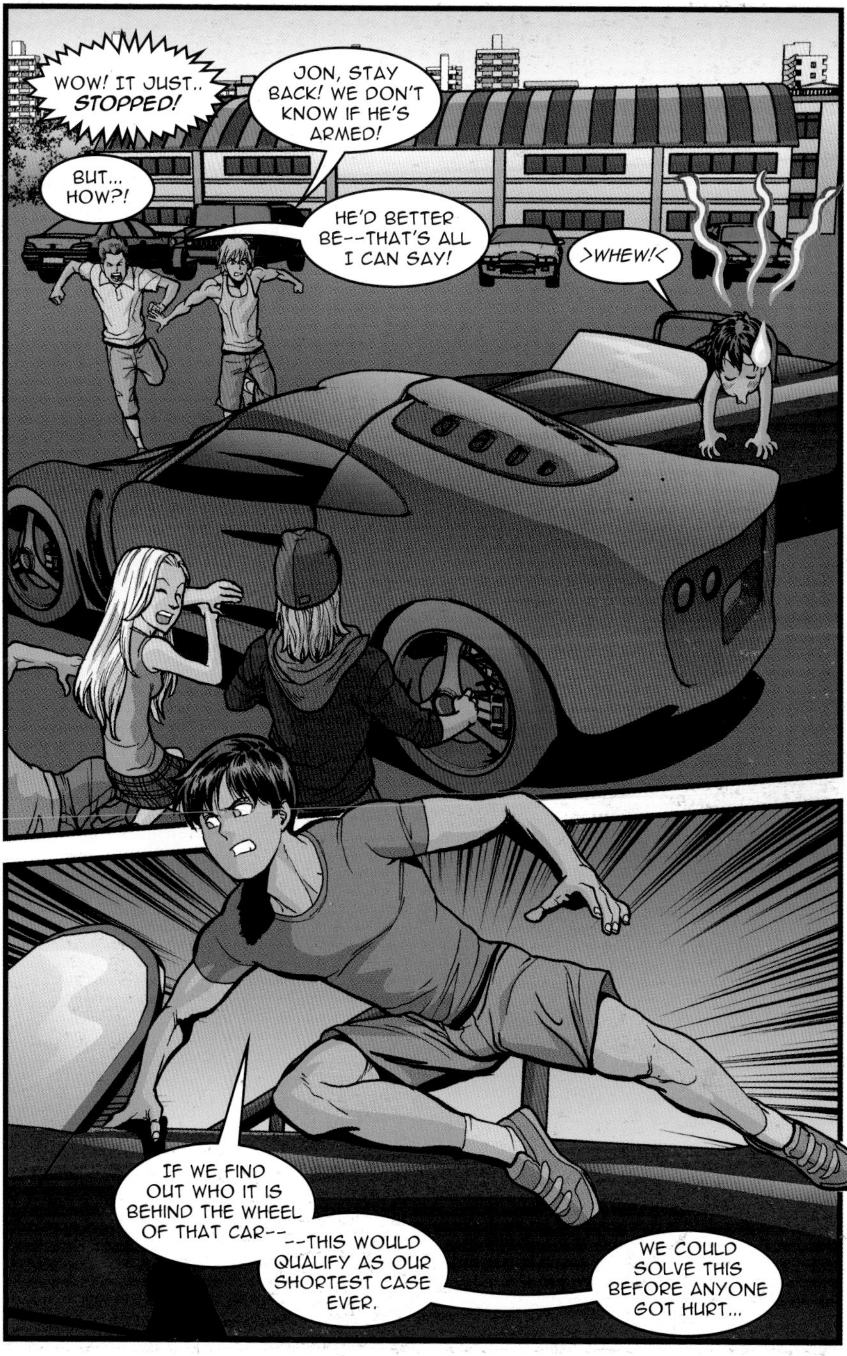

WOW! IT JUST.. STOPPED!
JON, STAY BACK! WE DON'T KNOW IF HE'S ARMED!
BUT... HOW?!
HE'D BETTER BE--THAT'S ALL I CAN SAY!
>WHEW!<
IF WE FIND OUT WHO IT IS BEHIND THE WHEEL OF THAT CAR--
--THIS WOULD QUALIFY AS OUR SHORTEST CASE EVER.
WE COULD SOLVE THIS BEFORE ANYONE GOT HURT...

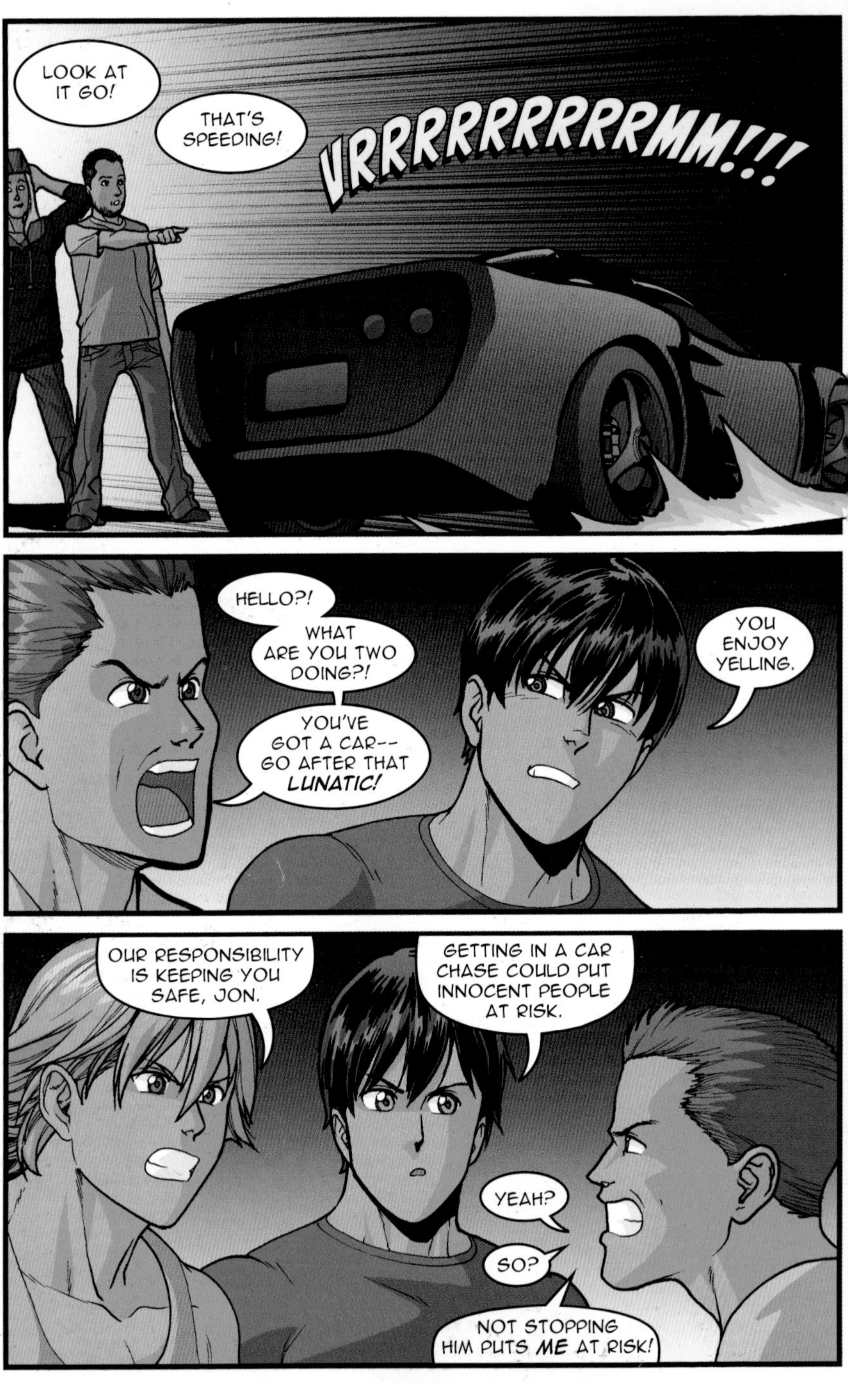
LOOK AT IT GO!
THAT'S SPEEDING!
VRRRRRRRRRMM!!!
HELLO?!
WHAT ARE YOU TWO DOING?!
YOU'VE GOT A CAR-- GO AFTER THAT LUNATIC!
YOU ENJOY YELLING.
OUR RESPONSIBILITY IS KEEPING YOU SAFE, JON.
GETTING IN A CAR CHASE COULD PUT INNOCENT PEOPLE AT RISK.
YEAH?
SO?
NOT STOPPING HIM PUTS ME AT RISK!

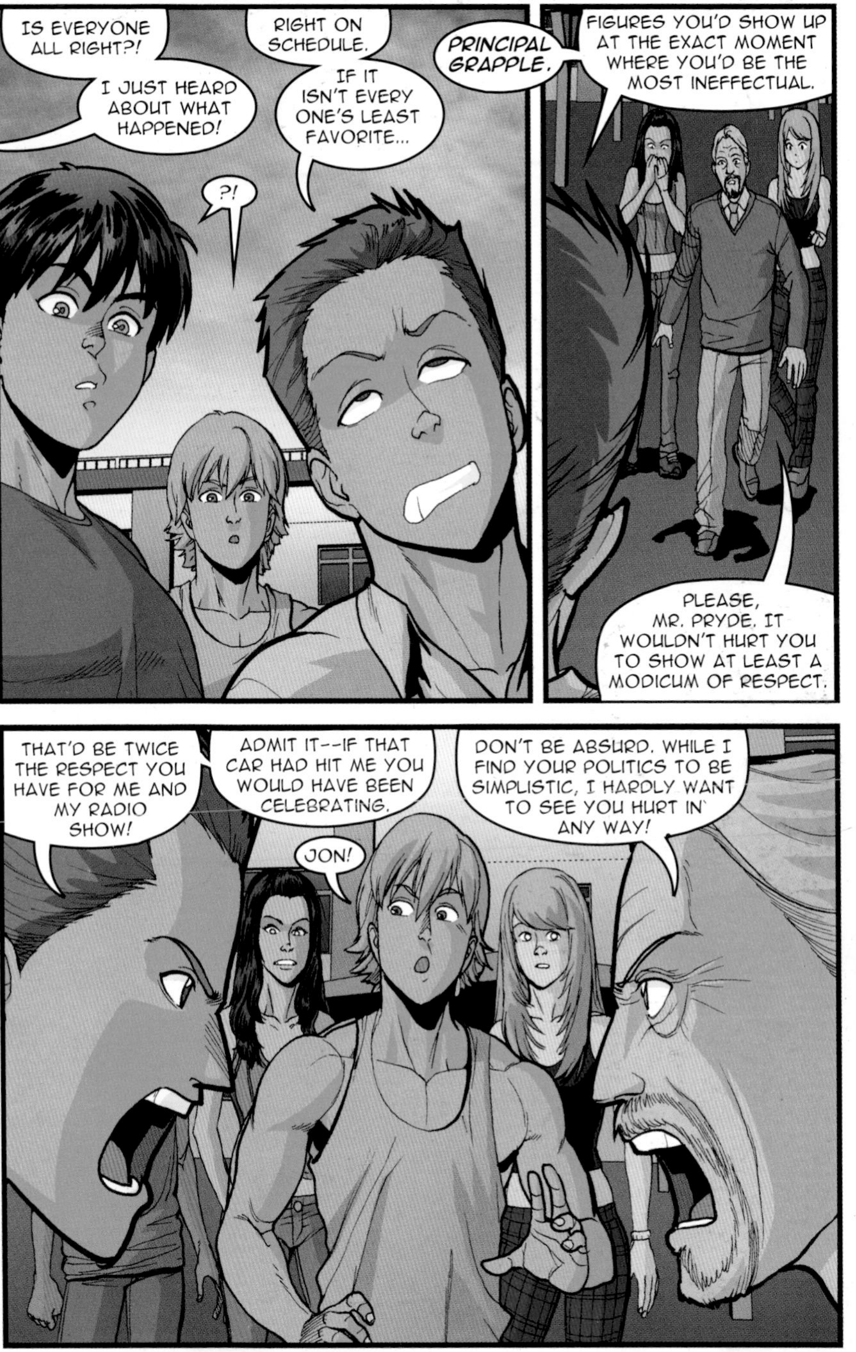
IS EVERYONE ALL RIGHT?!
I JUST HEARD ABOUT WHAT HAPPENED!
RIGHT ON SCHEDULE.
IF IT ISN'T EVERY ONE'S LEAST FAVORITE...
?!
PRINCIPAL GRAPPLE.
FIGURES YOU'D SHOW UP AT THE EXACT MOMENT WHERE YOU'D BE THE MOST INEFFECTUAL.
PLEASE, MR. PRYDE. IT WOULDN'T HURT YOU TO SHOW AT LEAST A MODICUM OF RESPECT.
THAT'D BE TWICE THE RESPECT YOU HAVE FOR ME AND MY RADIO SHOW!
ADMIT IT--IF THAT CAR HAD HIT ME YOU WOULD HAVE BEEN CELEBRATING.
JON!
DON'T BE ABSURD. WHILE I FIND YOUR POLITICS TO BE SIMPLISTIC, I HARDLY WANT TO SEE YOU HURT IN ANY WAY!

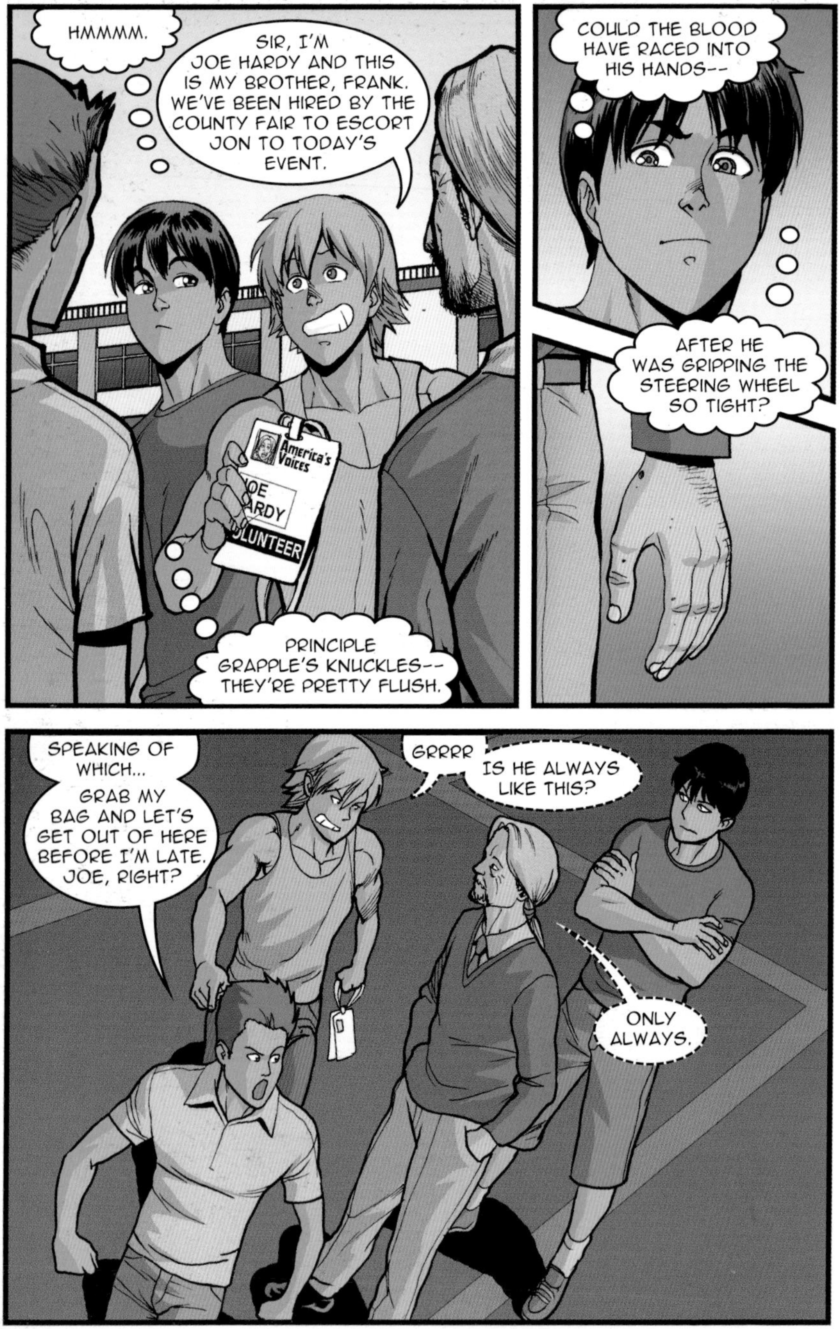
HMMMM.
SIR, I'M JOE HARDY AND THIS IS MY BROTHER, FRANK. WE'VE BEEN HIRED BY THE COUNTY FAIR TO ESCORT JON TO TODAY'S EVENT.
America's Voices
JOE HARDY
VOLUNTEER
PRINCIPLE GRAPPLE'S KNUCKLES-- THEY'RE PRETTY FLUSH.
COULD THE BLOOD HAVE RACED INTO HIS HANDS--
AFTER HE WAS GRIPPING THE STEERING WHEEL SO TIGHT?
SPEAKING OF WHICH...
GRAB MY BAG AND LET'S GET OUT OF HERE BEFORE I'M LATE. JOE, RIGHT?
GRRRR
IS HE ALWAYS LIKE THIS?
ONLY ALWAYS.

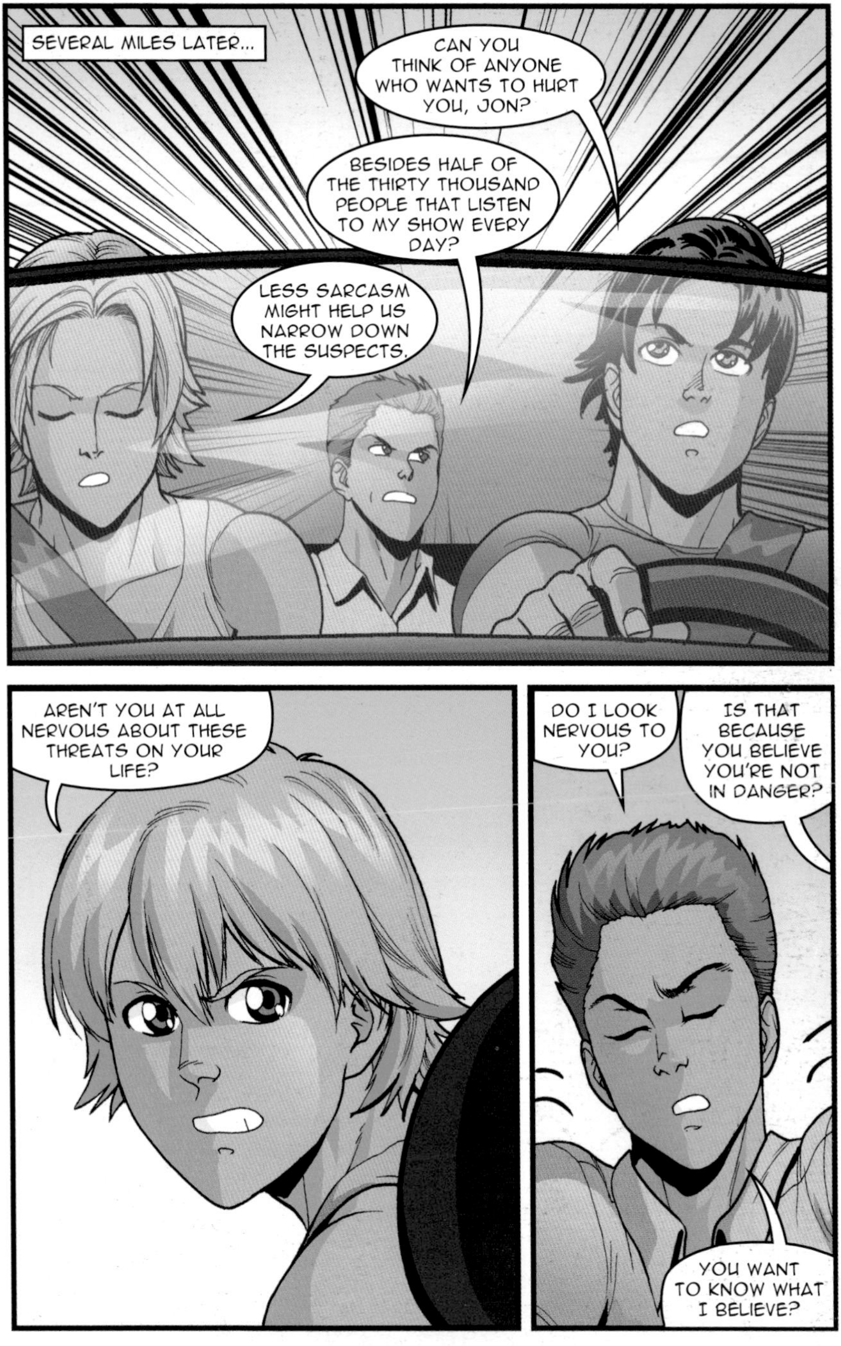
SEVERAL MILES LATER...
CAN YOU THINK OF ANYONE WHO WANTS TO HURT YOU, JON?
BESIDES HALF OF THE THIRTY THOUSAND PEOPLE THAT LISTEN TO MY SHOW EVERY DAY?
LESS SARCASM MIGHT HELP US NARROW DOWN THE SUSPECTS.
AREN'T YOU AT ALL NERVOUS ABOUT THESE THREATS ON YOUR LIFE?
DO I LOOK NERVOUS TO YOU?
IS THAT BECAUSE YOU BELIEVE YOU'RE NOT IN DANGER?
YOU WANT TO KNOW WHAT I BELIEVE?

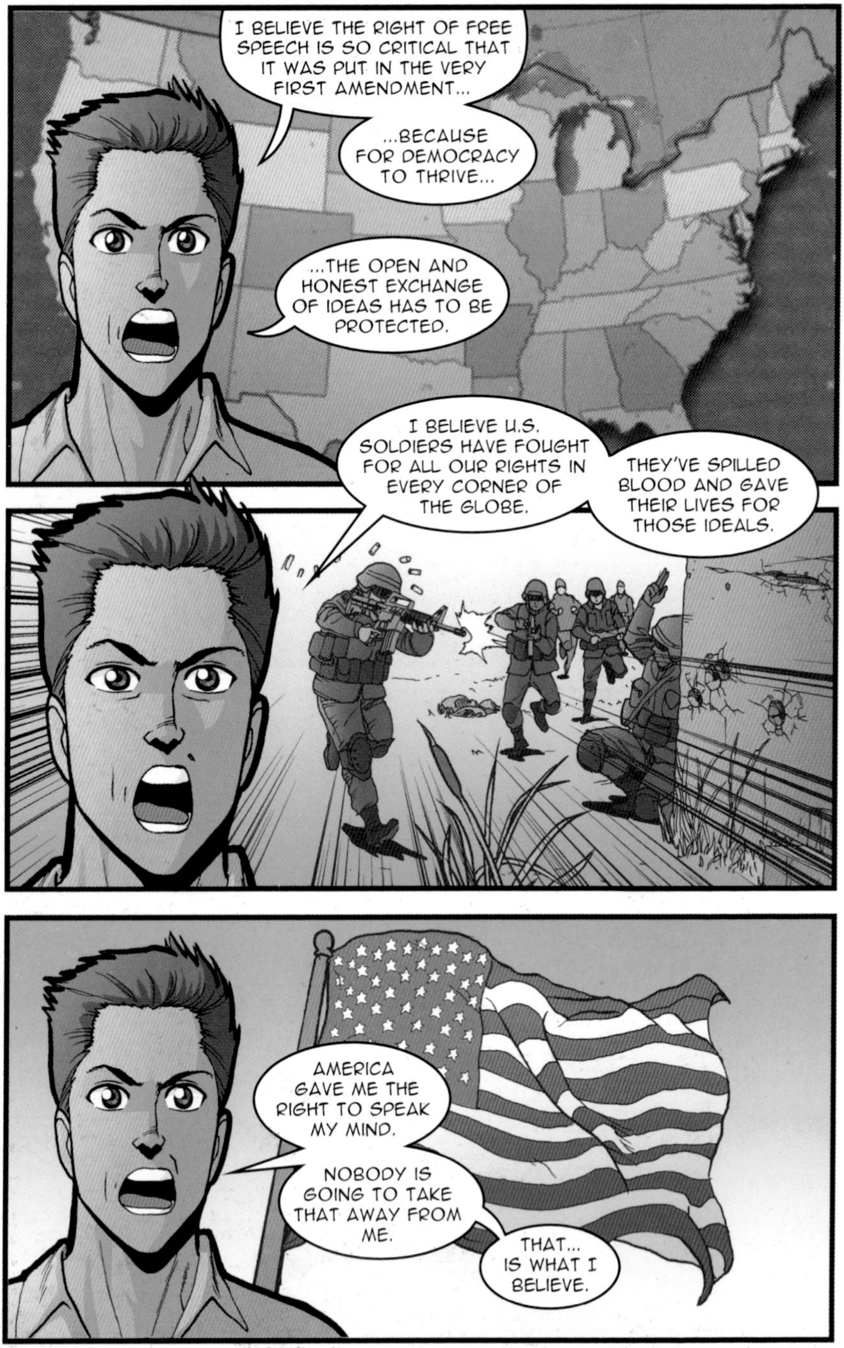
I BELIEVE THE RIGHT OF FREE SPEECH IS SO CRITICAL THAT IT WAS PUT IN THE VERY FIRST AMENDMENT...
...BECAUSE FOR DEMOCRACY TO THRIVE...
...THE OPEN AND HONEST EXCHANGE OF IDEAS HAS TO BE PROTECTED.
I BELIEVE U.S. SOLDIERS HAVE FOUGHT FOR ALL OUR RIGHTS IN EVERY CORNER OF THE GLOBE.
THEY'VE SPILLED BLOOD AND GAVE THEIR LIVES FOR THOSE IDEALS.
AMERICA GAVE ME THE RIGHT TO SPEAK MY MIND.
NOBODY IS GOING TO TAKE THAT AWAY FROM ME.
THAT... IS WHAT I BELIEVE.

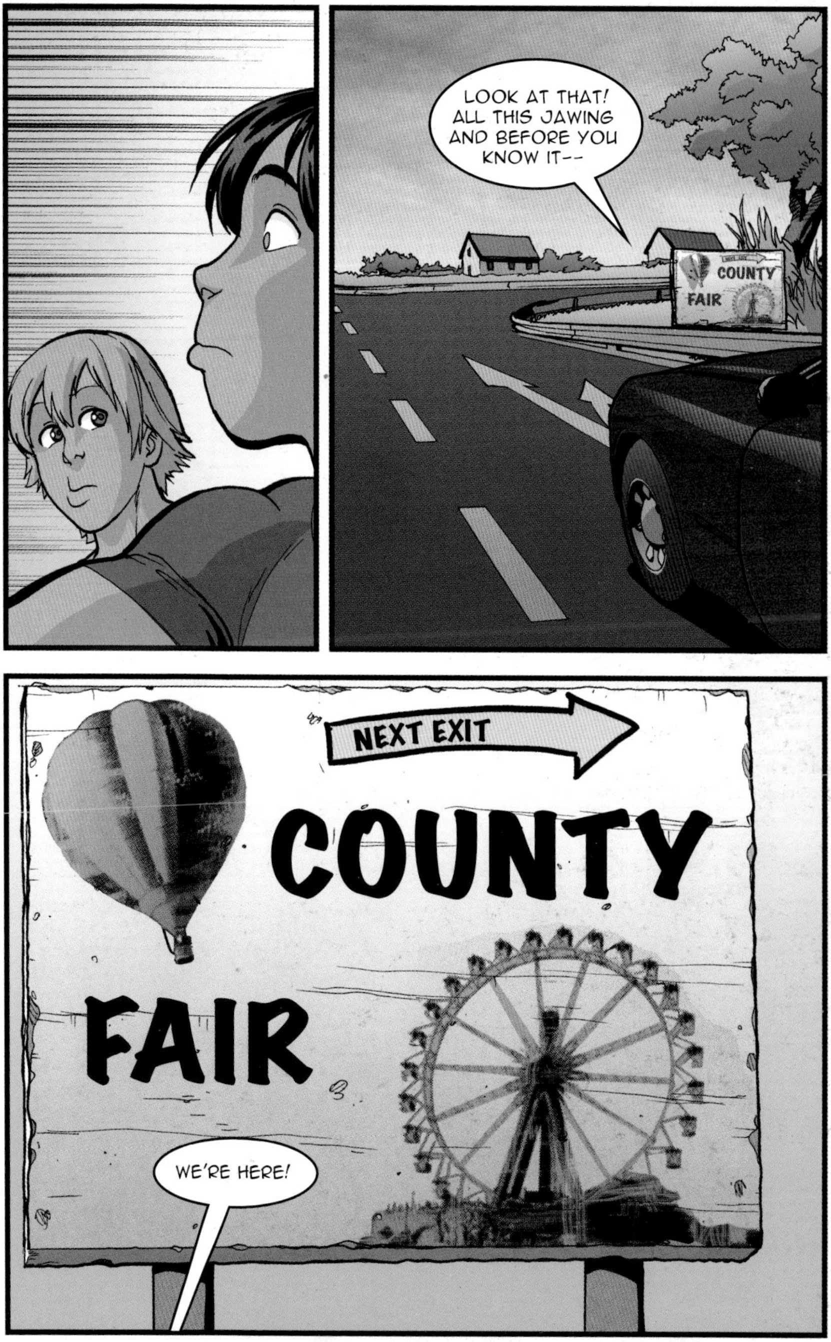
LOOK AT THAT! ALL THIS JAWING AND BEFORE YOU KNOW IT--
NEXT EXIT
COUNTY
FAIR
WE'RE HERE!

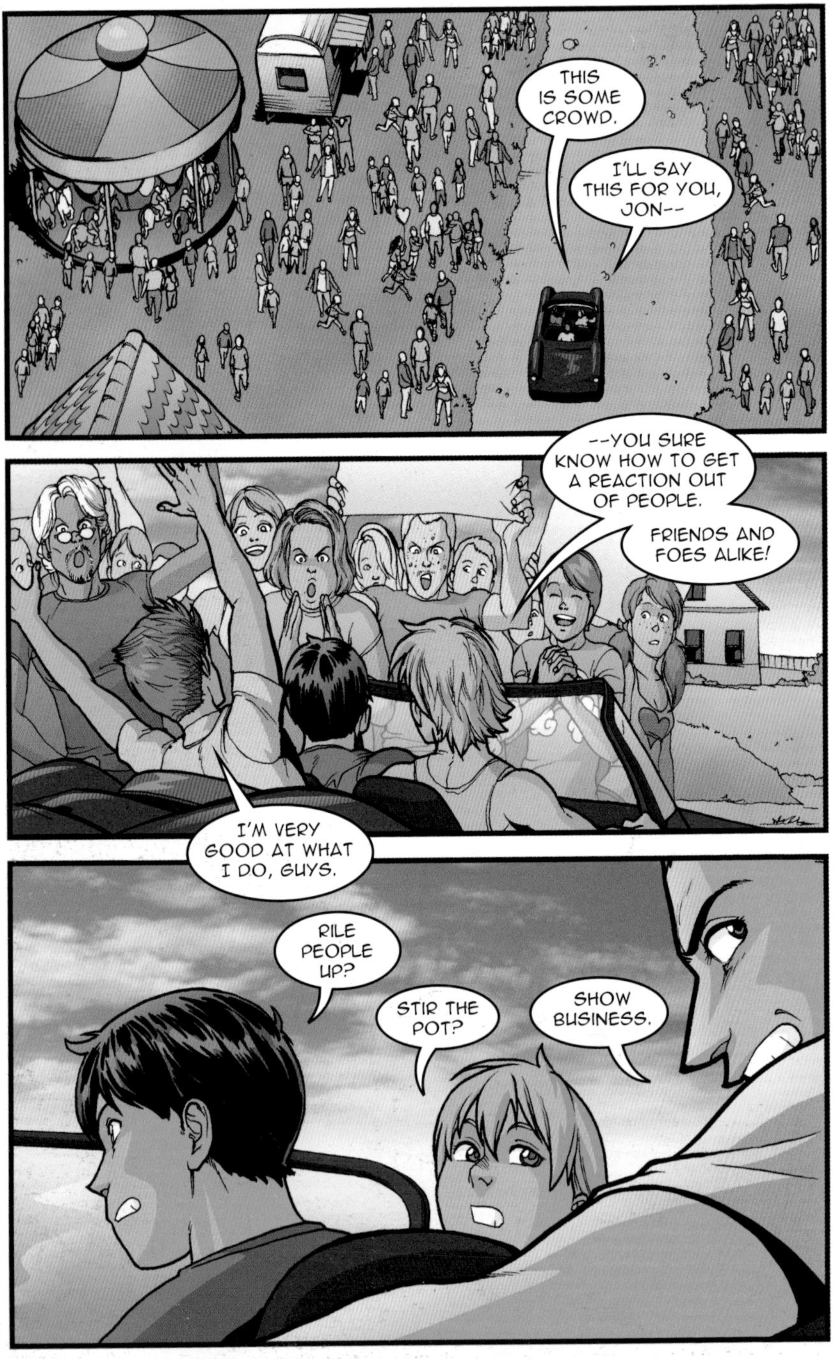
THIS IS SOME CROWD.
I'LL SAY THIS FOR YOU, JON--
--YOU SURE KNOW HOW TO GET A REACTION OUT OF PEOPLE.
FRIENDS AND FOES ALIKE!
I'M VERY GOOD AT WHAT I DO, GUYS.
RILE PEOPLE UP?
STIR THE POT?
SHOW BUSINESS.

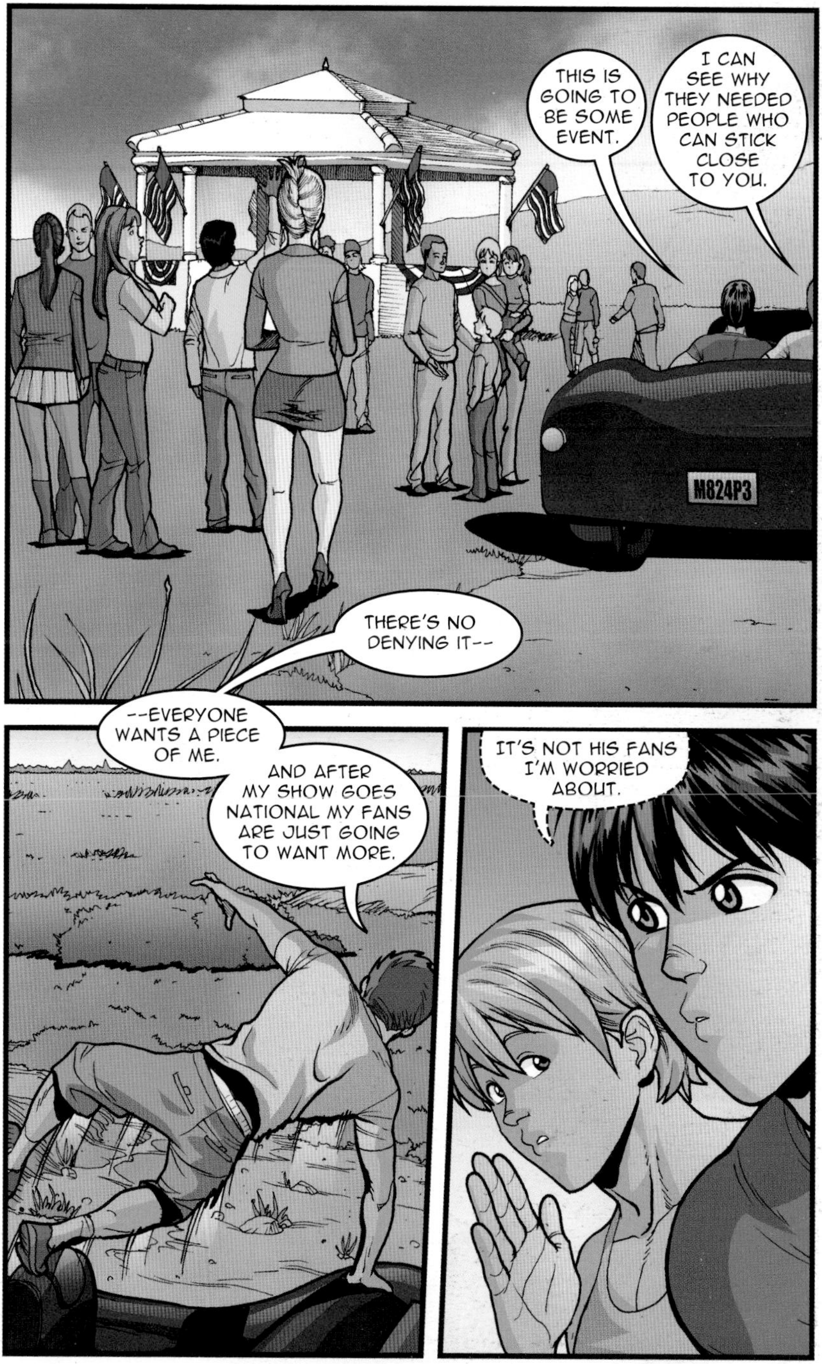

THIS IS GOING TO BE SOME EVENT.
I CAN SEE WHY THEY NEEDED PEOPLE WHO CAN STICK CLOSE TO YOU.
M824P3
THERE'S NO DENYING IT--
--EVERYONE WANTS A PIECE OF ME.
AND AFTER MY SHOW GOES NATIONAL MY FANS ARE JUST GOING TO WANT MORE.
IT'S NOT HIS FANS I'M WORRIED ABOUT.

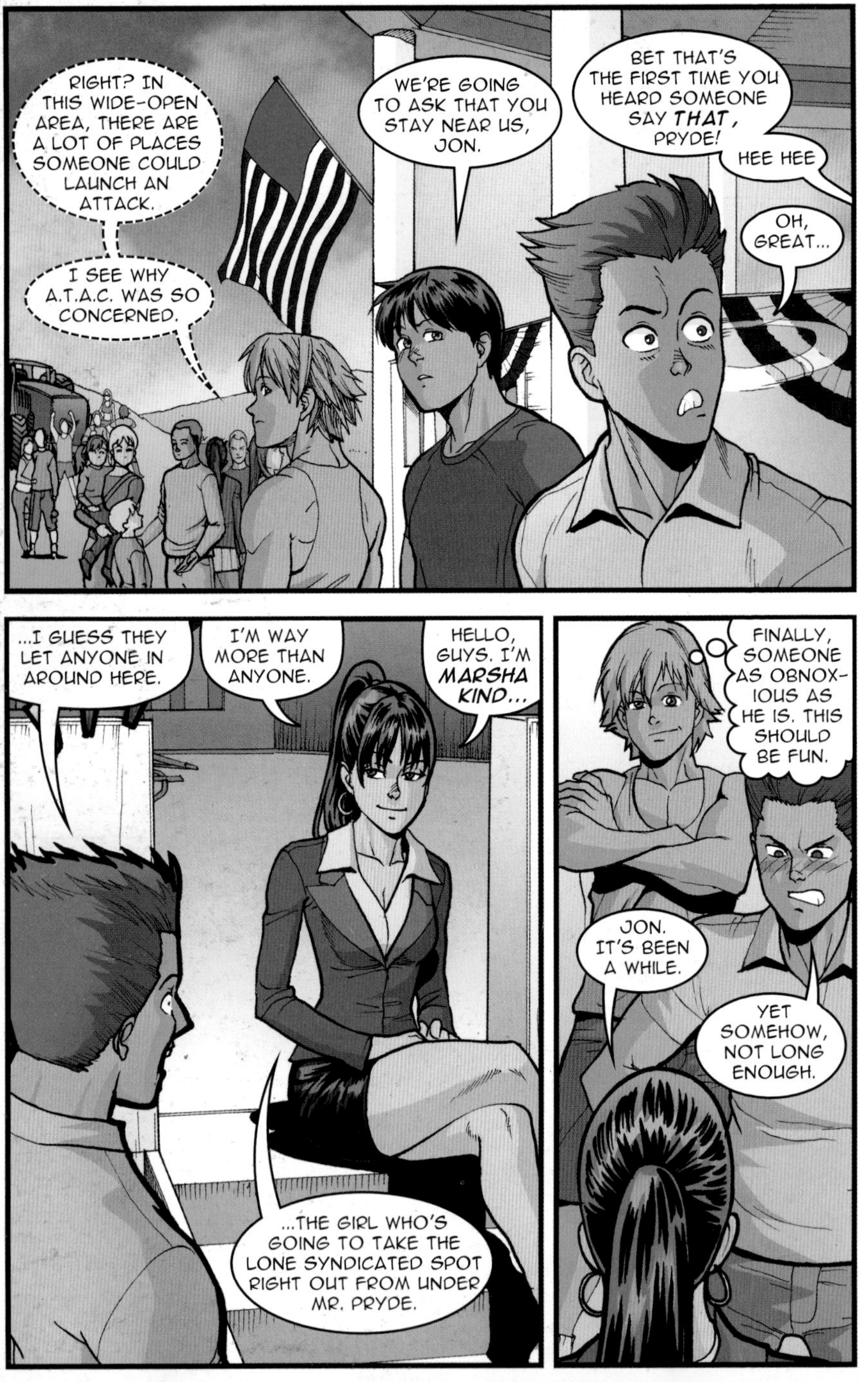
RIGHT? IN THIS WIDE-OPEN AREA, THERE ARE A LOT OF PLACES SOMEONE COULD LAUNCH AN ATTACK.
I SEE WHY A.T.A.C. WAS SO CONCERNED.
WE'RE GOING TO ASK THAT YOU STAY NEAR US, JON.
BET THAT'S THE FIRST TIME YOU HEARD SOMEONE SAY *THAT*, PRYDE!
HEE HEE
OH, GREAT...
...I GUESS THEY LET ANYONE IN AROUND HERE.
I'M WAY MORE THAN ANYONE.
HELLO, GUYS. I'M *MARSHA KIND*...
...THE GIRL WHO'S GOING TO TAKE THE LONE SYNDICATED SPOT RIGHT OUT FROM UNDER MR. PRYDE.
FINALLY, SOMEONE AS OBNOXIOUS AS HE IS. THIS SHOULD BE FUN.
JON. IT'S BEEN A WHILE.
YET SOMEHOW, NOT LONG ENOUGH.

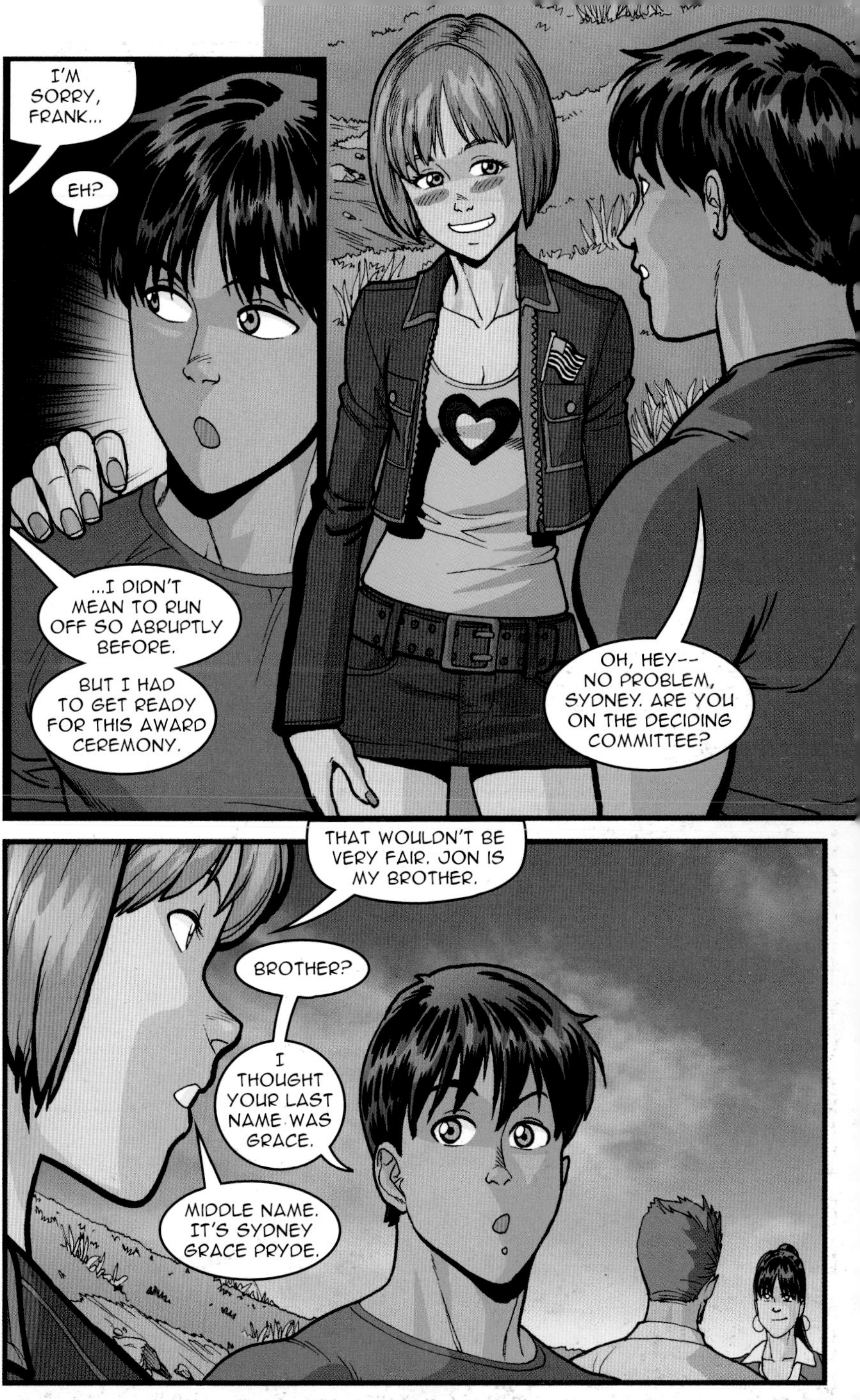
I'M SORRY, FRANK...
EH?
...I DIDN'T MEAN TO RUN OFF SO ABRUPTLY BEFORE.
BUT I HAD TO GET READY FOR THIS AWARD CEREMONY.
OH, HEY-- NO PROBLEM, SYDNEY. ARE YOU ON THE DECIDING COMMITTEE?
THAT WOULDN'T BE VERY FAIR. JON IS MY BROTHER.
BROTHER?
I THOUGHT YOUR LAST NAME WAS GRACE.
MIDDLE NAME. IT'S SYDNEY GRACE PRYDE.

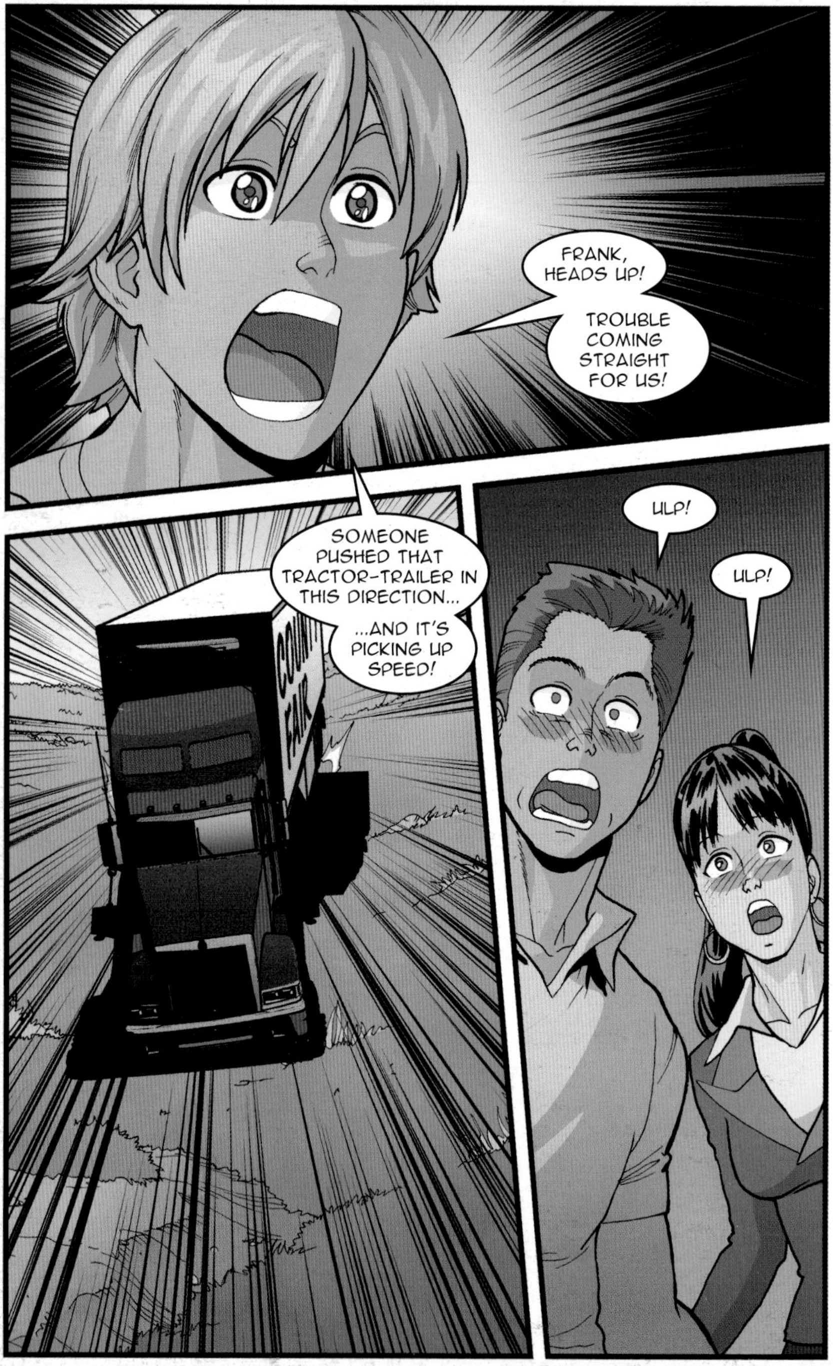
FRANK, HEADS UP!
TROUBLE COMING STRAIGHT FOR US!
SOMEONE PUSHED THAT TRACTOR-TRAILER IN THIS DIRECTION...
...AND IT'S PICKING UP SPEED!
COUNTY FAIR
ULP!
ULP!

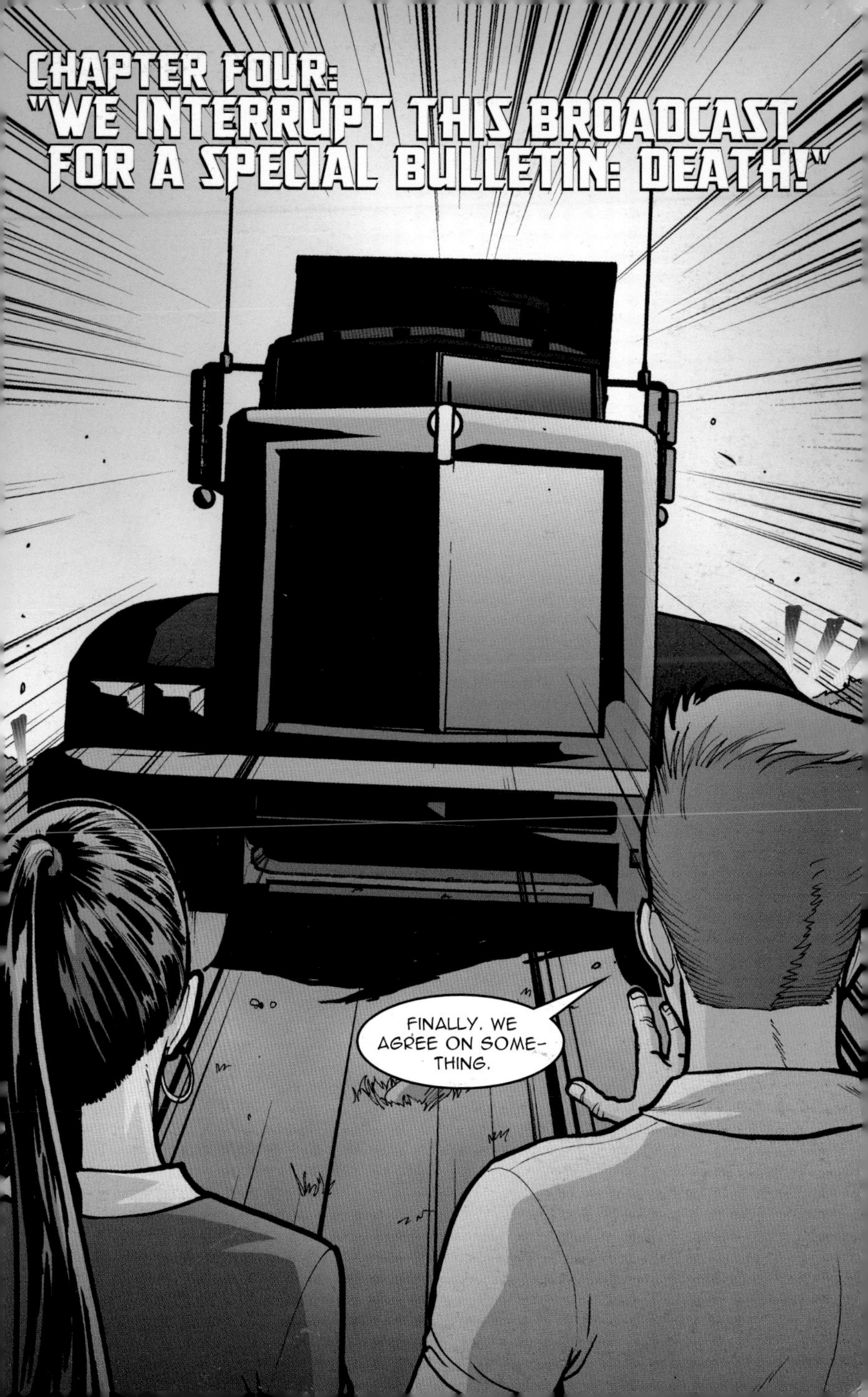
CHAPTER FOUR:
"WE INTERRUPT THIS BROADCAST FOR A SPECIAL BULLETIN: DEATH!"
FINALLY. WE AGREE ON SOME-THING.

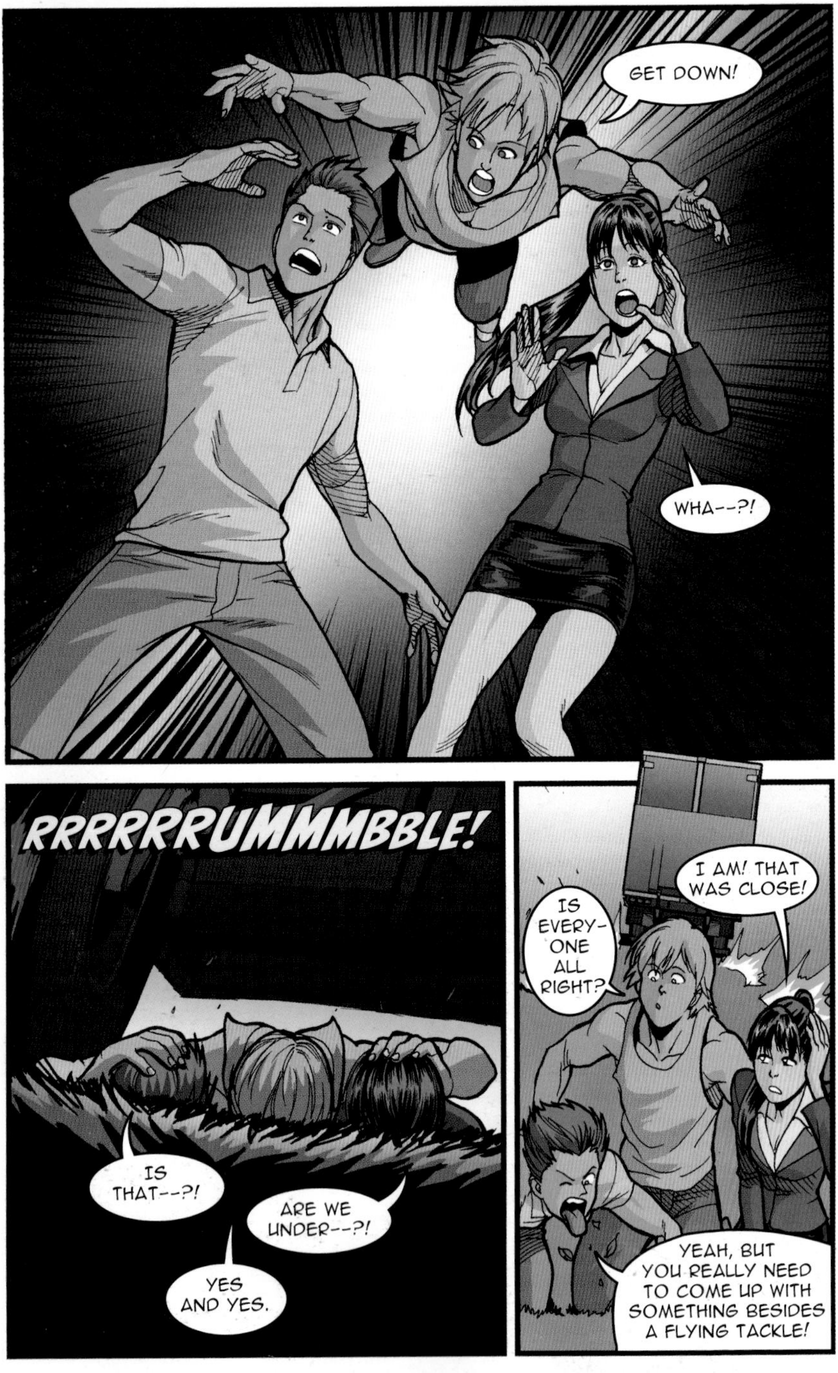
GET DOWN!
WHA--?!
RRRRRRUMMMMBBLE!
IS THAT--?!
ARE WE UNDER--?!
YES AND YES.
IS EVERY-ONE ALL RIGHT?
I AM! THAT WAS CLOSE!
YEAH, BUT YOU REALLY NEED TO COME UP WITH SOMETHING BESIDES A FLYING TACKLE!

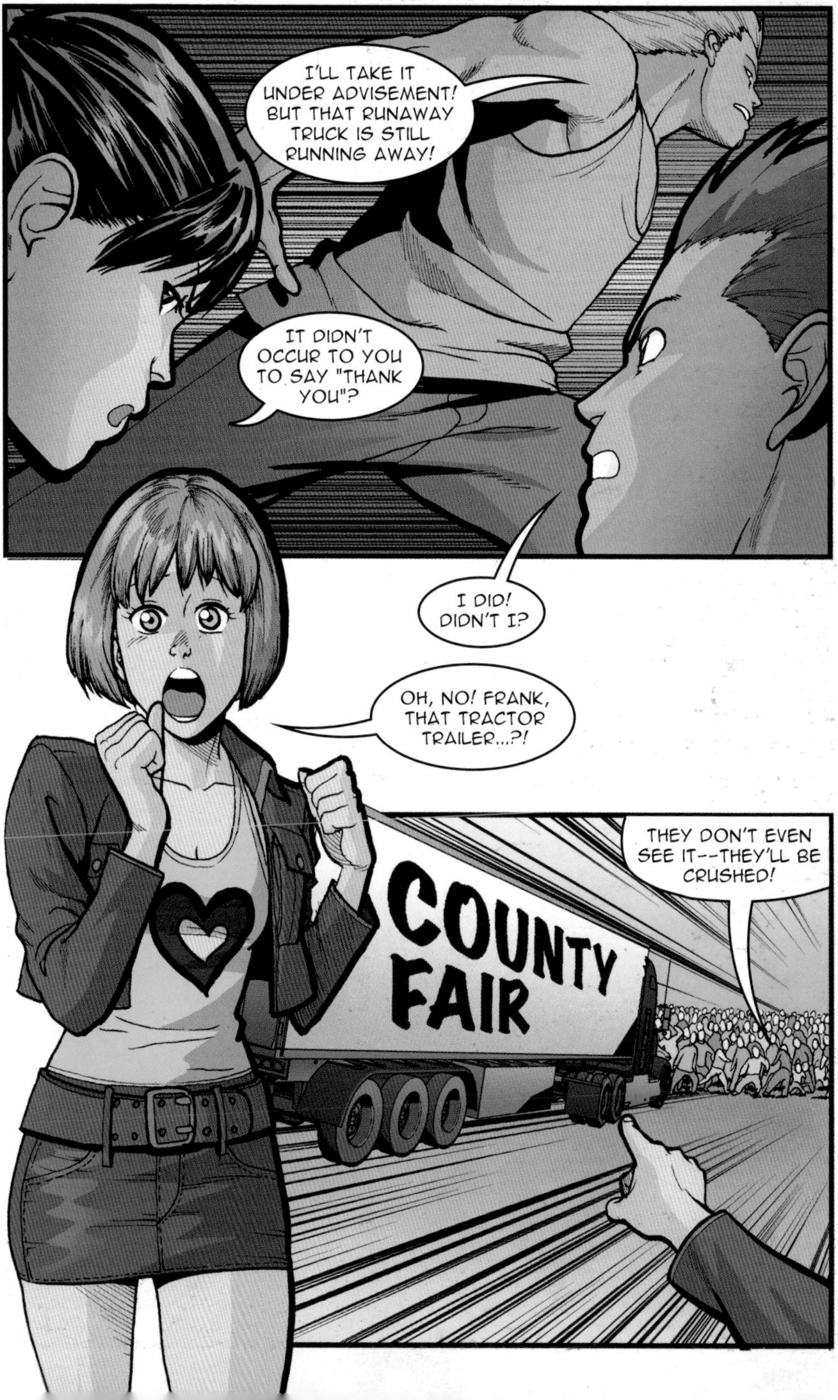
I'LL TAKE IT UNDER ADVISEMENT! BUT THAT RUNAWAY TRUCK IS STILL RUNNING AWAY!
IT DIDN'T OCCUR TO YOU TO SAY "THANK YOU"?
I DID! DIDN'T I?
OH, NO! FRANK, THAT TRACTOR TRAILER...?!
THEY DON'T EVEN SEE IT--THEY'LL BE CRUSHED!
COUNTY FAIR

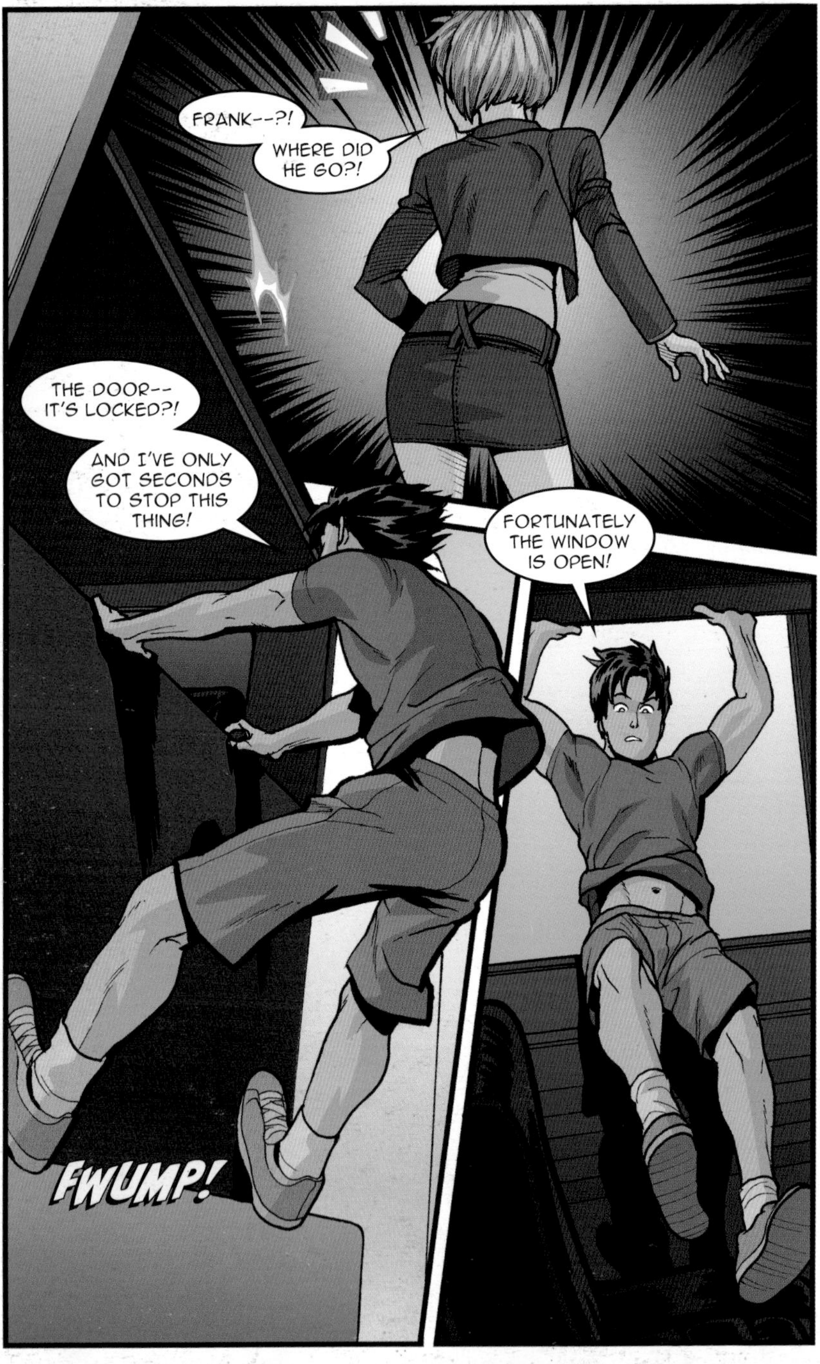
FRANK--?!
WHERE DID HE GO?!
THE DOOR-- IT'S LOCKED?!
AND I'VE ONLY GOT SECONDS TO STOP THIS THING!
FORTUNATELY THE WINDOW IS OPEN!
FWUMP!

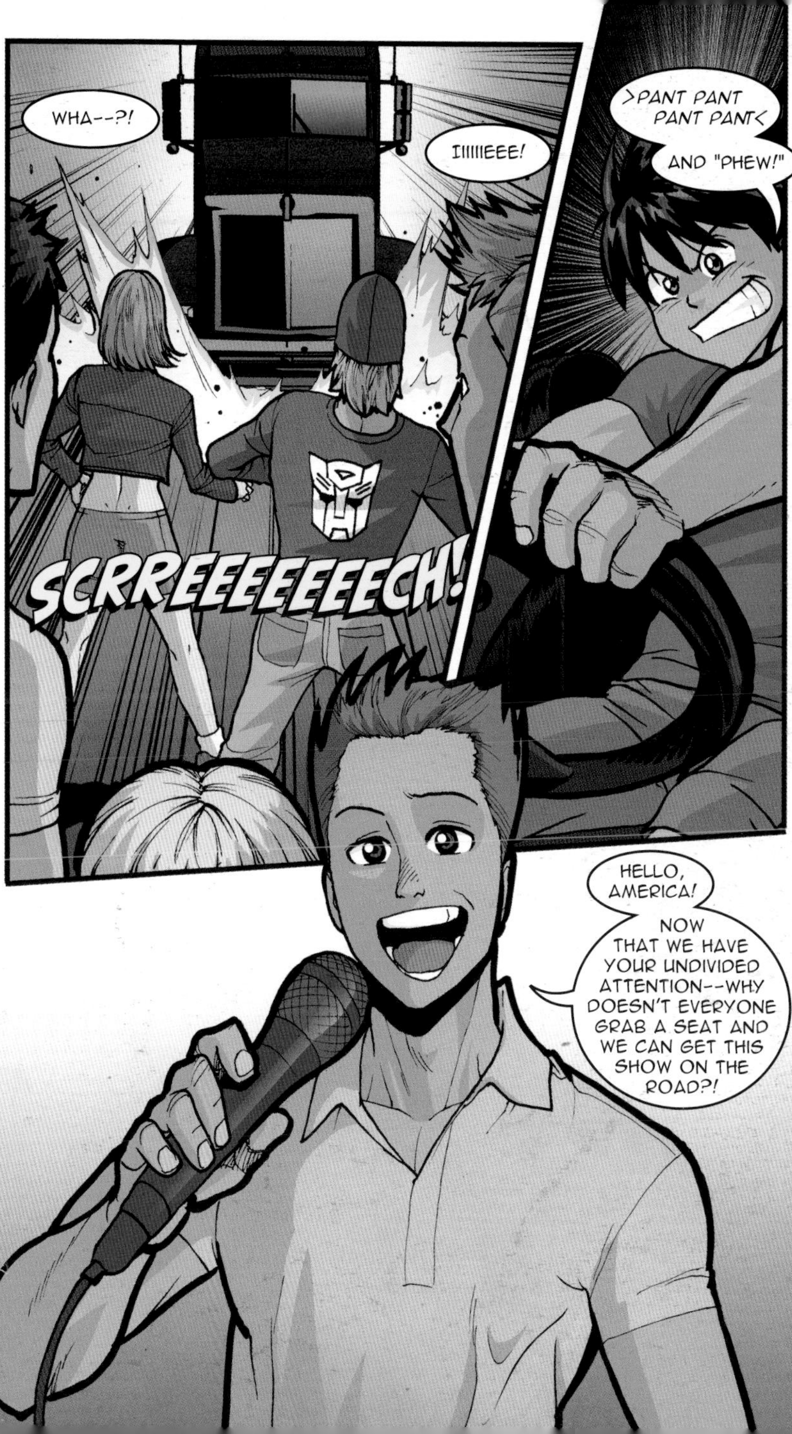

WHA--?!
IIIIIIEEE!
SCRREEEEEEEEECH!
>PANT PANT PANT PANT<
AND "PHEW!"
HELLO, AMERICA!
NOW THAT WE HAVE YOUR UNDIVIDED ATTENTION--WHY DOESN'T EVERYONE GRAB A SEAT AND WE CAN GET THIS SHOW ON THE ROAD?!

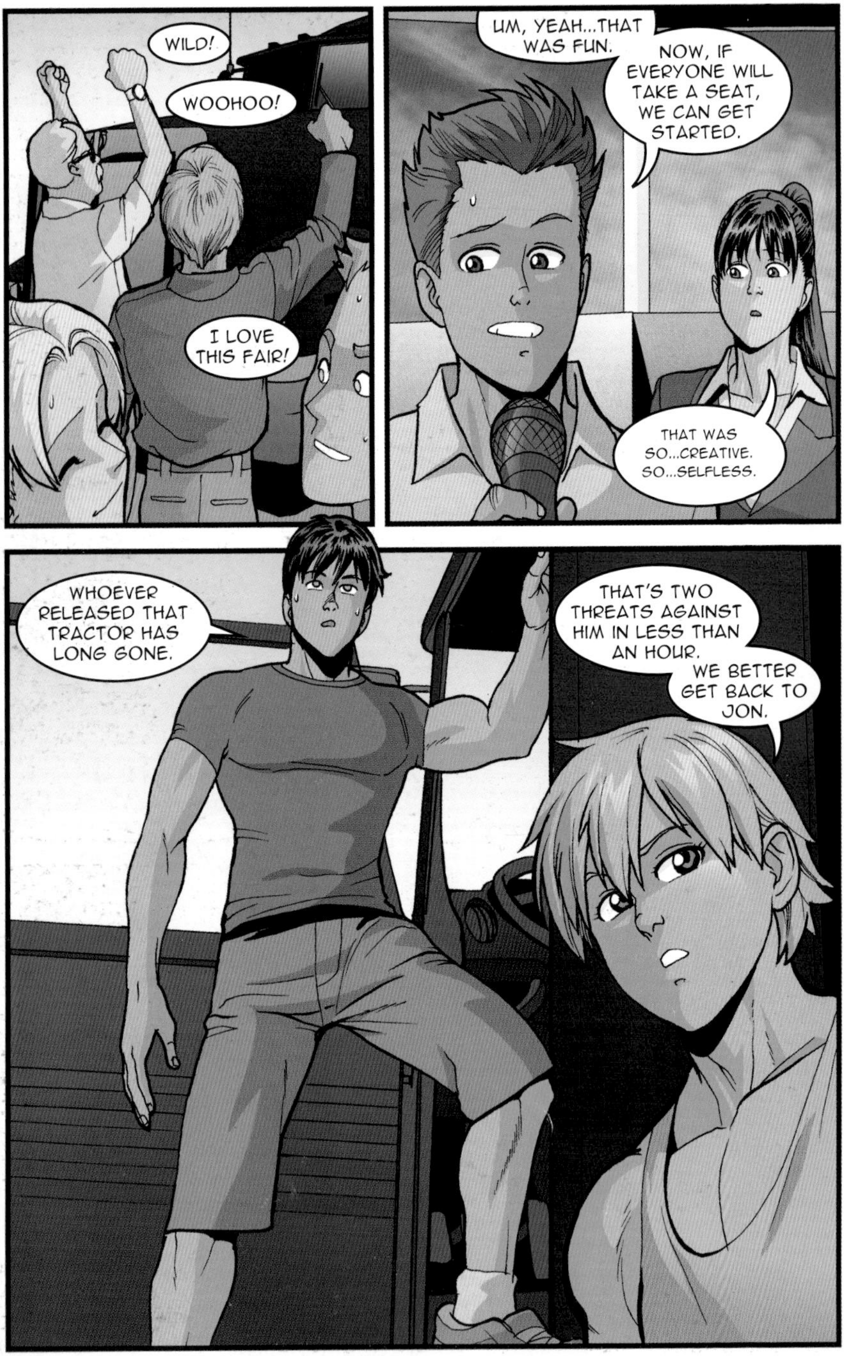
WILD!
WOOHOO!
I LOVE THIS FAIR!
UM, YEAH...THAT WAS FUN.
NOW, IF EVERYONE WILL TAKE A SEAT, WE CAN GET STARTED.
THAT WAS SO...CREATIVE. SO...SELFLESS.
WHOEVER RELEASED THAT TRACTOR HAS LONG GONE.
THAT'S TWO THREATS AGAINST HIM IN LESS THAN AN HOUR.
WE BETTER GET BACK TO JON.

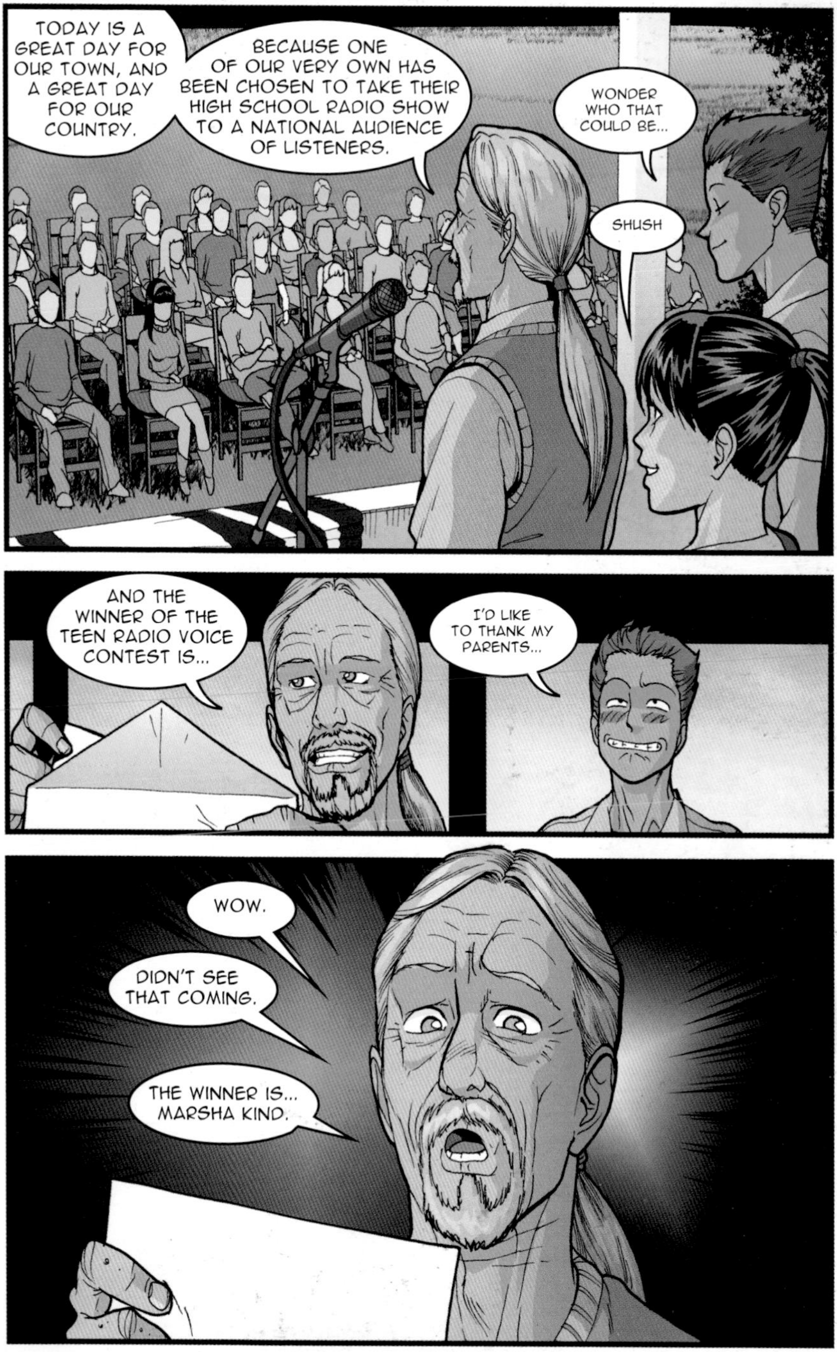
TODAY IS A GREAT DAY FOR OUR TOWN, AND A GREAT DAY FOR OUR COUNTRY.
BECAUSE ONE OF OUR VERY OWN HAS BEEN CHOSEN TO TAKE THEIR HIGH SCHOOL RADIO SHOW TO A NATIONAL AUDIENCE OF LISTENERS.
WONDER WHO THAT COULD BE...
SHUSH
AND THE WINNER OF THE TEEN RADIO VOICE CONTEST IS...
I'D LIKE TO THANK MY PARENTS...
WOW.
DIDN'T SEE THAT COMING.
THE WINNER IS... MARSHA KIND.

CHAPTER FIVE:

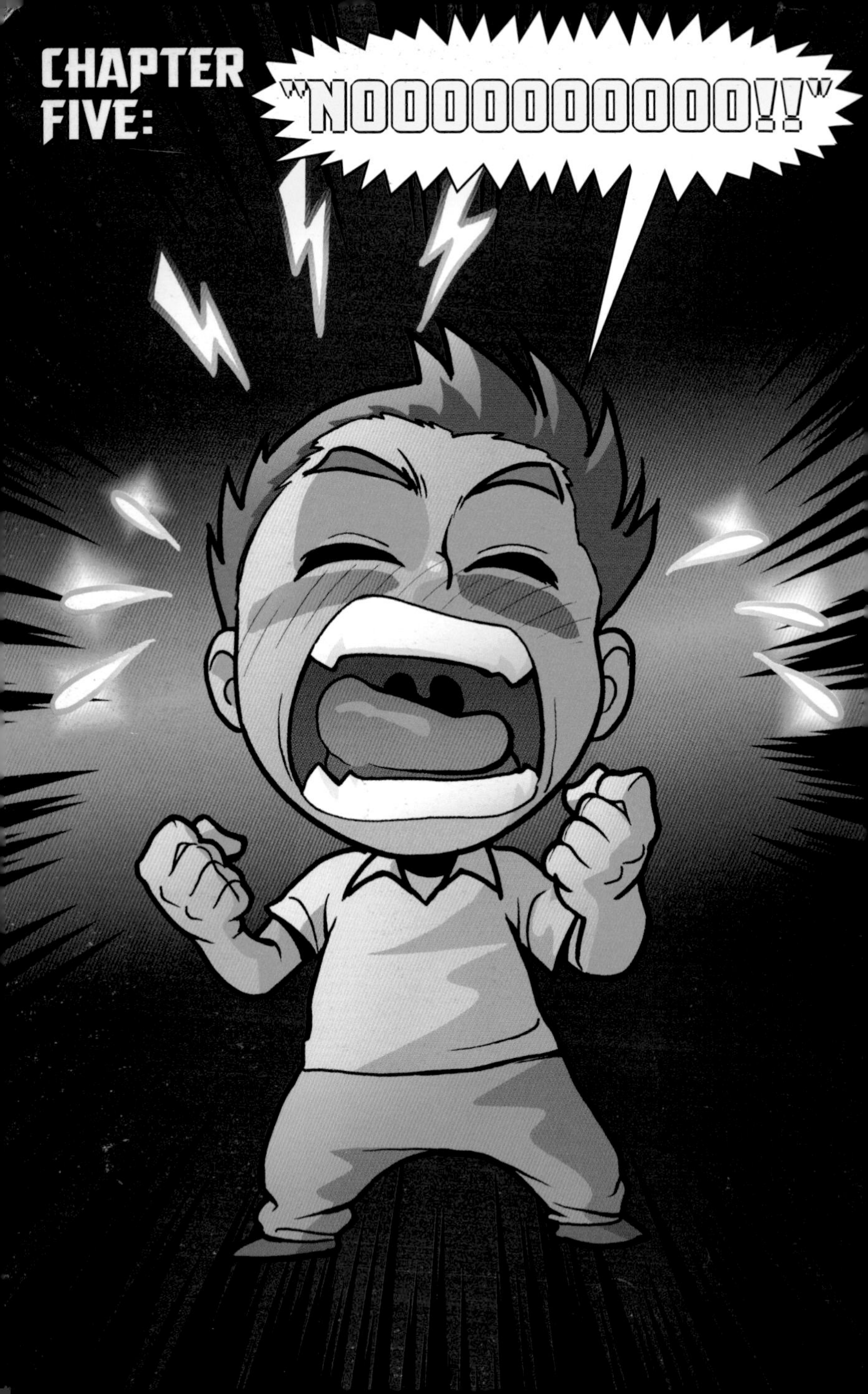
"NOOOOOOOOOO!!"

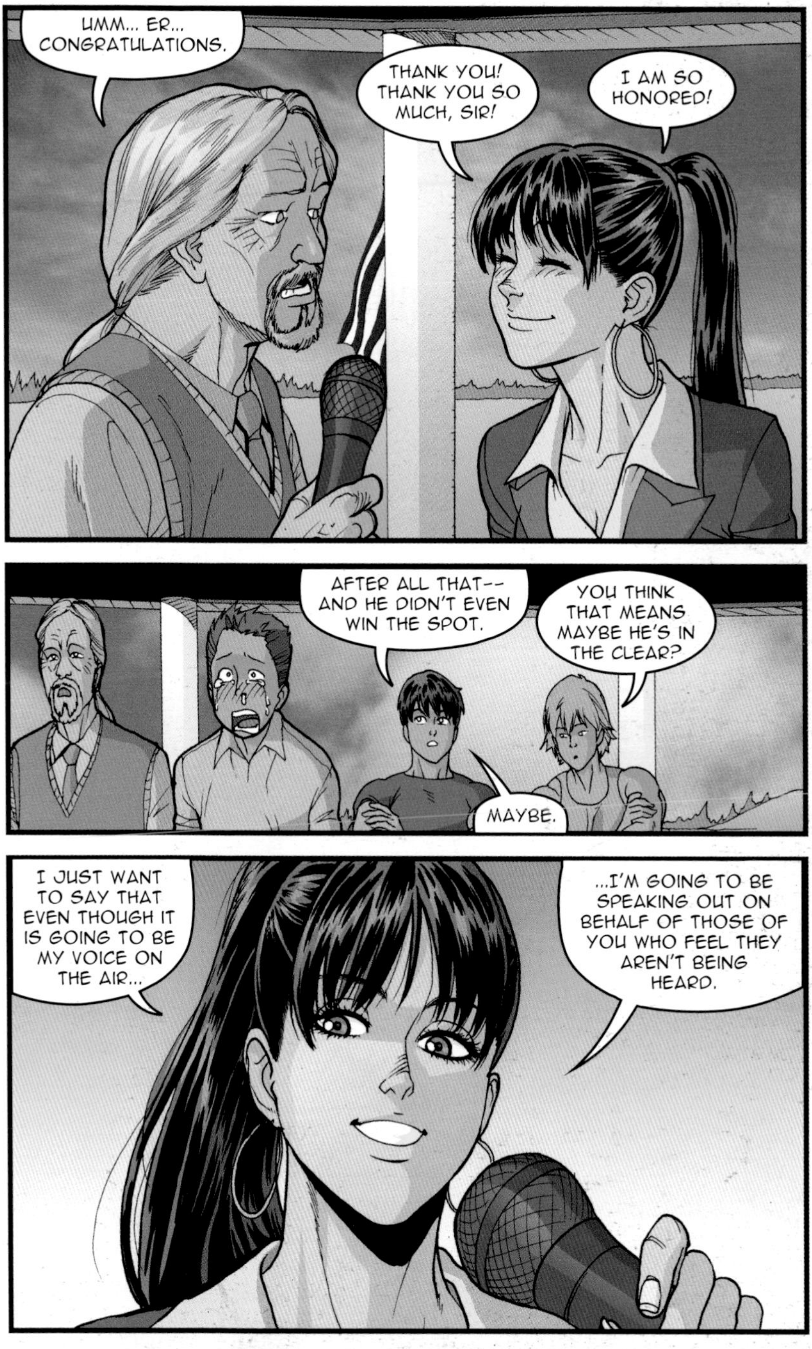
UMM... ER... CONGRATULATIONS.
THANK YOU! THANK YOU SO MUCH, SIR!
I AM SO HONORED!
AFTER ALL THAT-- AND HE DIDN'T EVEN WIN THE SPOT.
YOU THINK THAT MEANS MAYBE HE'S IN THE CLEAR?
MAYBE.
I JUST WANT TO SAY THAT EVEN THOUGH IT IS GOING TO BE MY VOICE ON THE AIR...
...I'M GOING TO BE SPEAKING OUT ON BEHALF OF THOSE OF YOU WHO FEEL THEY AREN'T BEING HEARD.

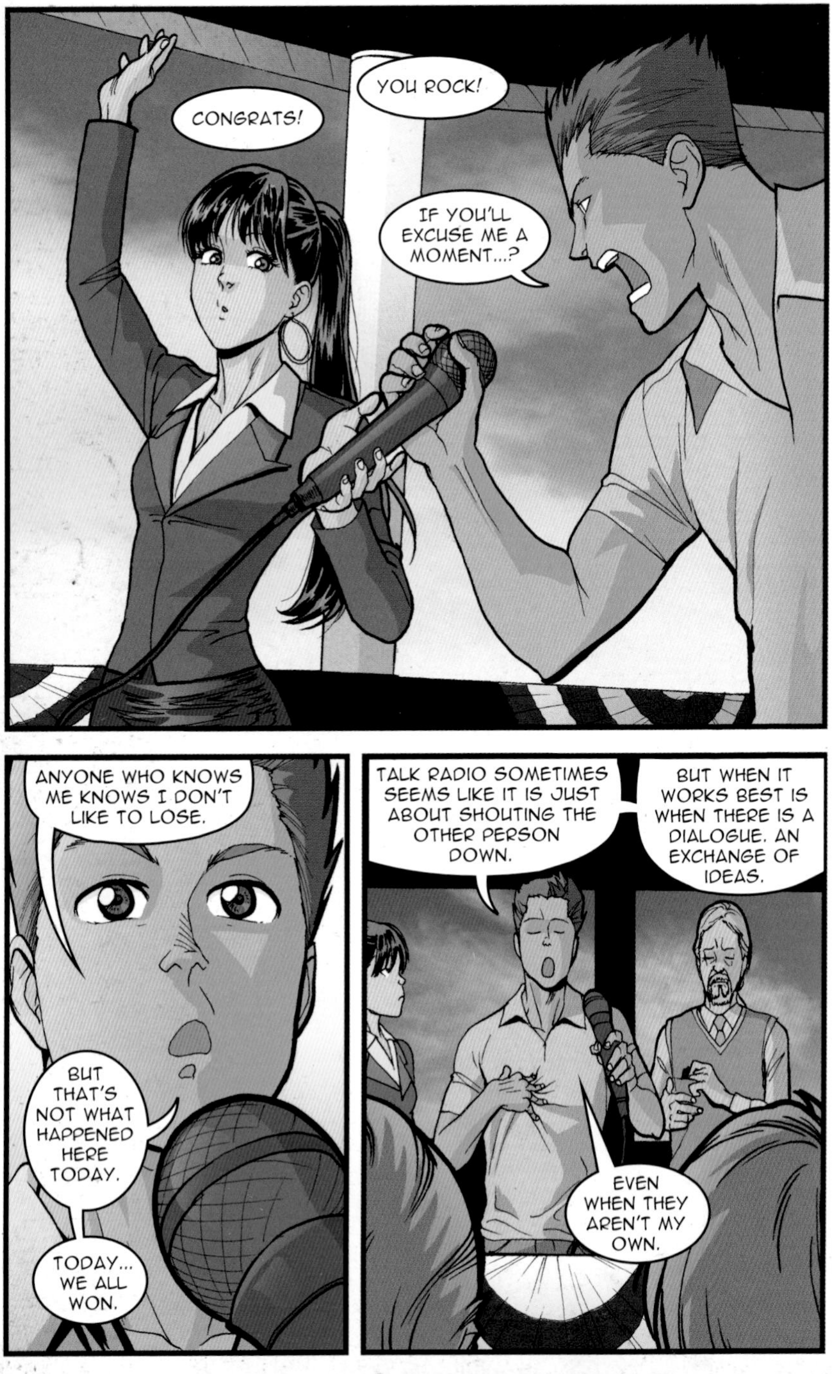
CONGRATS!
YOU ROCK!
IF YOU'LL EXCUSE ME A MOMENT...?
ANYONE WHO KNOWS ME KNOWS I DON'T LIKE TO LOSE.
BUT THAT'S NOT WHAT HAPPENED HERE TODAY.
TODAY... WE ALL WON.
TALK RADIO SOMETIMES SEEMS LIKE IT IS JUST ABOUT SHOUTING THE OTHER PERSON DOWN.
BUT WHEN IT WORKS BEST IS WHEN THERE IS A DIALOGUE. AN EXCHANGE OF IDEAS.
EVEN WHEN THEY AREN'T MY OWN.

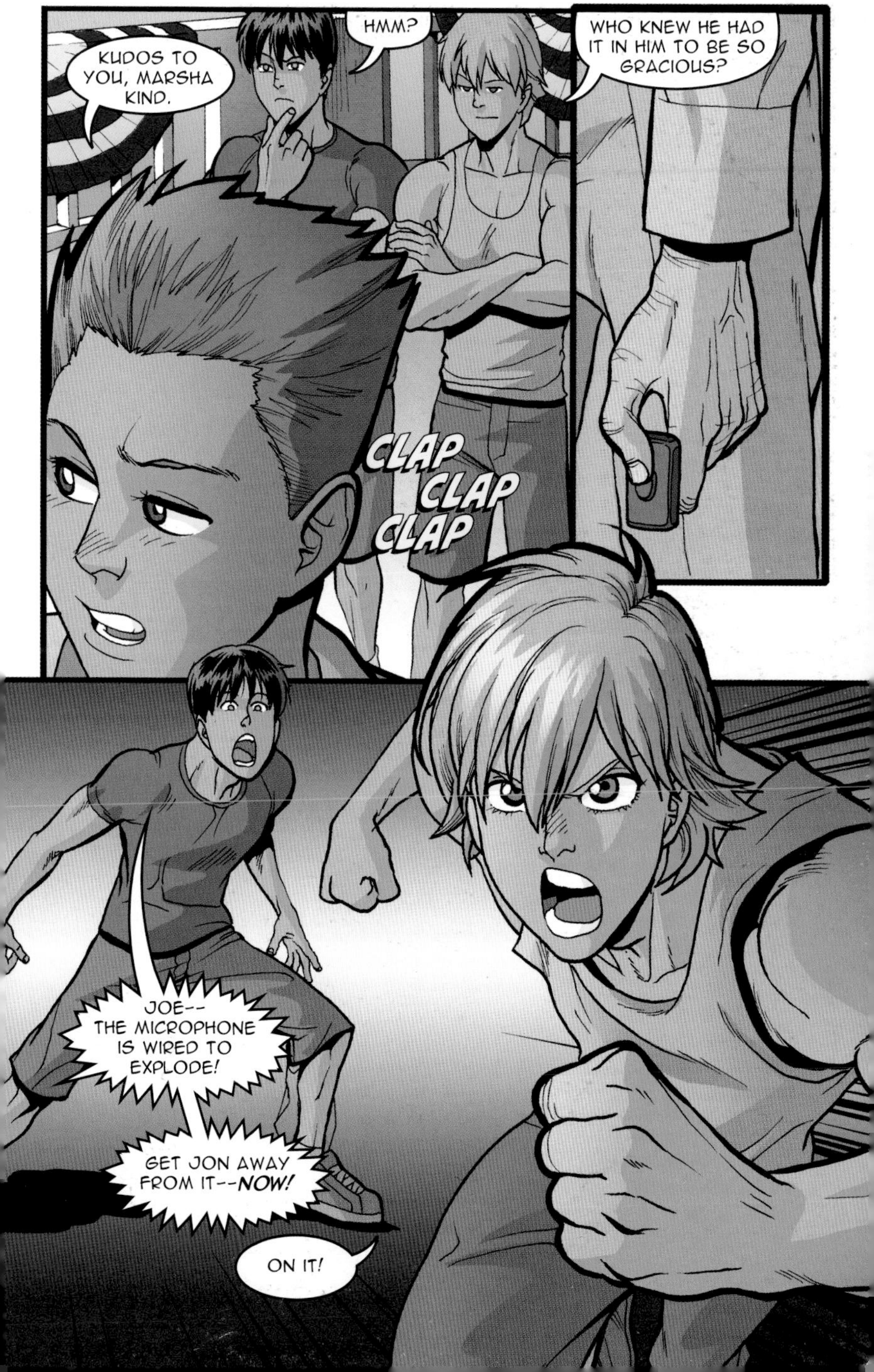
KUDOS TO YOU, MARSHA KIND.
HMM?
WHO KNEW HE HAD IT IN HIM TO BE SO GRACIOUS?
CLAP CLAP CLAP
JOE-- THE MICROPHONE IS WIRED TO EXPLODE!
GET JON AWAY FROM IT--NOW!
ON IT!

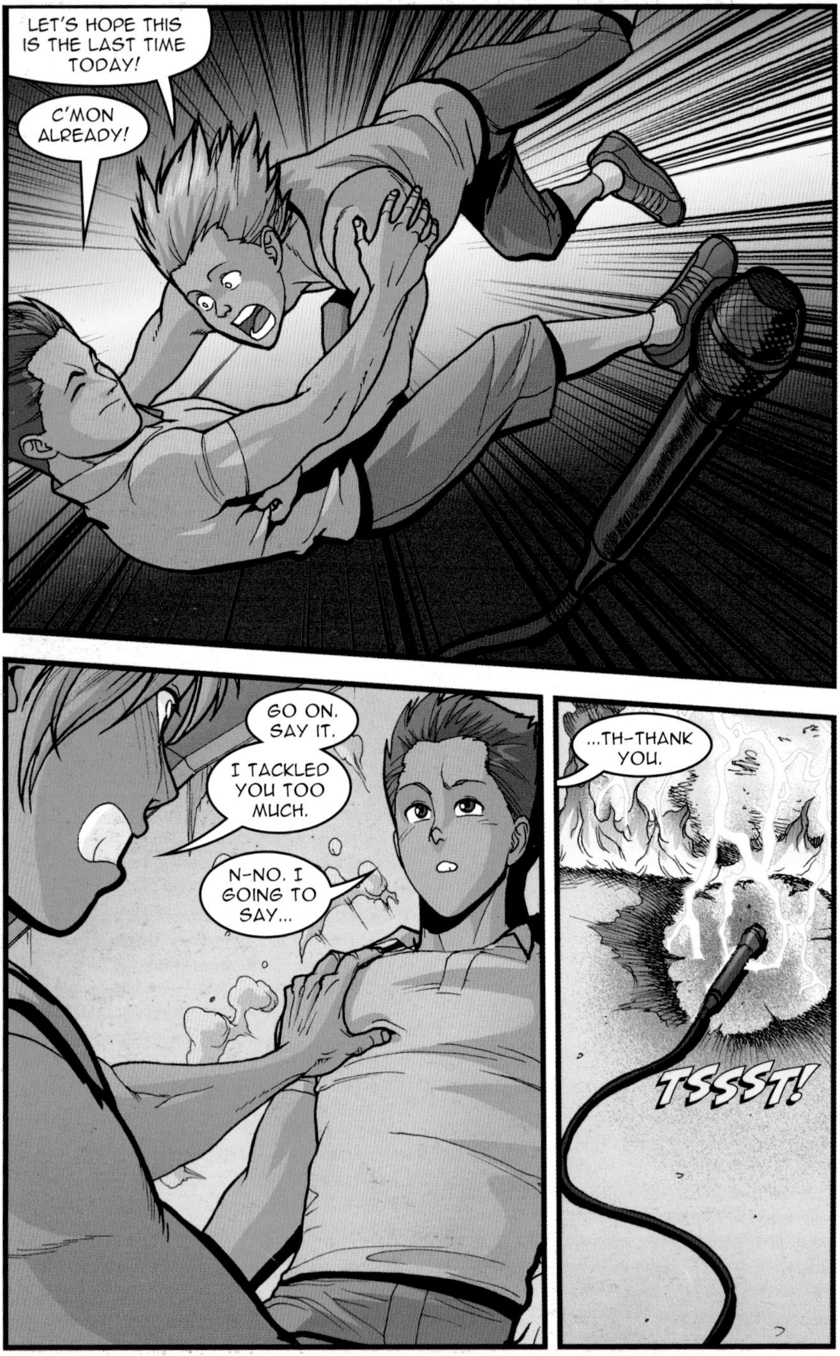
LET'S HOPE THIS IS THE LAST TIME TODAY!
C'MON ALREADY!
GO ON. SAY IT.
I TACKLED YOU TOO MUCH.
N-NO. I GOING TO SAY...
...TH-THANK YOU.
TSSST!

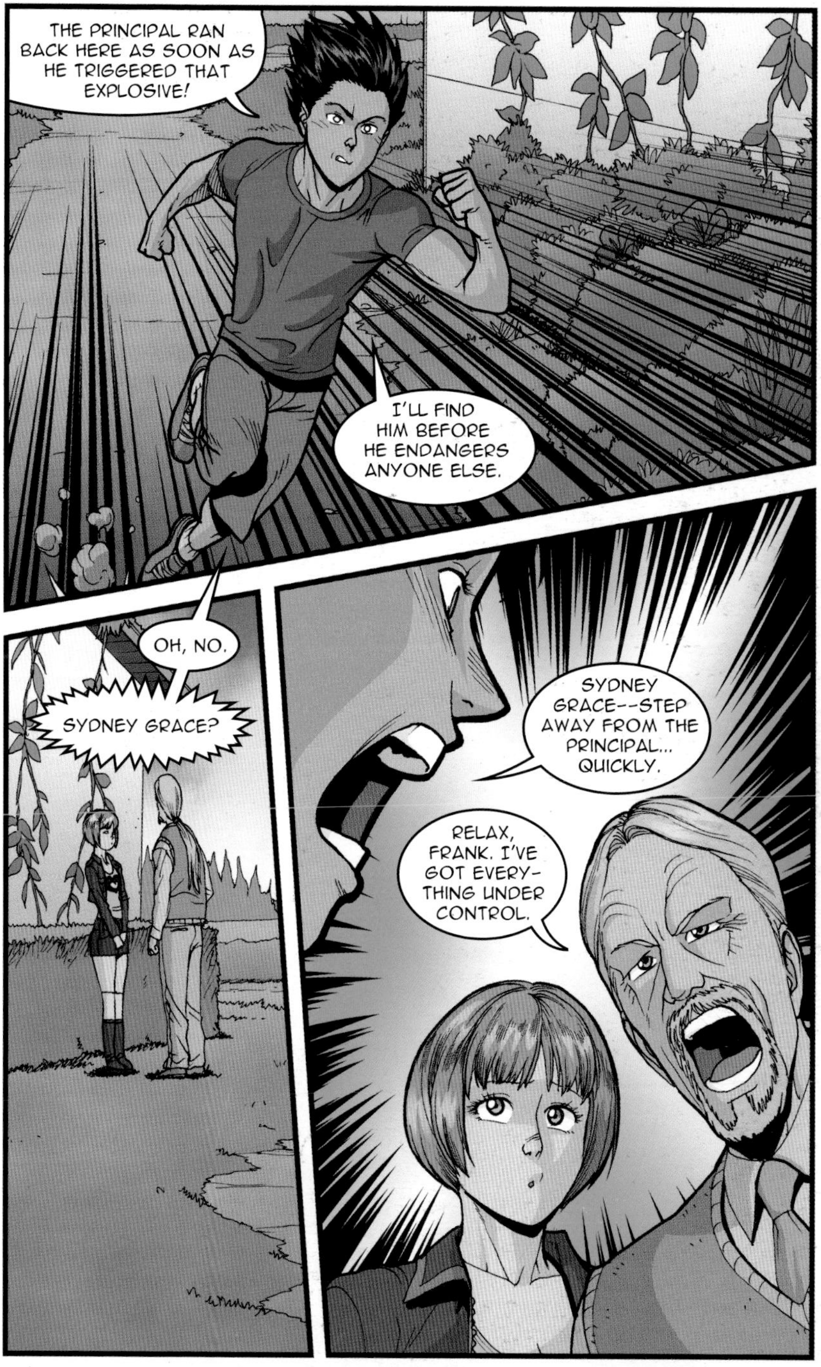
THE PRINCIPAL RAN BACK HERE AS SOON AS HE TRIGGERED THAT EXPLOSIVE!
I'LL FIND HIM BEFORE HE ENDANGERS ANYONE ELSE.
OH, NO.
SYDNEY GRACE?
SYDNEY GRACE--STEP AWAY FROM THE PRINCIPAL... QUICKLY.
RELAX, FRANK. I'VE GOT EVERY-THING UNDER CONTROL.

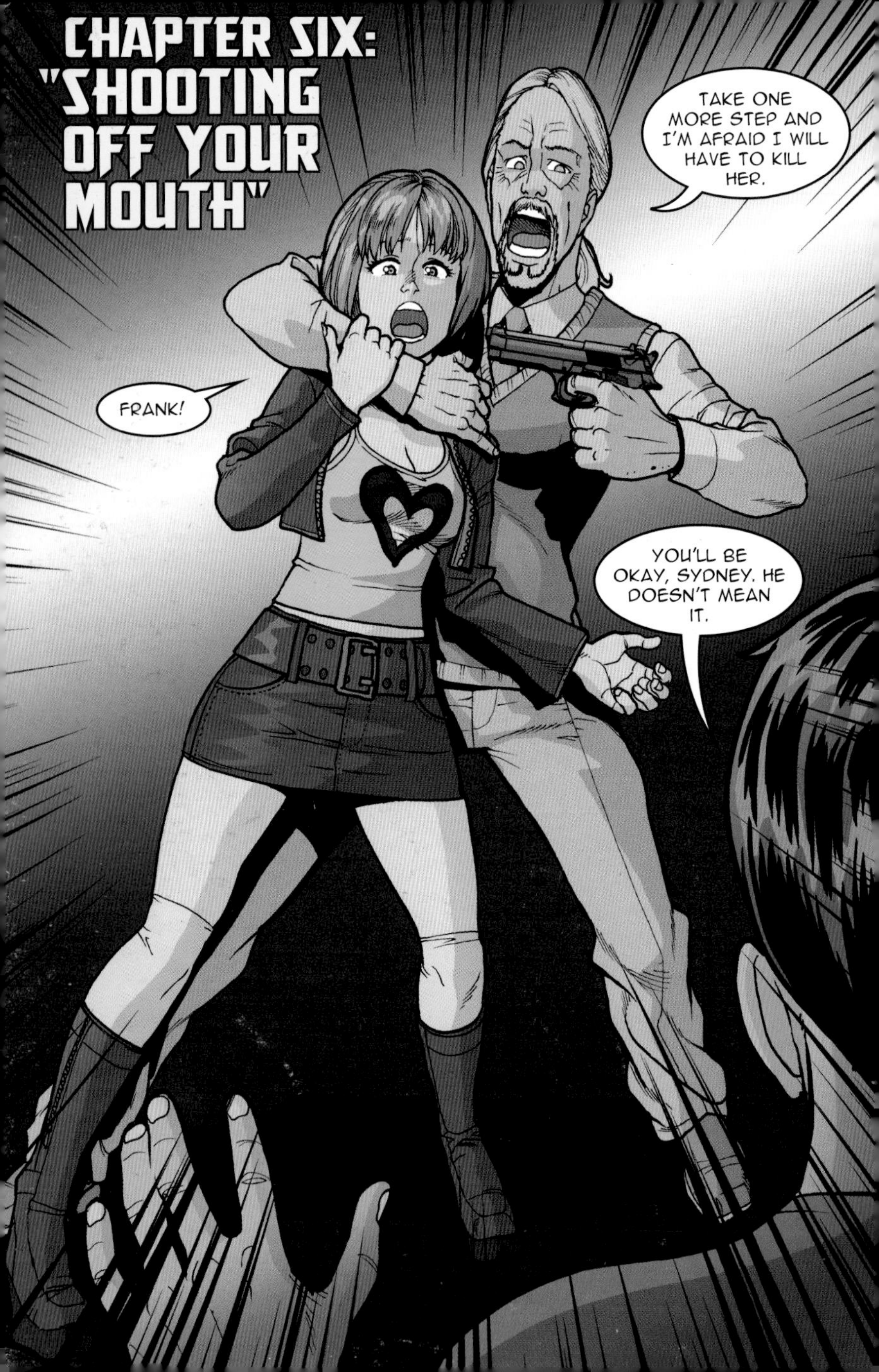
CHAPTER SIX: "SHOOTING OFF YOUR MOUTH"
TAKE ONE MORE STEP AND I'M AFRAID I WILL HAVE TO KILL HER.
FRANK!
YOU'LL BE OKAY, SYDNEY. HE DOESN'T MEAN IT.

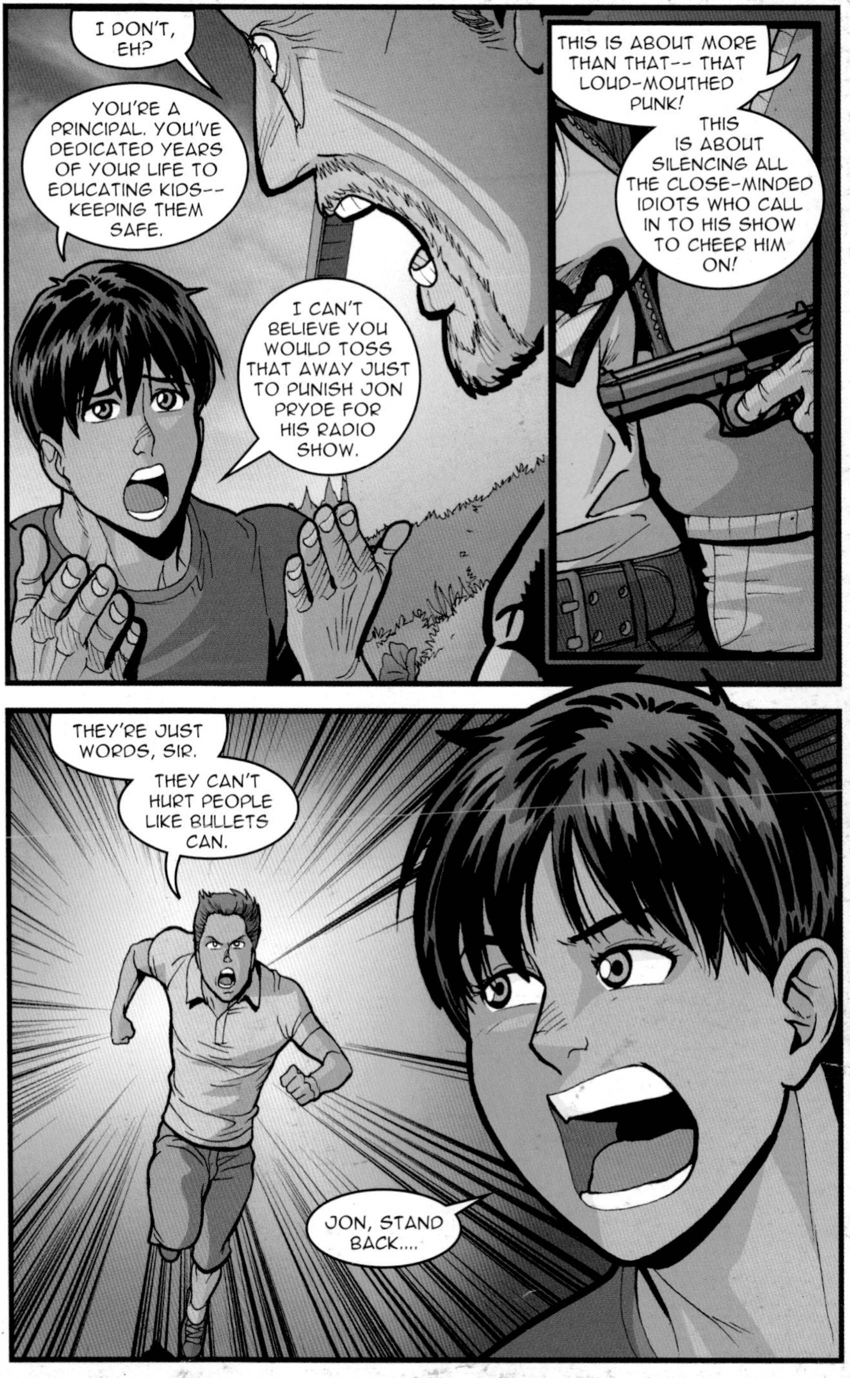
I DON'T, EH?
YOU'RE A PRINCIPAL. YOU'VE DEDICATED YEARS OF YOUR LIFE TO EDUCATING KIDS-- KEEPING THEM SAFE.
I CAN'T BELIEVE YOU WOULD TOSS THAT AWAY JUST TO PUNISH JON PRYDE FOR HIS RADIO SHOW.
THIS IS ABOUT MORE THAN THAT-- THAT LOUD-MOUTHED PUNK!
THIS IS ABOUT SILENCING ALL THE CLOSE-MINDED IDIOTS WHO CALL IN TO HIS SHOW TO CHEER HIM ON!
THEY'RE JUST WORDS, SIR.
THEY CAN'T HURT PEOPLE LIKE BULLETS CAN.
JON, STAND BACK....

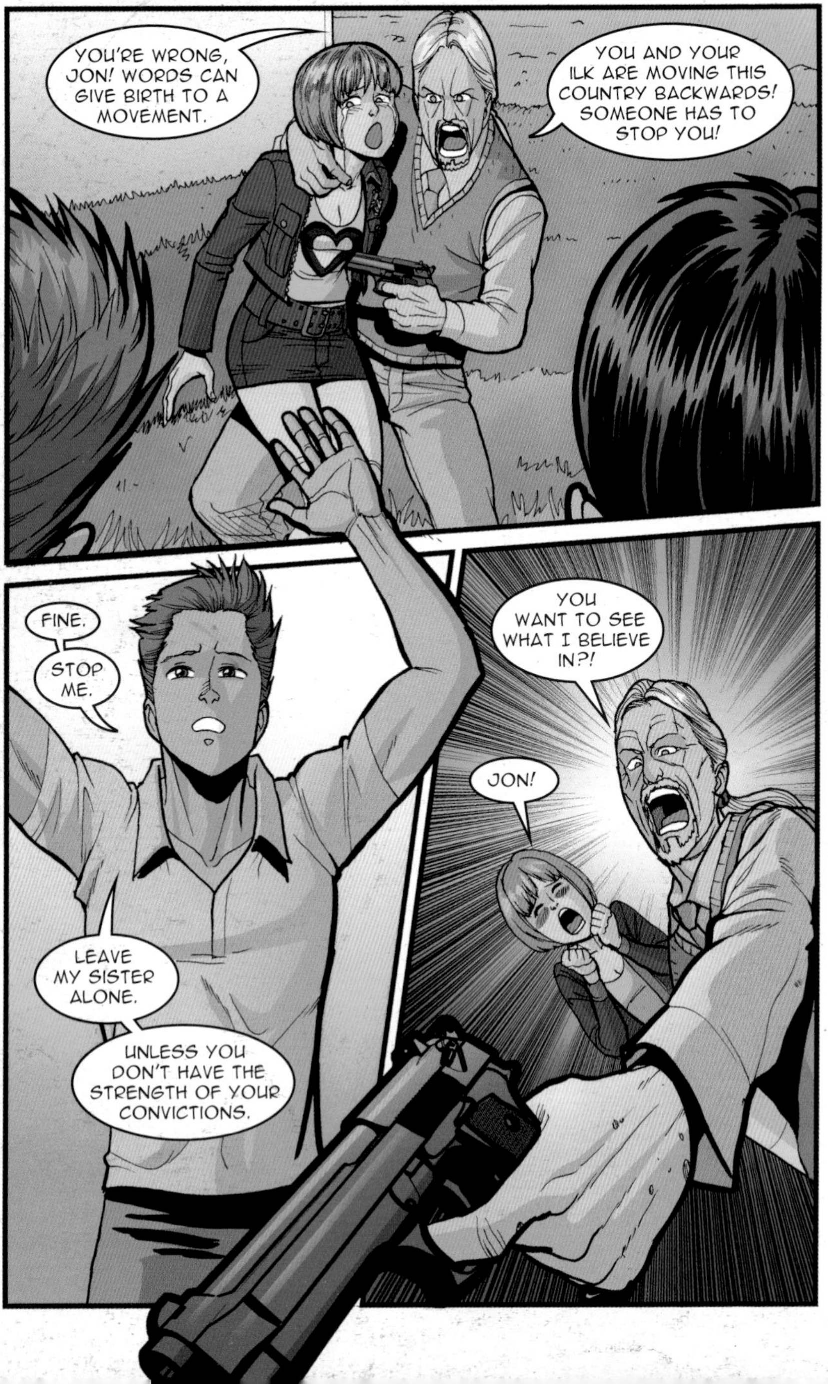
YOU'RE WRONG, JON! WORDS CAN GIVE BIRTH TO A MOVEMENT.
YOU AND YOUR ILK ARE MOVING THIS COUNTRY BACKWARDS! SOMEONE HAS TO STOP YOU!
FINE.
STOP ME.
LEAVE MY SISTER ALONE.
UNLESS YOU DON'T HAVE THE STRENGTH OF YOUR CONVICTIONS.
YOU WANT TO SEE WHAT I BELIEVE IN?!
JON!

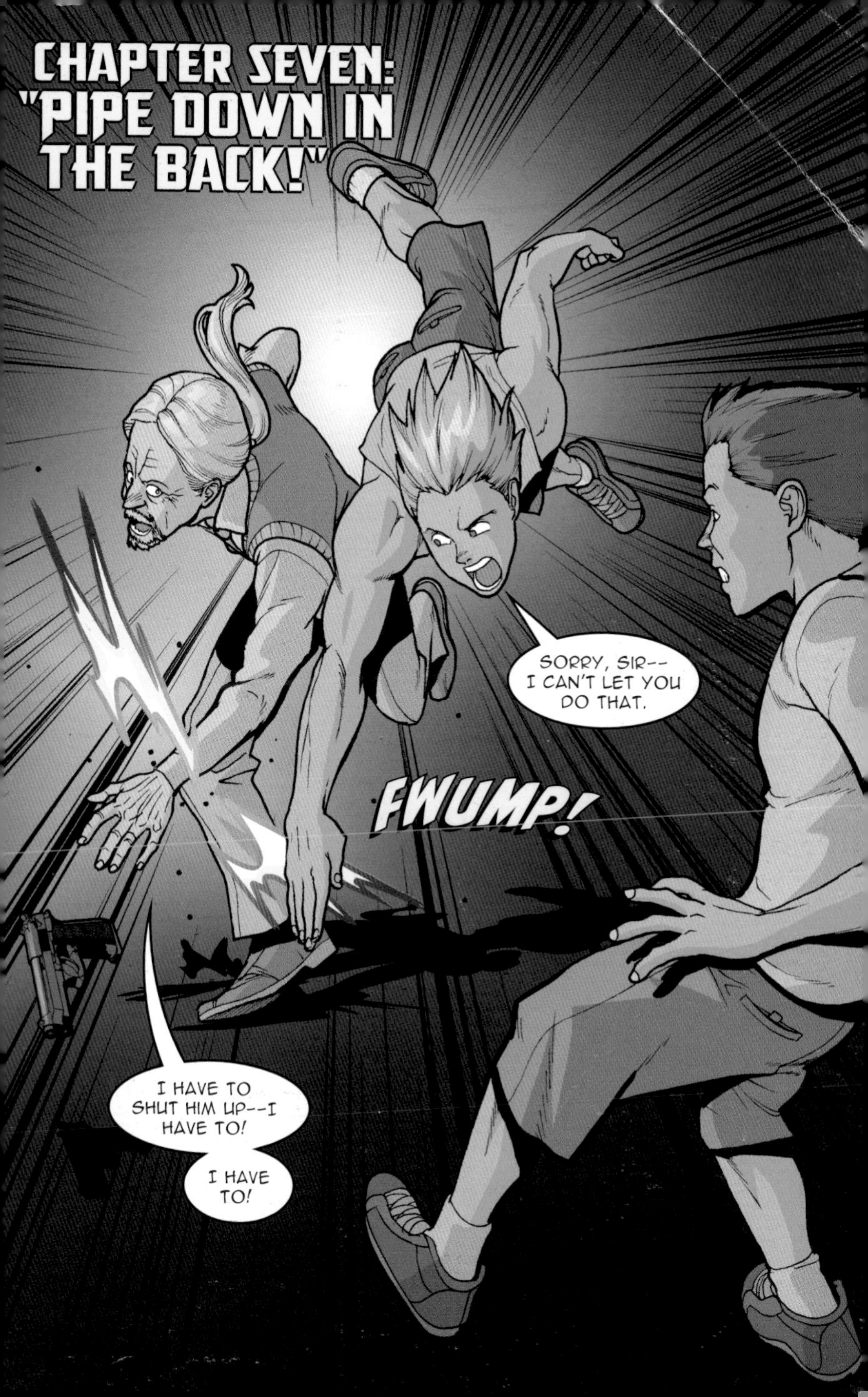
CHAPTER SEVEN: "PIPE DOWN IN THE BACK!"
SORRY, SIR-- I CAN'T LET YOU DO THAT.
FWUMP!
I HAVE TO SHUT HIM UP--I HAVE TO!
I HAVE TO!

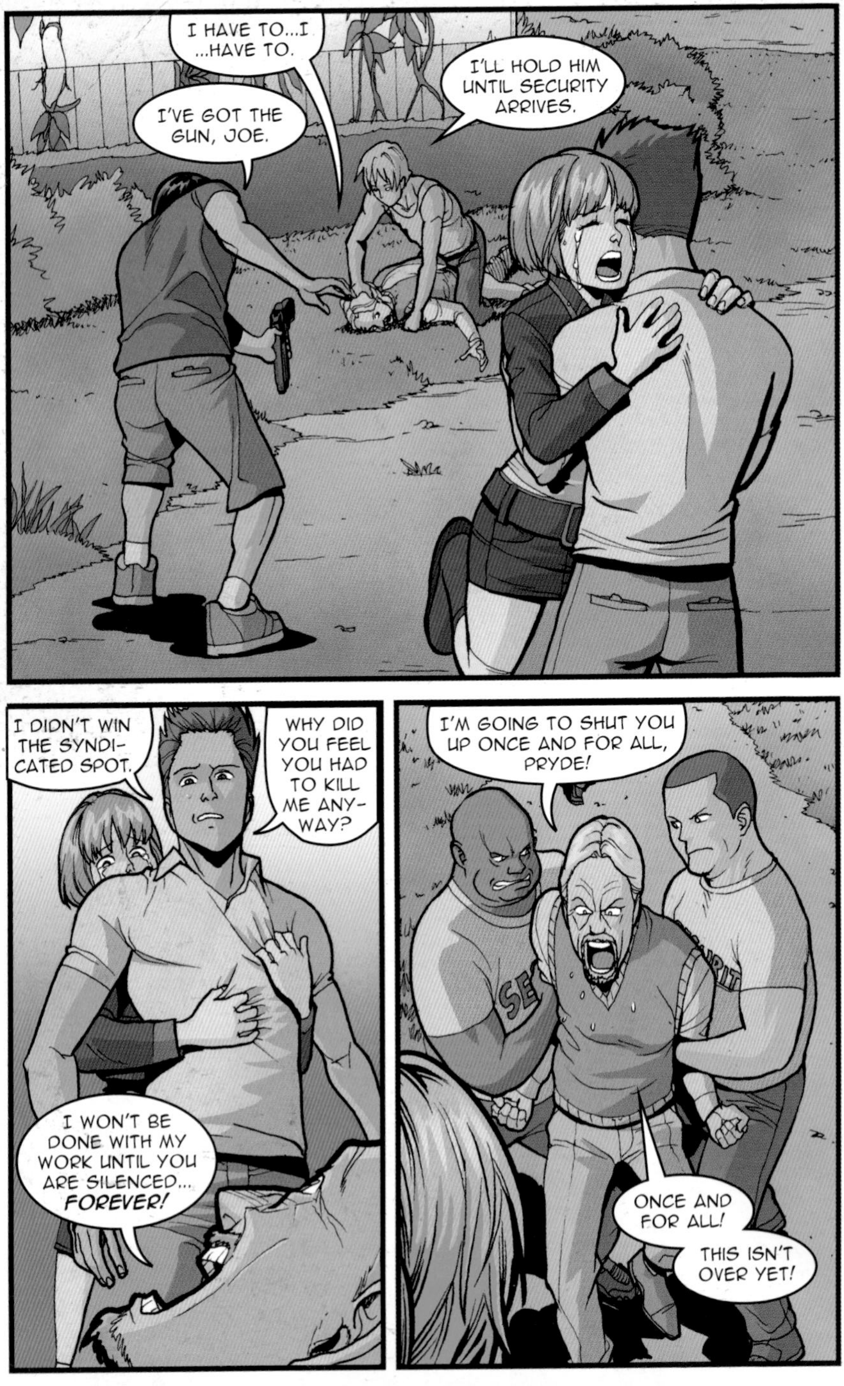
I HAVE TO...I ...HAVE TO.
I'VE GOT THE GUN, JOE.
I'LL HOLD HIM UNTIL SECURITY ARRIVES.
I DIDN'T WIN THE SYNDI-CATED SPOT.
WHY DID YOU FEEL YOU HAD TO KILL ME ANY-WAY?
I WON'T BE DONE WITH MY WORK UNTIL YOU ARE SILENCED... ***FOREVER!***
I'M GOING TO SHUT YOU UP ONCE AND FOR ALL, PRYDE!
ONCE AND FOR ALL!
THIS ISN'T OVER YET!

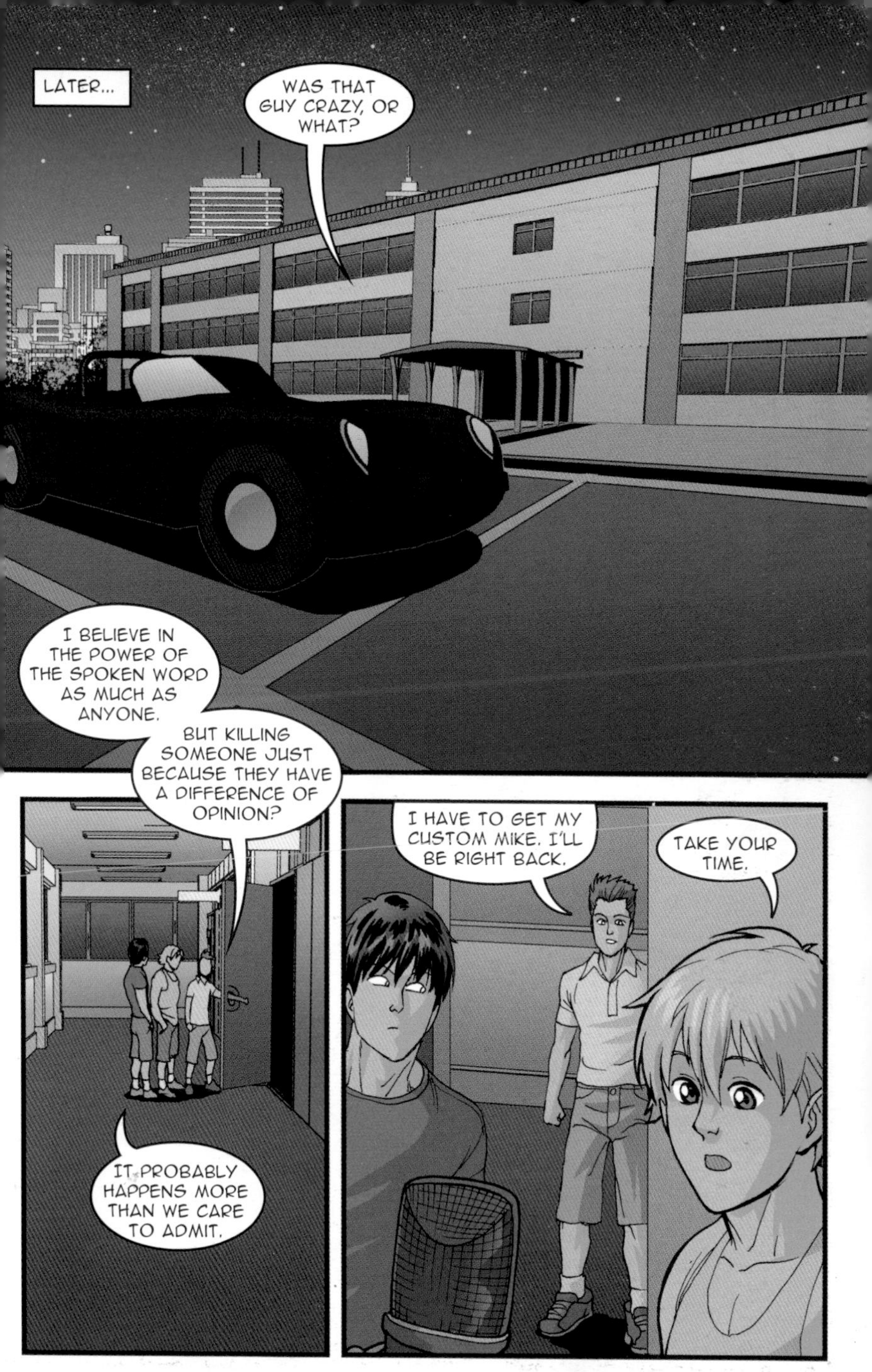
LATER...
WAS THAT GUY CRAZY, OR WHAT?
I BELIEVE IN THE POWER OF THE SPOKEN WORD AS MUCH AS ANYONE.
BUT KILLING SOMEONE JUST BECAUSE THEY HAVE A DIFFERENCE OF OPINION?
IT PROBABLY HAPPENS MORE THAN WE CARE TO ADMIT.
I HAVE TO GET MY CUSTOM MIKE. I'LL BE RIGHT BACK.
TAKE YOUR TIME.

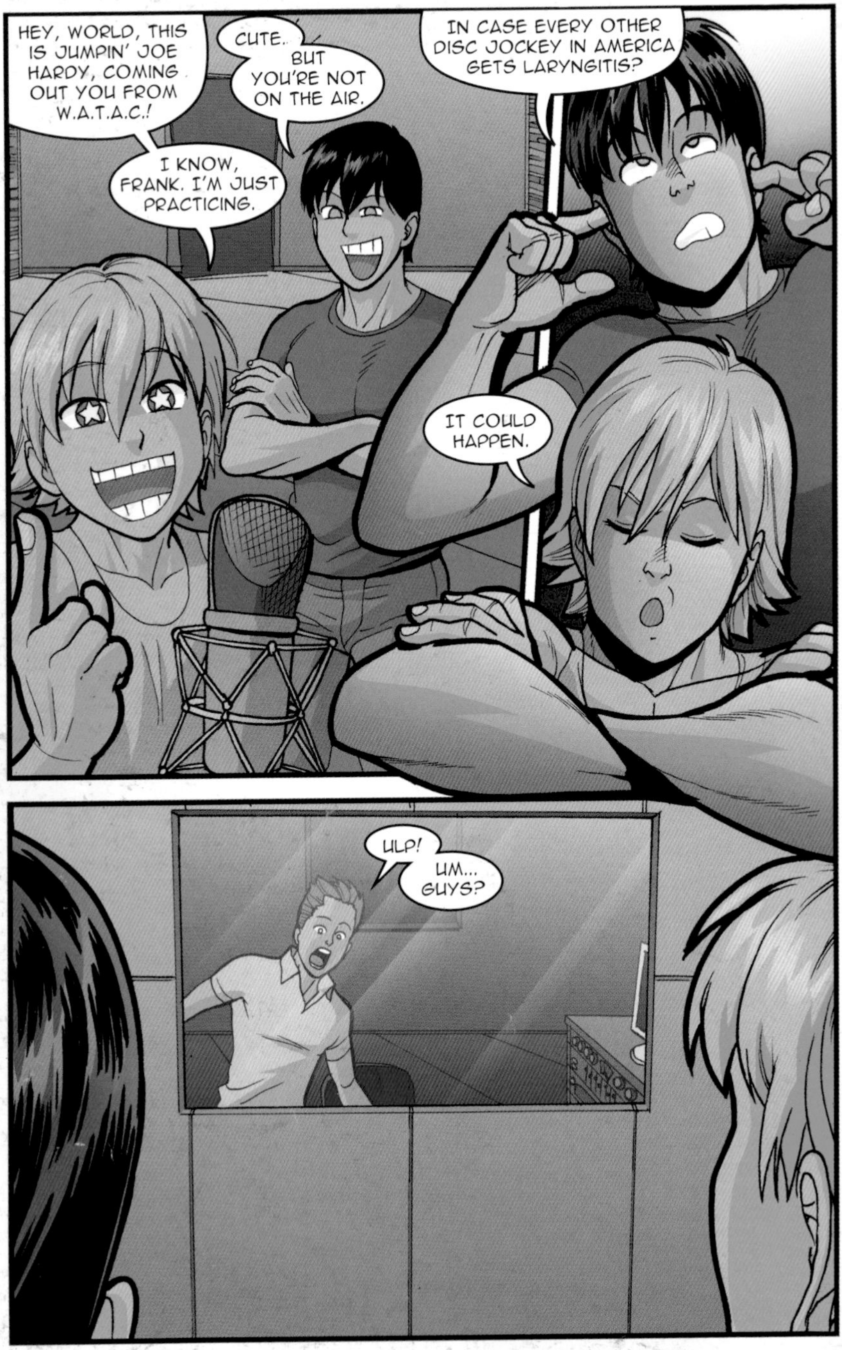
HEY, WORLD, THIS IS JUMPIN' JOE HARDY, COMING OUT YOU FROM W.A.T.A.C.!
CUTE.. BUT YOU'RE NOT ON THE AIR.
I KNOW, FRANK. I'M JUST PRACTICING.
IN CASE EVERY OTHER DISC JOCKEY IN AMERICA GETS LARYNGITIS?
IT COULD HAPPEN.
ULP!
UM... GUYS?

CHAPTER EIGHT: "EXPLODING IN RAGE!"

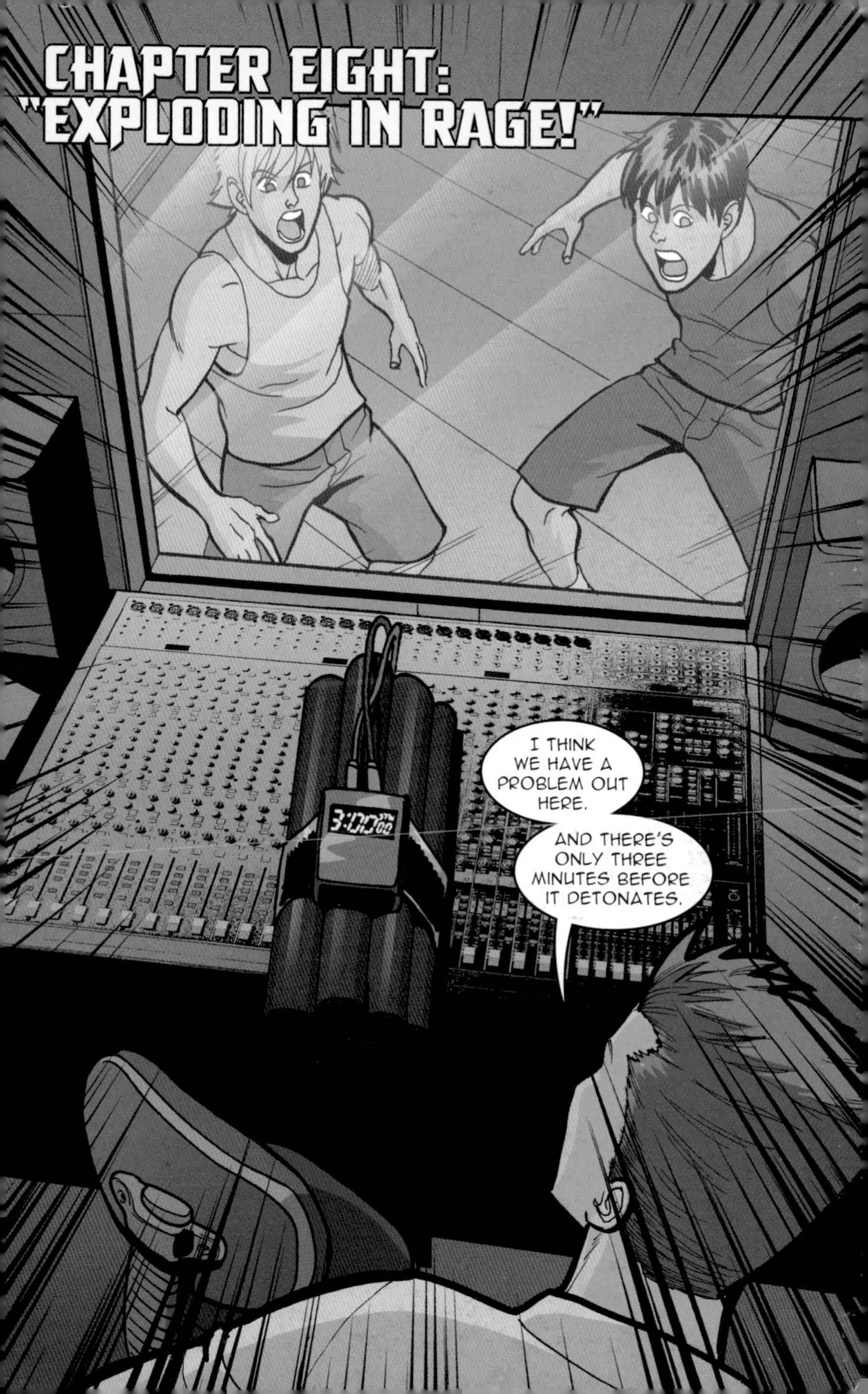
3:00
I THINK WE HAVE A PROBLEM OUT HERE.
AND THERE'S ONLY THREE MINUTES BEFORE IT DETONATES.

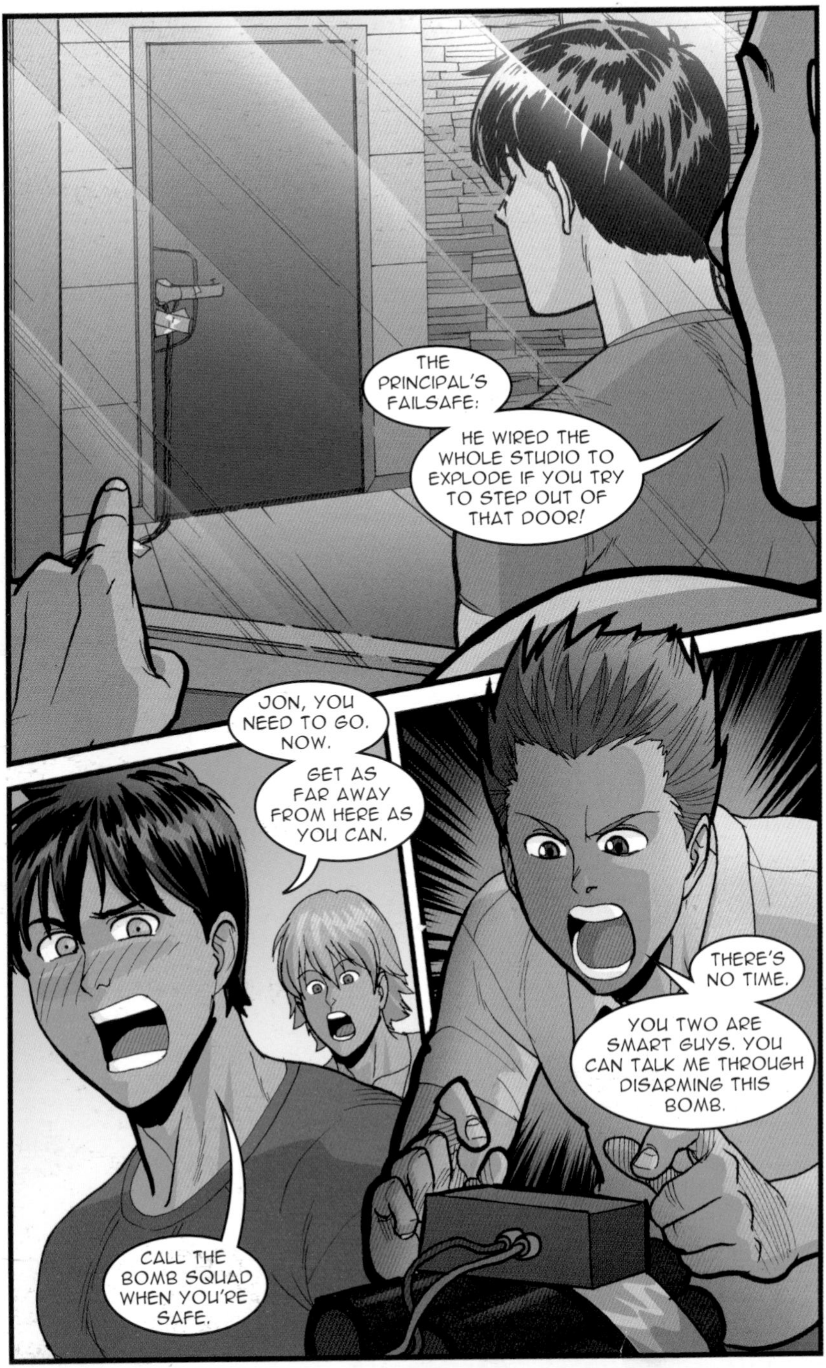
THE PRINCIPAL'S FAILSAFE:
HE WIRED THE WHOLE STUDIO TO EXPLODE IF YOU TRY TO STEP OUT OF THAT DOOR!
JON, YOU NEED TO GO. NOW.
GET AS FAR AWAY FROM HERE AS YOU CAN.
CALL THE BOMB SQUAD WHEN YOU'RE SAFE.
THERE'S NO TIME.
YOU TWO ARE SMART GUYS. YOU CAN TALK ME THROUGH DISARMING THIS BOMB.

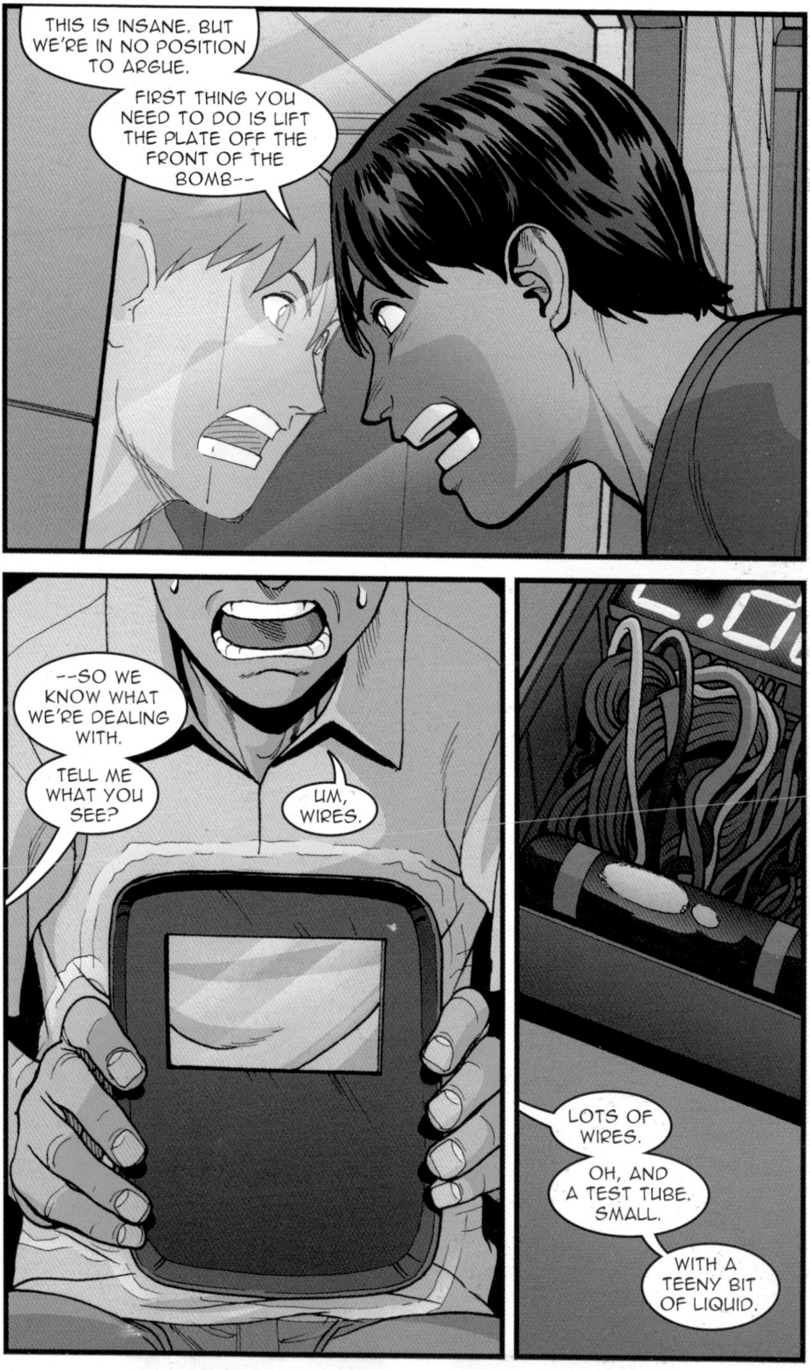
THIS IS INSANE. BUT WE'RE IN NO POSITION TO ARGUE.
FIRST THING YOU NEED TO DO IS LIFT THE PLATE OFF THE FRONT OF THE BOMB--
--SO WE KNOW WHAT WE'RE DEALING WITH.
TELL ME WHAT YOU SEE?
UM, WIRES.
LOTS OF WIRES.
OH, AND A TEST TUBE. SMALL.
WITH A TEENY BIT OF LIQUID.

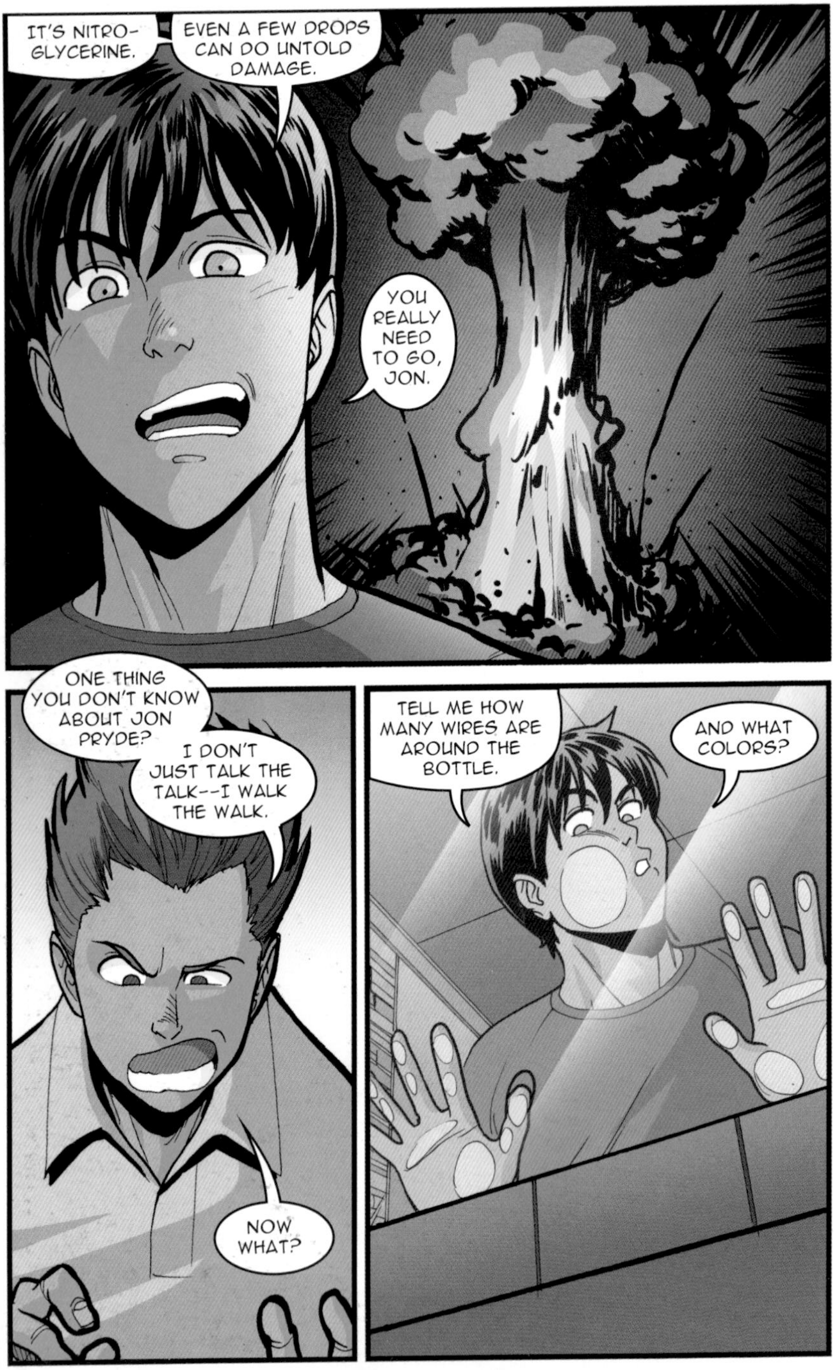
IT'S NITRO-GLYCERINE.
EVEN A FEW DROPS CAN DO UNTOLD DAMAGE.
YOU REALLY NEED TO GO, JON.
ONE THING YOU DON'T KNOW ABOUT JON PRYDE?
I DON'T JUST TALK THE TALK--I WALK THE WALK.
NOW WHAT?
TELL ME HOW MANY WIRES ARE AROUND THE BOTTLE.
AND WHAT COLORS?

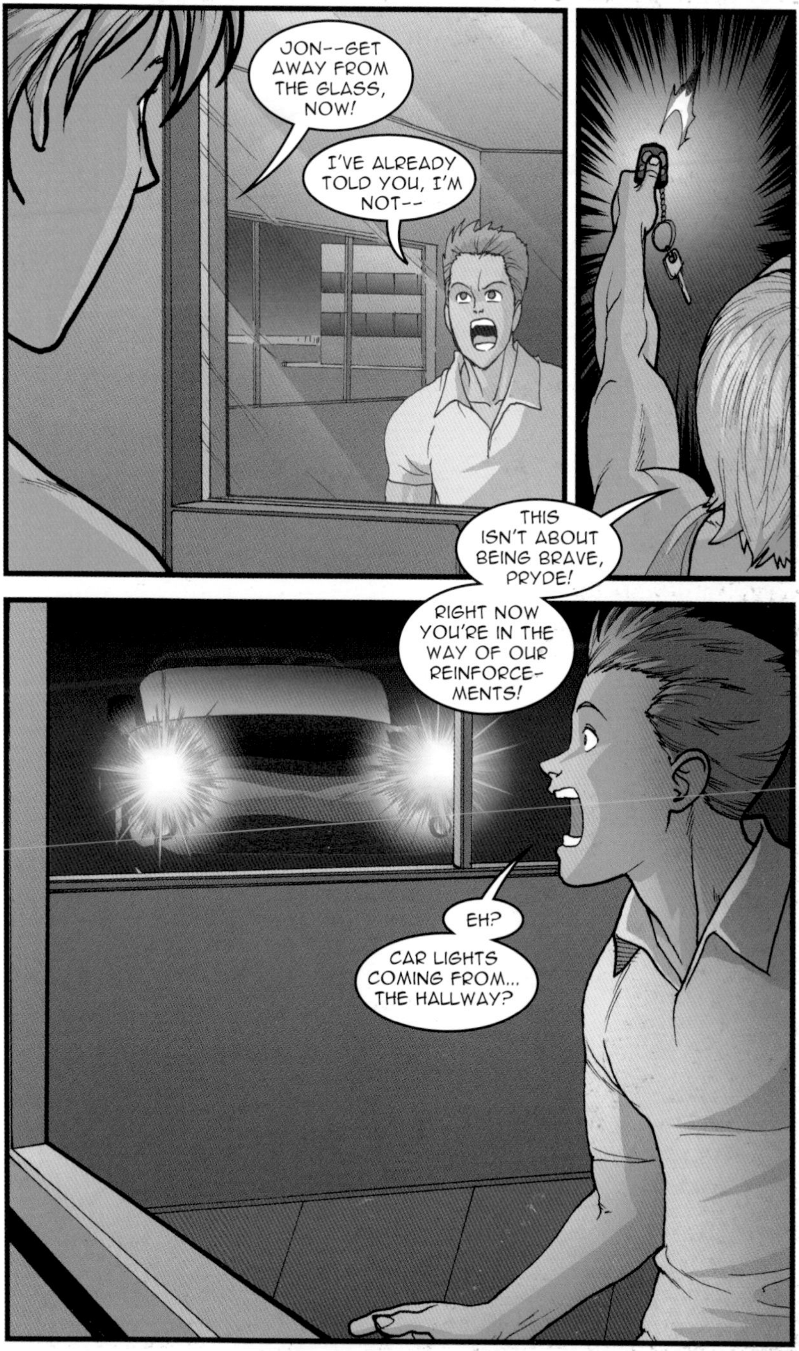
JON--GET AWAY FROM THE GLASS, NOW!
I'VE ALREADY TOLD YOU, I'M NOT--
THIS ISN'T ABOUT BEING BRAVE, PRYDE!
RIGHT NOW YOU'RE IN THE WAY OF OUR REINFORCE-MENTS!
EH?
CAR LIGHTS COMING FROM... THE HALLWAY?

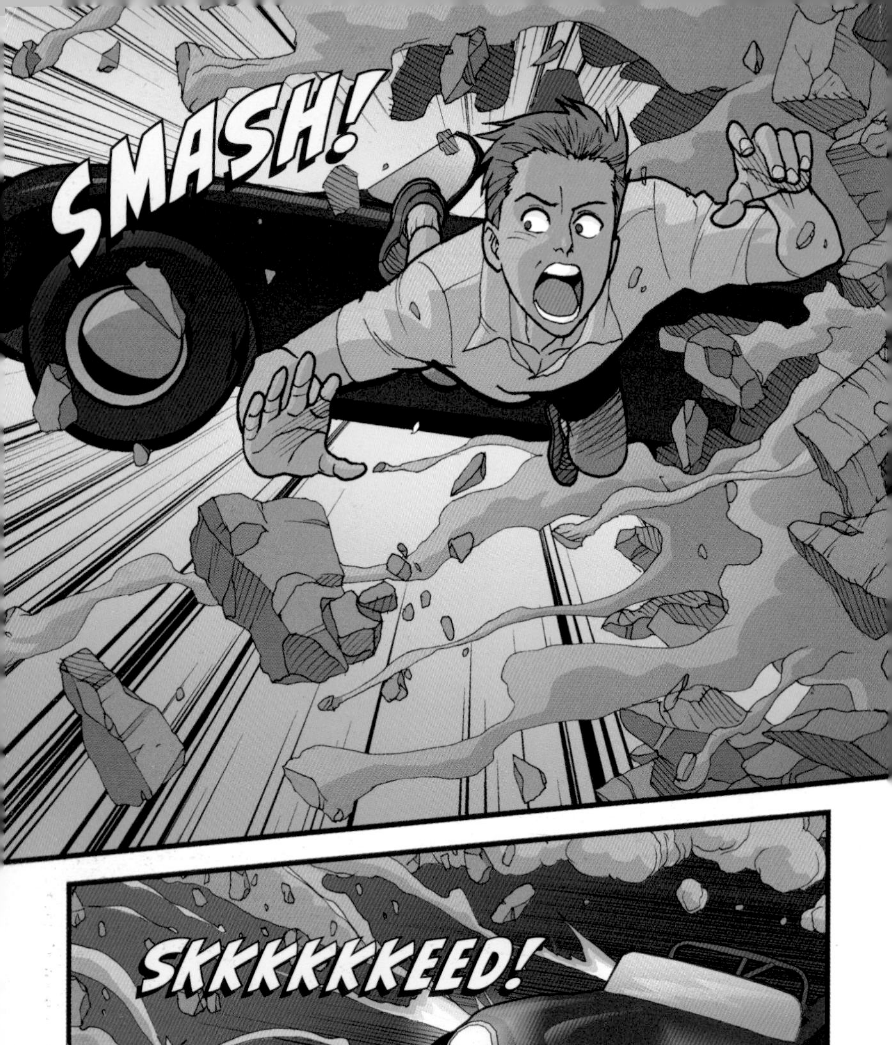
SMASH!
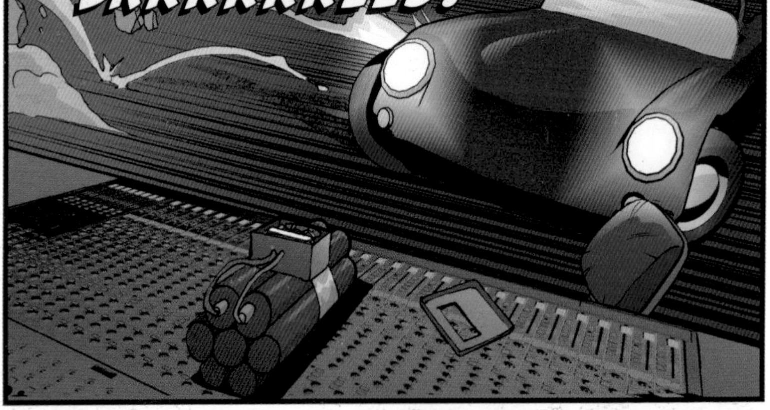
SKKKKKKEED!

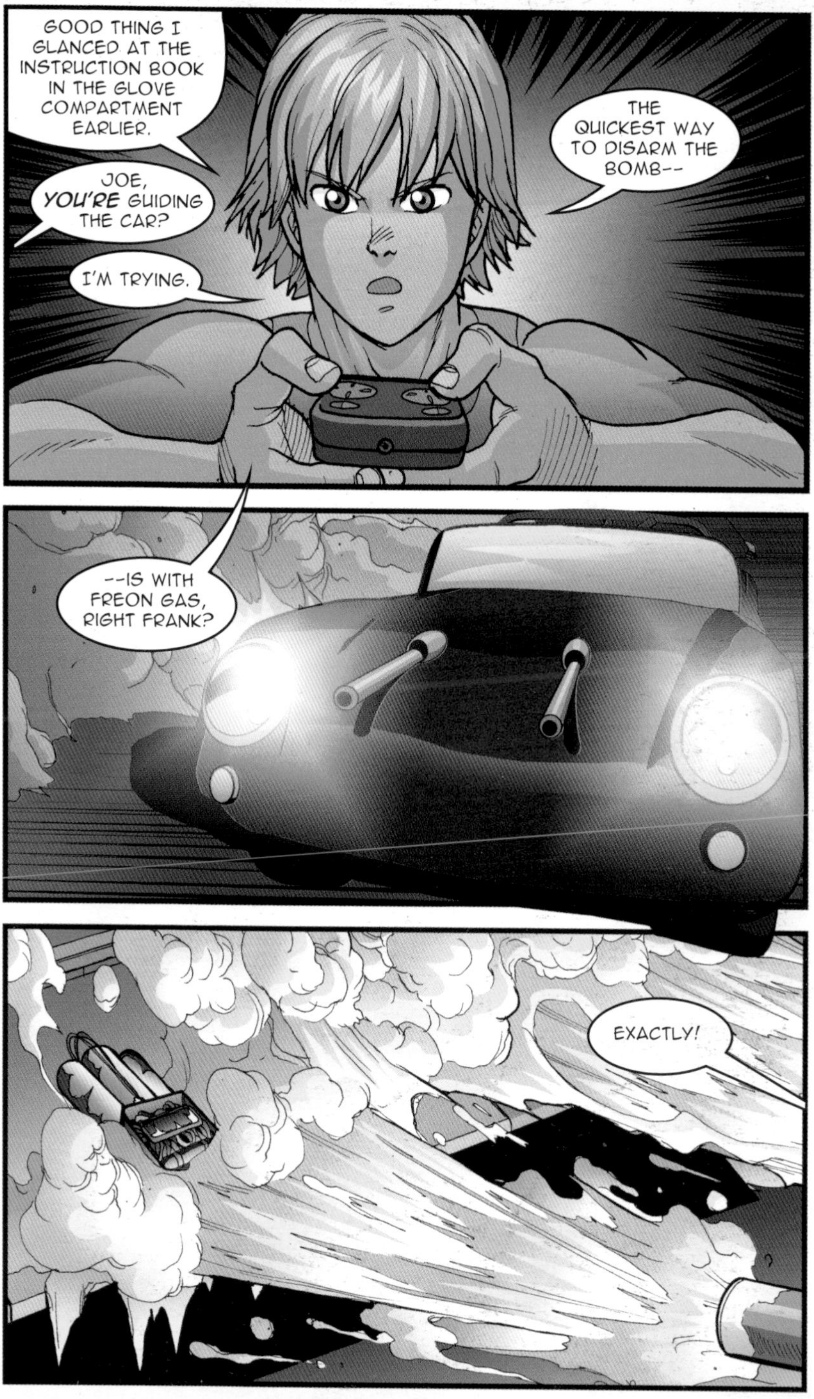
GOOD THING I GLANCED AT THE INSTRUCTION BOOK IN THE GLOVE COMPARTMENT EARLIER.
THE QUICKEST WAY TO DISARM THE BOMB--
JOE, *YOU'RE* GUIDING THE CAR?
I'M TRYING.
--IS WITH FREON GAS, RIGHT FRANK?
EXACTLY!

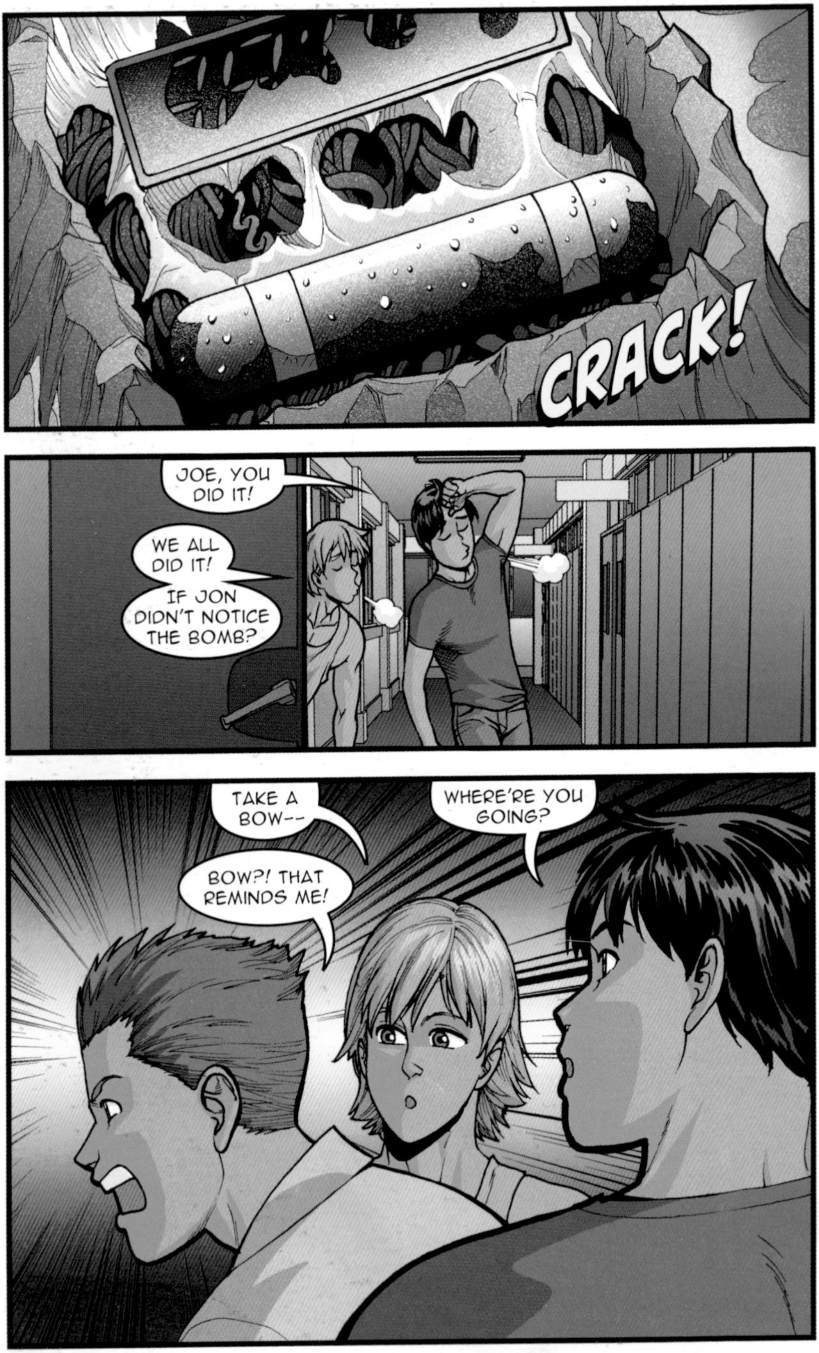
CRACK!
JOE, YOU DID IT!
WE ALL DID IT!
IF JON DIDN'T NOTICE THE BOMB?
TAKE A BOW--
WHERE'RE YOU GOING?
BOW?! THAT REMINDS ME!

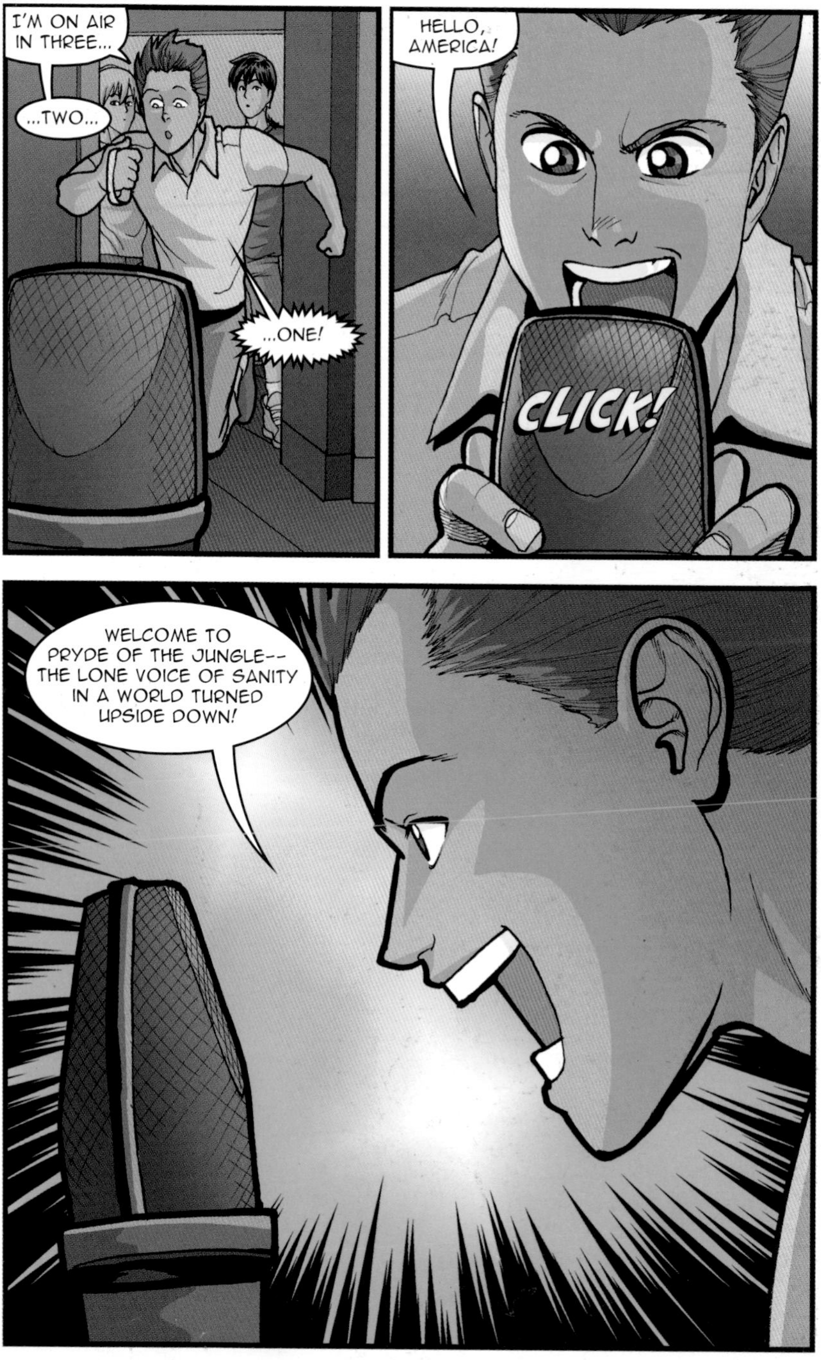
I'M ON AIR IN THREE...
...TWO...
...ONE!
HELLO, AMERICA!
CLICK!
WELCOME TO PRYDE OF THE JUNGLE-- THE LONE VOICE OF SANITY IN A WORLD TURNED UPSIDE DOWN!

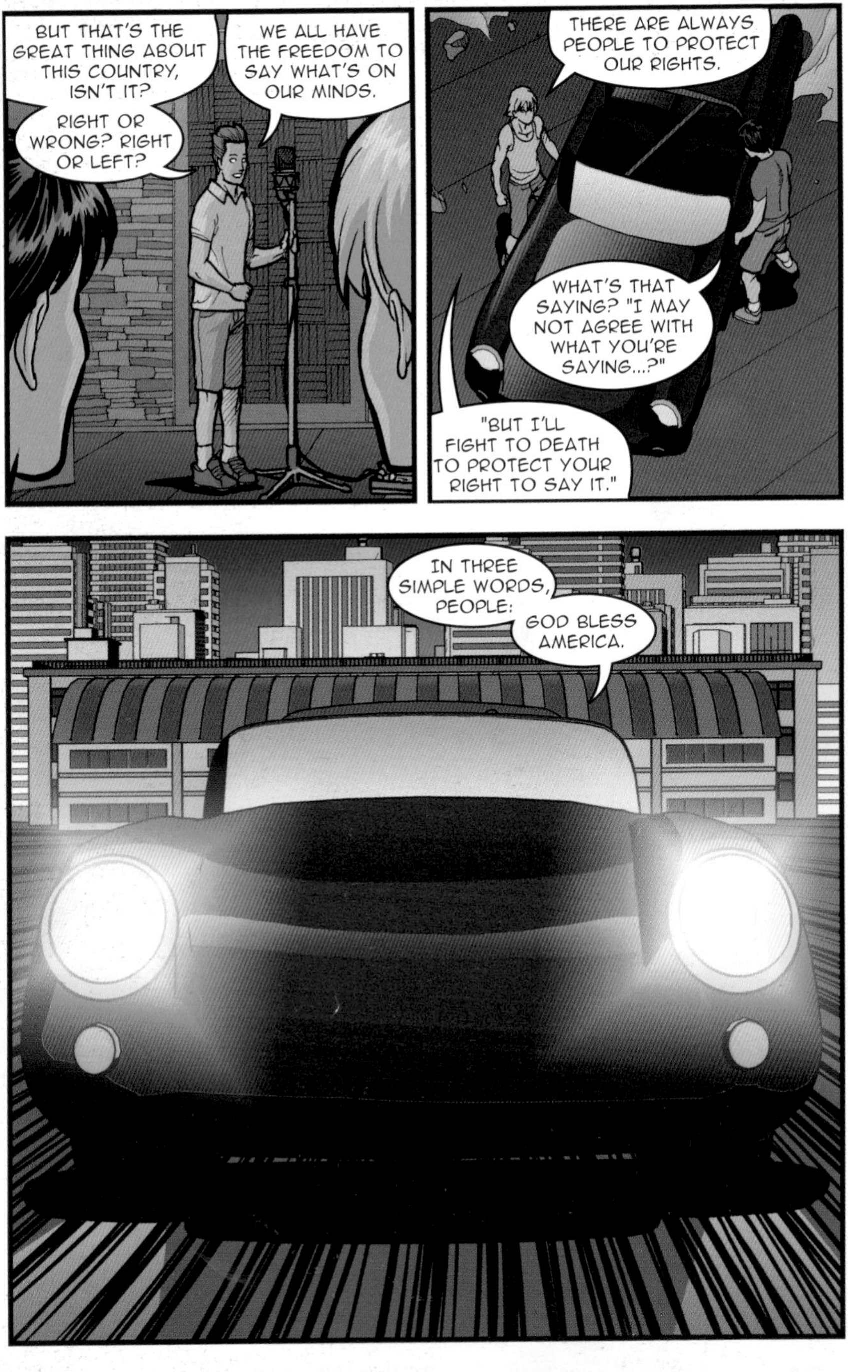
BUT THAT'S THE GREAT THING ABOUT THIS COUNTRY, ISN'T IT?
RIGHT OR WRONG? RIGHT OR LEFT?
WE ALL HAVE THE FREEDOM TO SAY WHAT'S ON OUR MINDS.
THERE ARE ALWAYS PEOPLE TO PROTECT OUR RIGHTS.
WHAT'S THAT SAYING? "I MAY NOT AGREE WITH WHAT YOU'RE SAYING...?"
"BUT I'LL FIGHT TO DEATH TO PROTECT YOUR RIGHT TO SAY IT."
IN THREE SIMPLE WORDS, PEOPLE:
GOD BLESS AMERICA.

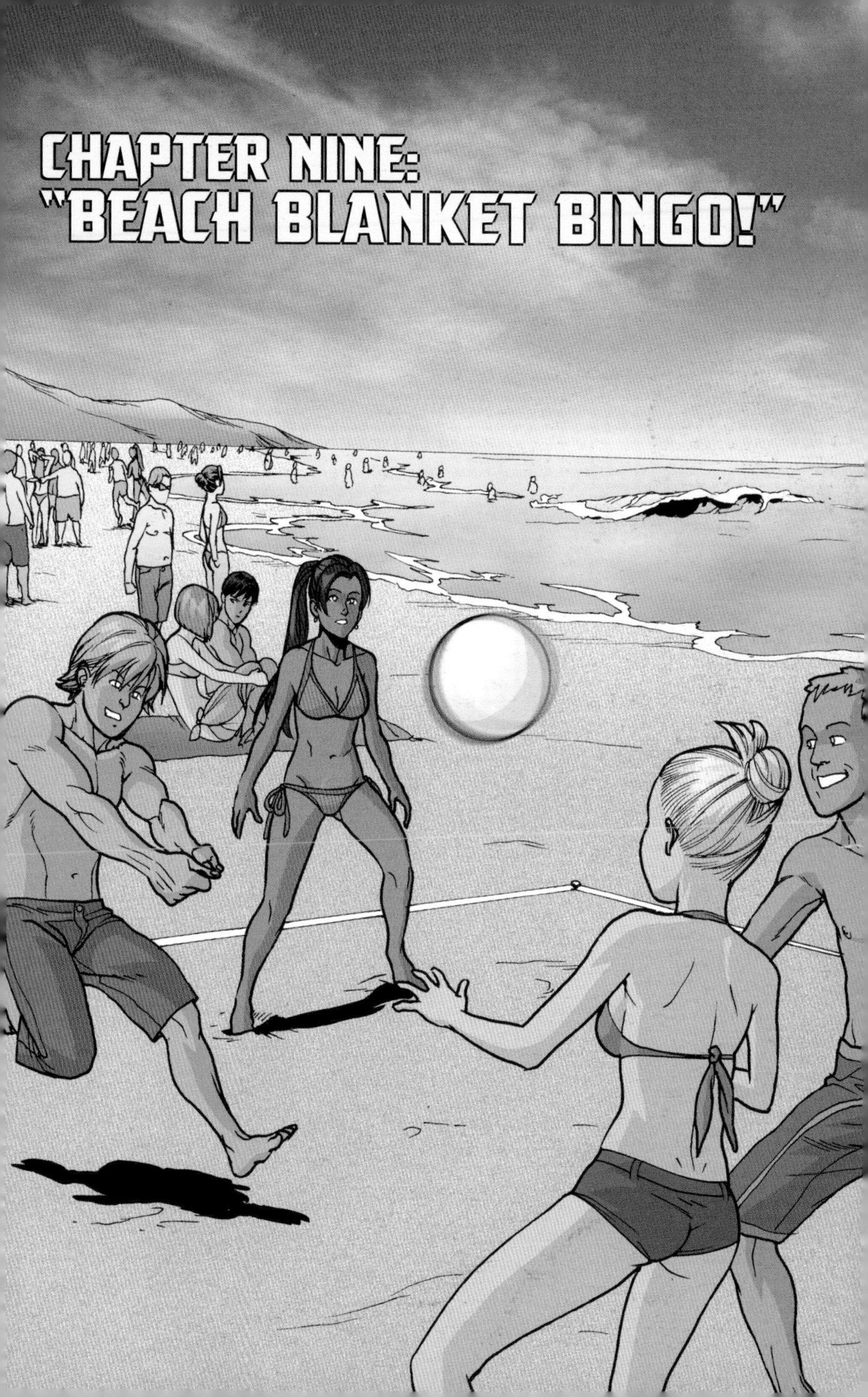
CHAPTER NINE:
"BEACH BLANKET BINGO!"

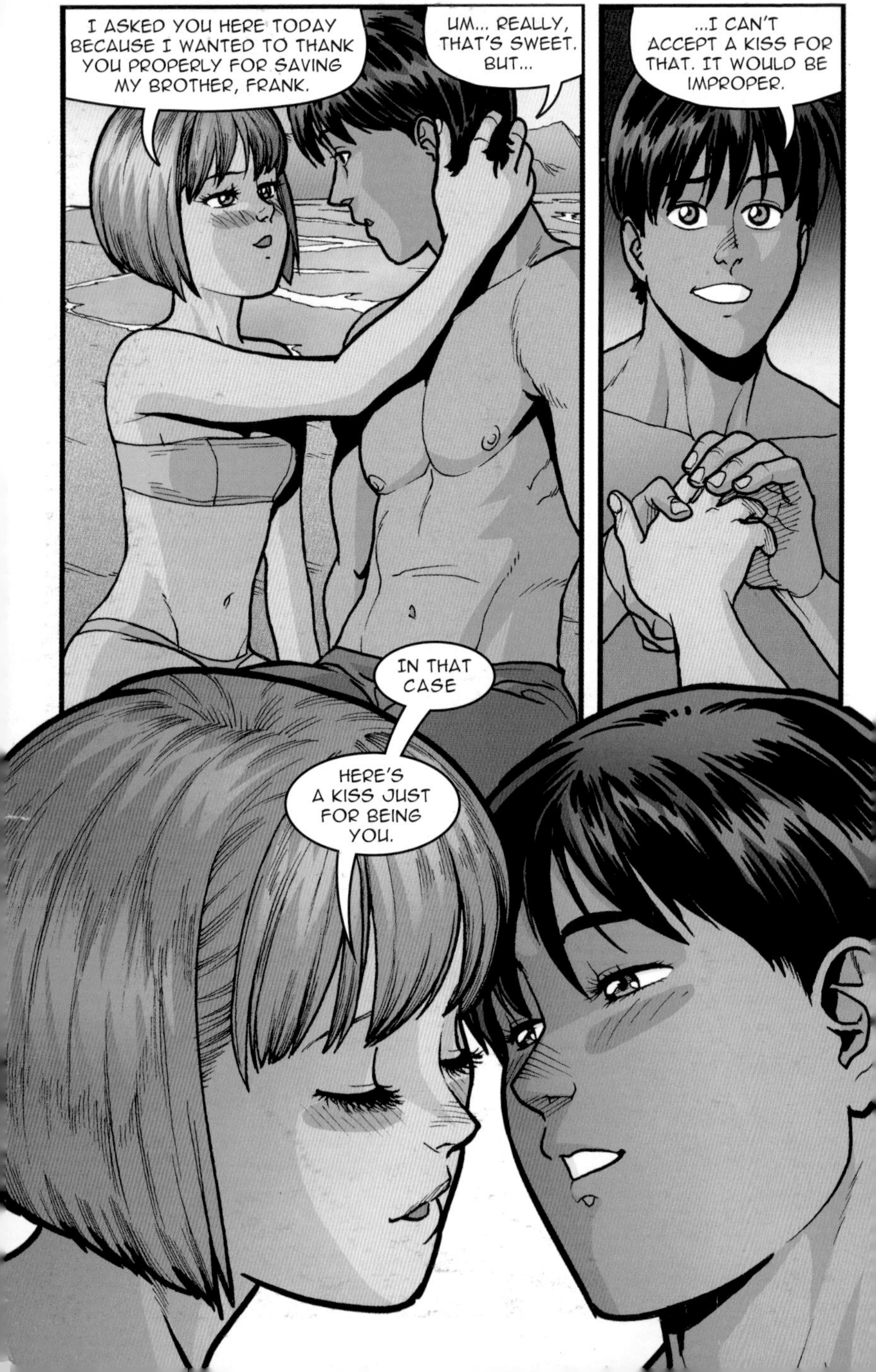
I ASKED YOU HERE TODAY BECAUSE I WANTED TO THANK YOU PROPERLY FOR SAVING MY BROTHER, FRANK.
UM... REALLY, THAT'S SWEET. BUT...
...I CAN'T ACCEPT A KISS FOR THAT. IT WOULD BE IMPROPER.
IN THAT CASE
HERE'S A KISS JUST FOR BEING YOU.

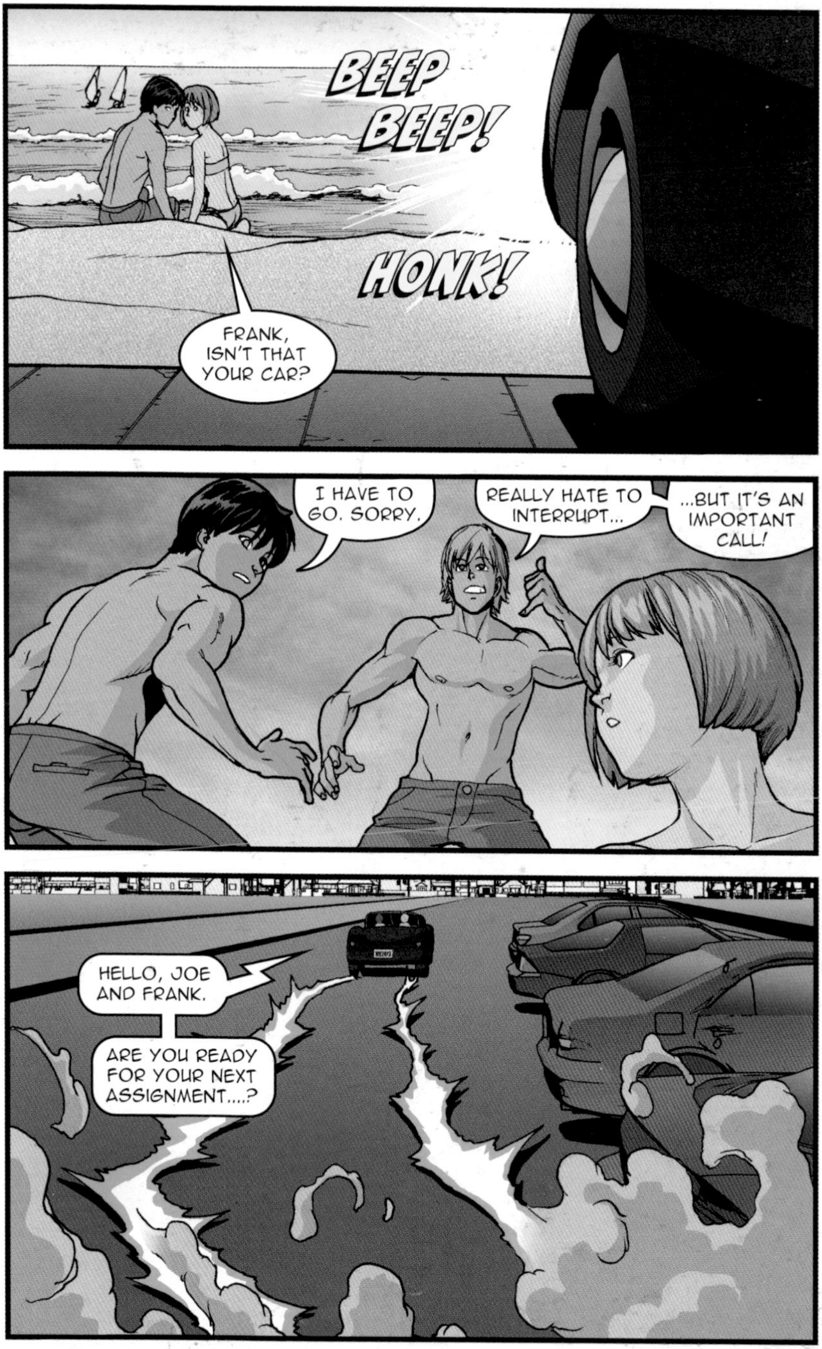
BEEP BEEP!
HONK!
FRANK, ISN'T THAT YOUR CAR?
I HAVE TO GO. SORRY.
REALLY HATE TO INTERRUPT...
...BUT IT'S AN IMPORTANT CALL!
HELLO, JOE AND FRANK.
ARE YOU READY FOR YOUR NEXT ASSIGNMENT....?

NANCY DREW

A NEW GRAPHIC NOVEL EVERY 3 MONTHS!

NEW!

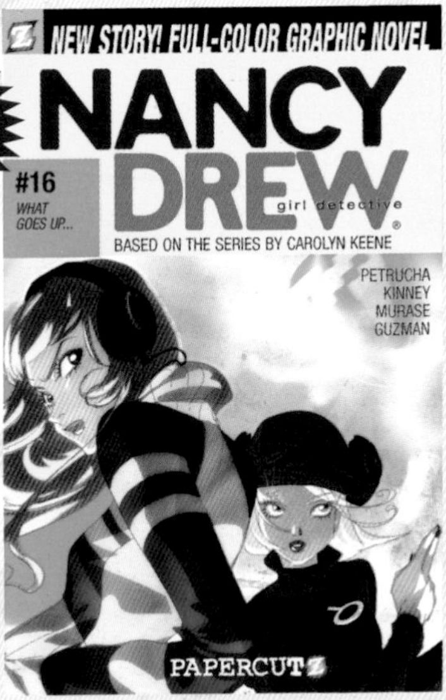
NEW STORY! FULL-COLOR GRAPHIC NOVEL
NANCY DREW
girl detective
#16
WHAT GOES UP...
BASED ON THE SERIES BY CAROLYN KEENE
PETRUCHA
KINNEY
MURASE
GUZMAN
PAPERCUTZ

#12 – "Dress Reversal"
ISBN – 978-1-59707-086-7
#13 – "Doggone Town"
ISBN – 978-1-59707-098-0
#14 – "Sleight of Dan"
ISBN – 978-1-59707-107-9
#15 – "Tiger Counter"
ISBN – 978-1-59707-118-5
NEW! #16 – "What Goes Up..."
ISBN – 978-1-59707-134-5
Also available – Nancy Drew #1-11
All: Pocket-sized, 96-112 pp., full-color $7.95
Also available in hardcover for $12.95 each

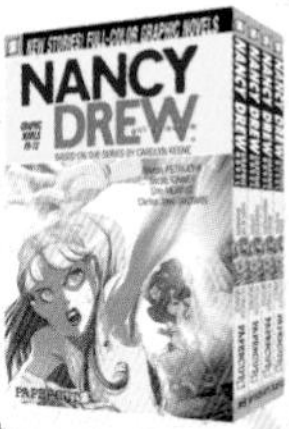
NEW STORIES! FULL-COLOR GRAPHIC NOVELS
NANCY DREW

NANCY DREW
Graphic Novels #1-4 Boxed Set
ISBN – 978-1-59707-038-6
NANCY DREW
Graphic Novels #5-8 Boxed Set
ISBN – 978-1-59707-074-4
NANCY DREW
Graphic Novels #9-12 Boxed Set
ISBN – 978-1-59707-126-0
All: full-color, $29.95 each

CLASSICS Illustrated Deluxe

NEW!

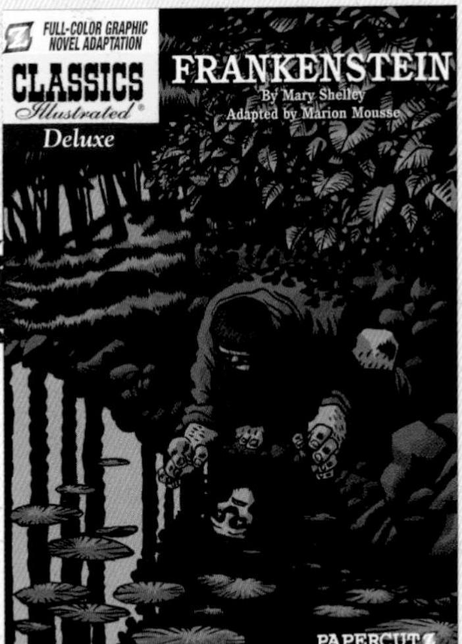
FULL-COLOR GRAPHIC NOVEL ADAPTATION
CLASSICS Illustrated Deluxe
FRANKENSTEIN
By Mary Shelley
Adapted by Marion Mousse
PAPERCUTZ

#1 "The Wind in the Willows"
ISBN – 978-159707-096-6
#2 "Tales from the Brothers Grimm"
ISBN – 978-159707-100-0
NEW! #3 "Frankenstein"
ISBN – 978-159707-131-4
All: 6 1/2 x 9, 144 pp. full-color, $13.95
Also available in hardcover for $17.95 each

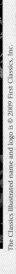

Please add $4.00 postage and handling. Add $1.00 for each additional item.
Make check payable to NBM publishing. Send to:
Papercutz, 40 Exchange Place, Suite 1308,
New York, New York 10005, 1-800-886-1223

www.papercutz.com

Special Preview of THE HARDY BOYS Graphic Novel #18 –
"D.A.N.G.E.R. Spells the Hangman"

CHAPTER ONE: "PAINT THAT A SHAME!"

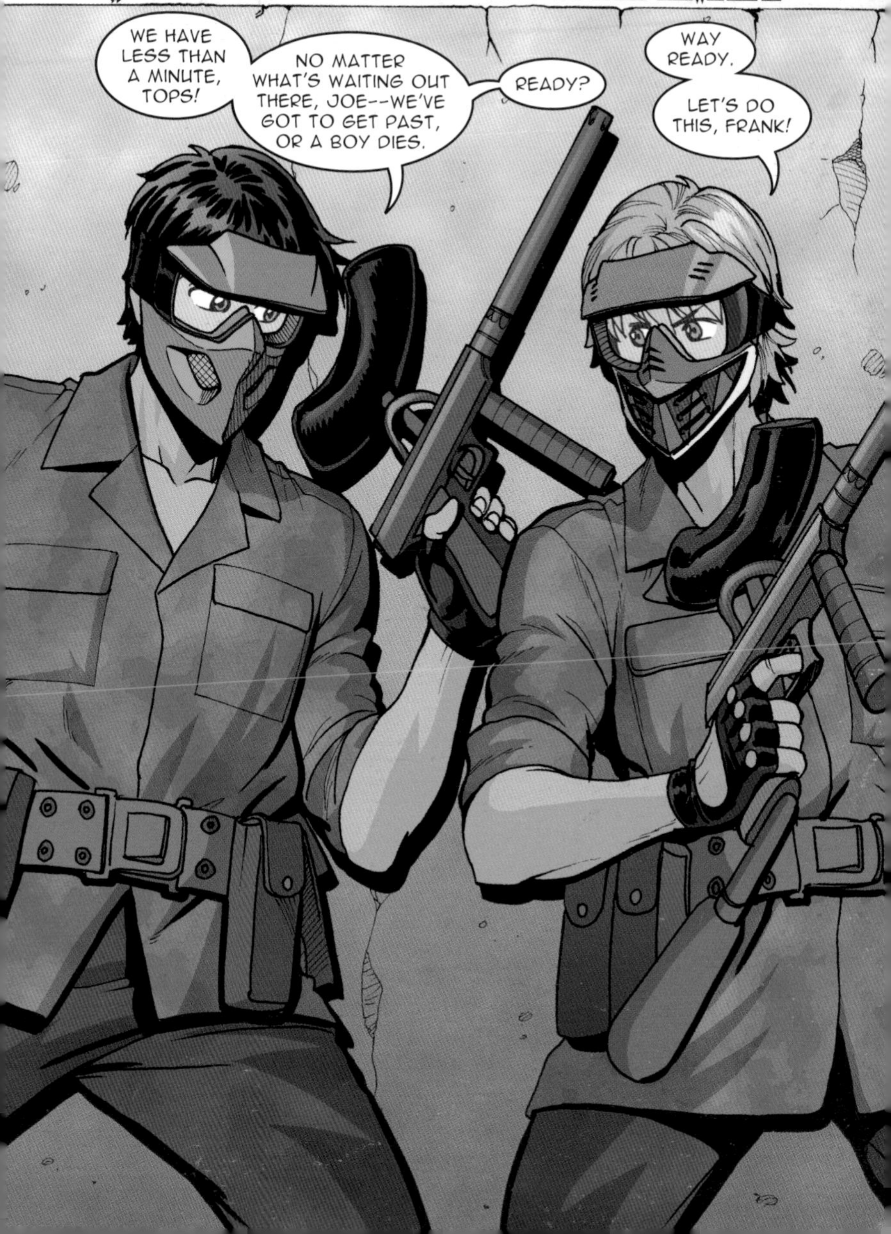

WE HAVE LESS THAN A MINUTE, TOPS!
NO MATTER WHAT'S WAITING OUT THERE, JOE--WE'VE GOT TO GET PAST, OR A BOY DIES.
READY?
WAY READY.
LET'S DO THIS, FRANK!

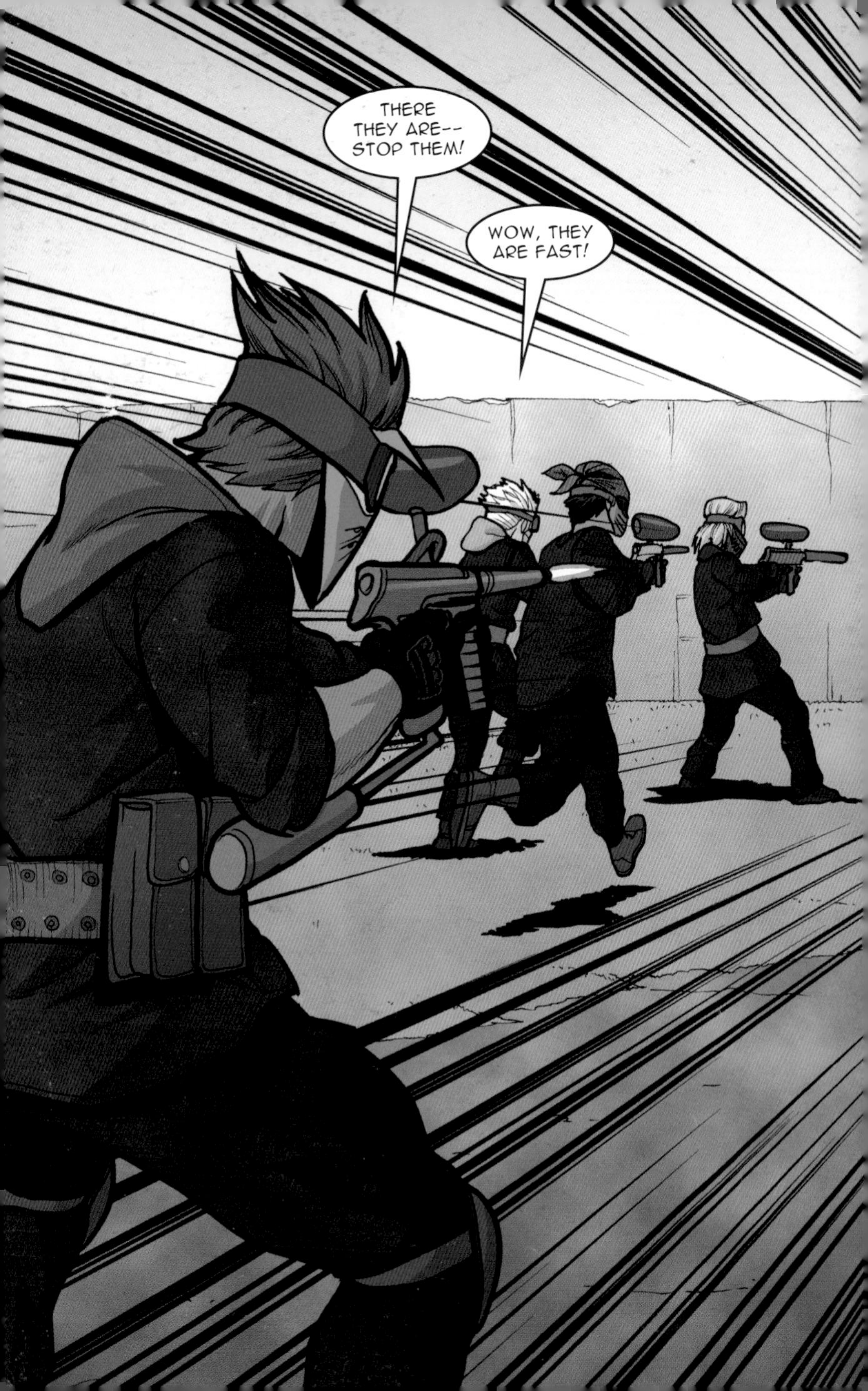
THERE THEY ARE-- STOP THEM!
WOW, THEY ARE FAST!

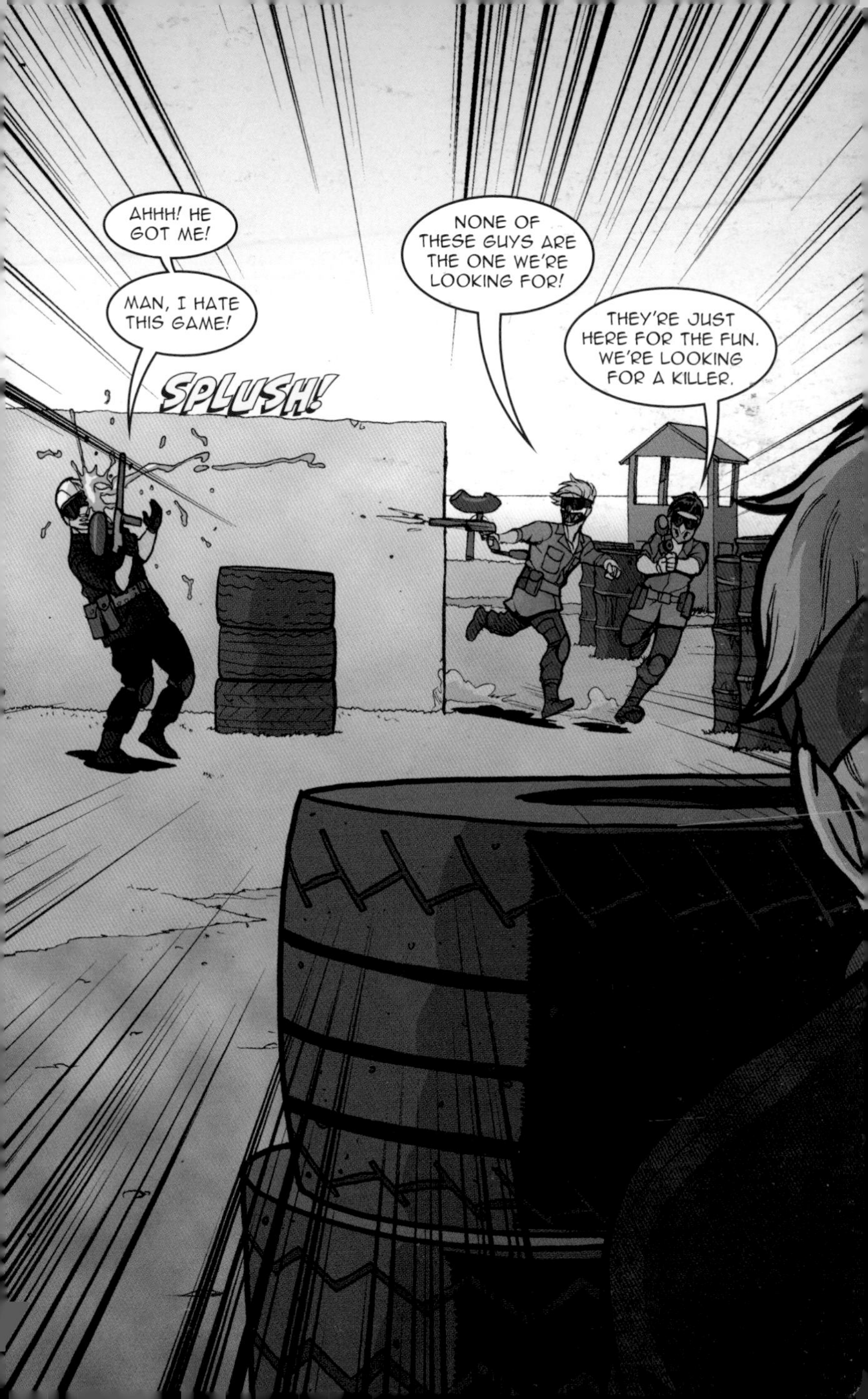
AHHH! HE GOT ME!
MAN, I HATE THIS GAME!
SPLUSH!
NONE OF THESE GUYS ARE THE ONE WE'RE LOOKING FOR!
THEY'RE JUST HERE FOR THE FUN. WE'RE LOOKING FOR A KILLER.

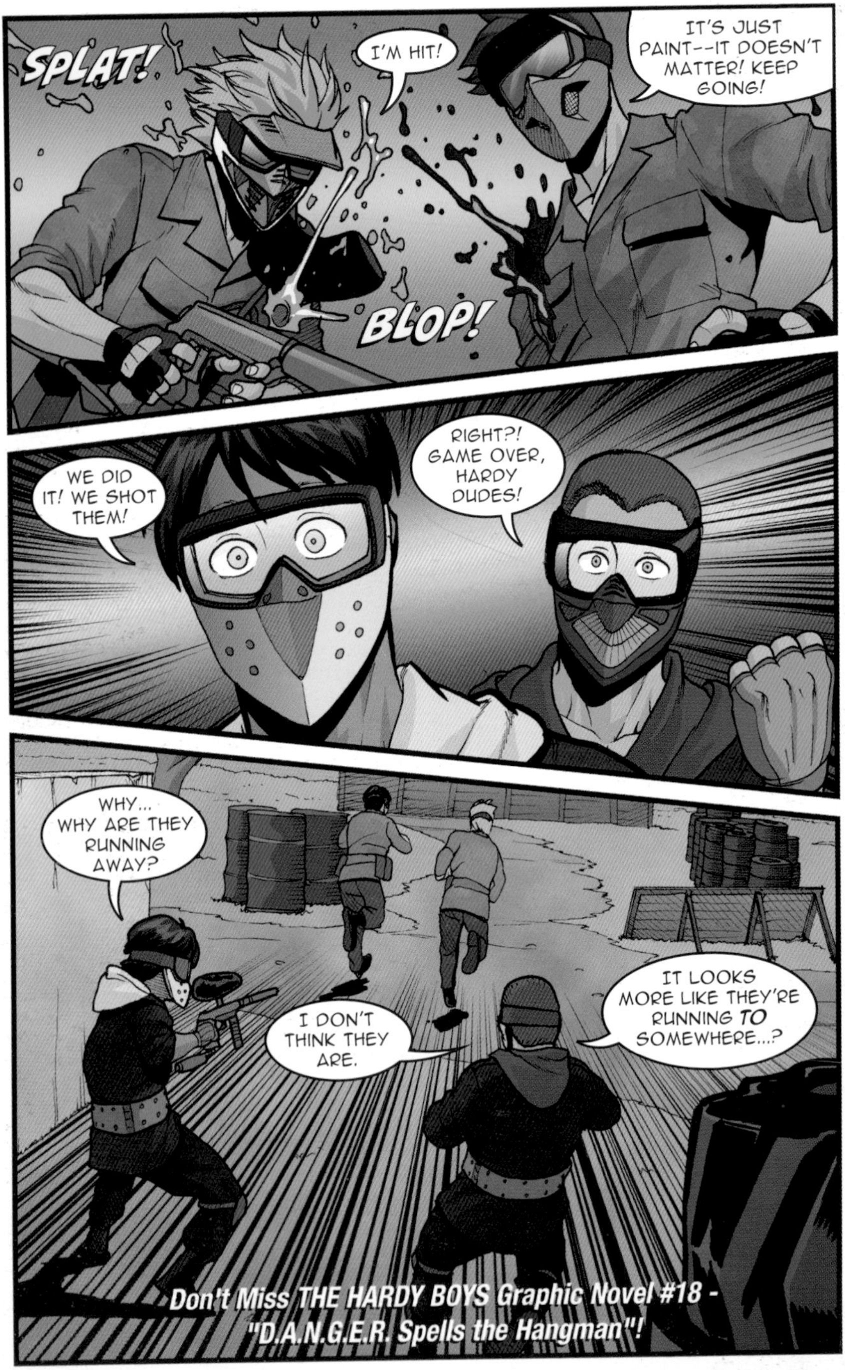
SPLAT!
I'M HIT!
IT'S JUST PAINT--IT DOESN'T MATTER! KEEP GOING!
BLOP!
WE DID IT! WE SHOT THEM!
RIGHT?! GAME OVER, HARDY DUDES!
WHY... WHY ARE THEY RUNNING AWAY?
I DON'T THINK THEY ARE.
IT LOOKS MORE LIKE THEY'RE RUNNING *TO* SOMEWHERE...?
Don't Miss THE HARDY BOYS Graphic Novel #18 - "D.A.N.G.E.R. Spells the Hangman"!

WATCH OUT FOR PAPERCUTZ™

Hey, Welcome to the Papercutz Backpages. I'm Jim Salicrup, Papercutz Editor-in-Chief, here to serve as your guide to the wondrous world of Papercutz. Not only do we bring you all-new exciting HARDY BOYS graphic novels every three months, but we also publish all-new graphic novels starring NANCY DREW, GIRL DETECTIVE, and comics adaptations of stories by the world's greatest authors in CLASSICS ILLUSTRATED and CLASSICS ILLUSTRATED DELUXE (the DELUXE means there's over twice as many pages). The best way to keep up with what is new and exciting at Papercutz is to visit our website at www.papercutz.com, and not that long ago we started up a Papercutz blog, with entries by all your favorite Papercutz creators.

The Papercutz blog is a perfect opportunity to tell the creators exactly what you liked about this graphic novel, as well as a great chance to ask them any questions you might have. Here's part of the introduction I wrote in my first entry, where I introduce you to the blogs of Scott Lobdell and Paulo Henrique. I also included the intro for Greg Farshtey's blog, as we're also previewing BIONICLE and a TALES FROM THE CRYPT story by the prolific Mr. Farshtey in this special installment of the Papercutz Backpages...

Scott Lobdell, is the well-known comics writer that took over Marvel's top-selling UNCANNY X-MEN title after long-time legendary X-scribe Chris Claremont originally left the series. Talk about having big shoes to fill! Scott has already done a great job introducing himself on his blog, that there's little left for me to say, except that Scott has always been a real true friend. We first met when he was breaking in at Marvel Comics, and I've always known he was destined for greatness. Scott has done it all, everything from movie screenplays to creating TV series, and we're so lucky that he still manages to find time to chronicle the all-new continuing adventures of the Hardy Boys for us. With Paulo Henrique drawing the Undercover Brother's exploits, the series is looking more exciting than ever. And I can say with total confidence, the best is yet to come from this talented team!

Greg Farshtey, BIONICLE author and expert, also does a great job of introducing himself, and although we haven't known each other very long and we've only worked together on his terror-tale "Murder M.A.I.D." for TALES FROM THE CRYPT #6, I have tremendous respect for him. He's created a universe for the BIONICLE series that's as fantastic as it is impressive. Collecting his BIONICLE comicbooks, beautifully illustrated by Carlos D'Anda, Randy Elliot and Stuart Sayger, as a Papercutz graphic novel series has turned out to be one of our best decisions ever. BIONICLE is currently our best-selling title. Our heartfelt thanks to the many loyal BIONICLE fans.

FULL-COLOR GRAPHIC NOVEL
BIONICLE
#5: THE BATTLE OF VOYA NUI
LEGO
PAPERCUTZ

So, there you have it! Enjoy the previews, and we'll see you online at the Papercutz blog!

Thanks,

Jim

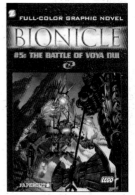

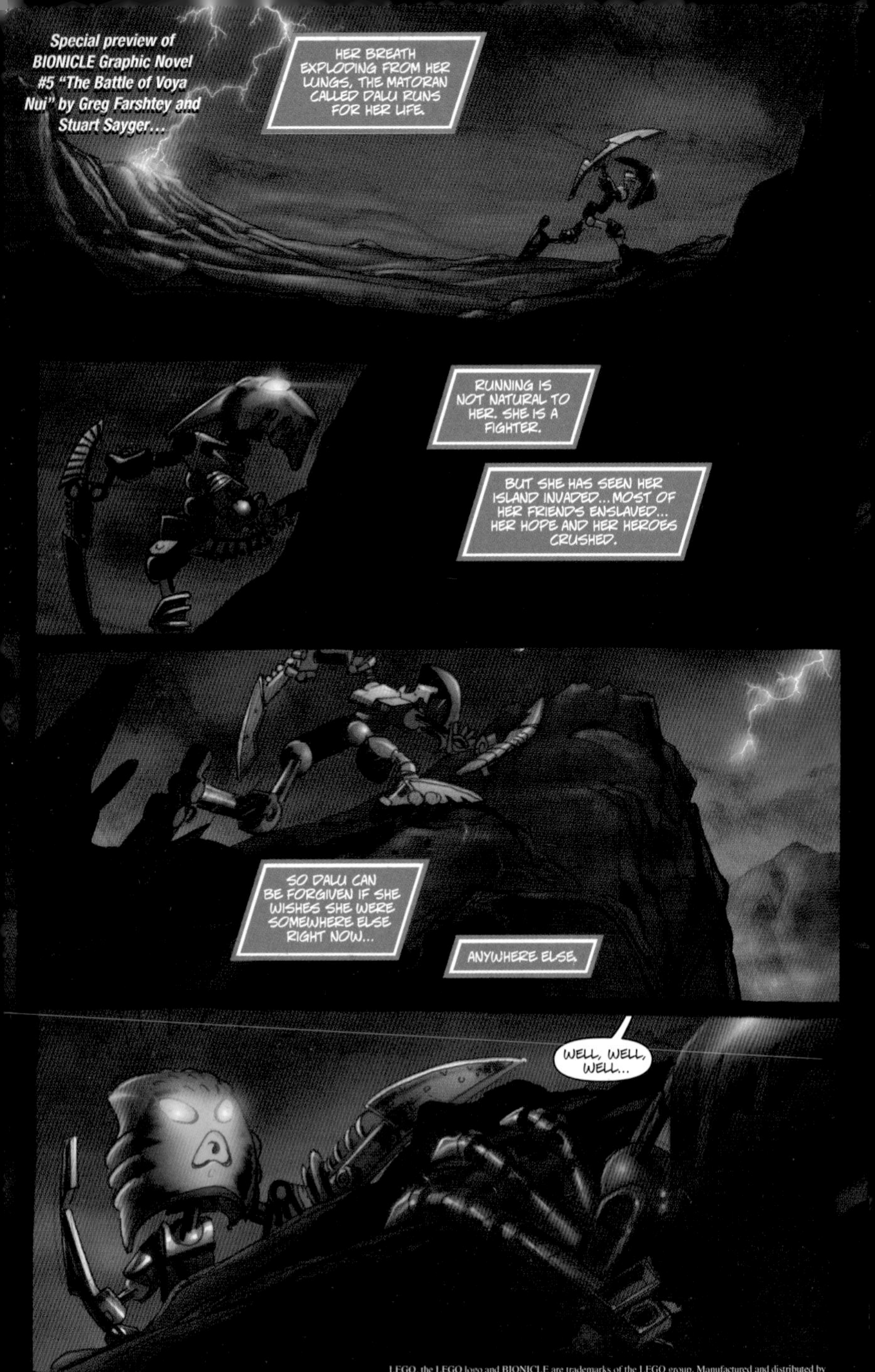
Special preview of BIONICLE Graphic Novel #5 "The Battle of Voya Nui" by Greg Farshtey and Stuart Sayger…
HER BREATH EXPLODING FROM HER LUNGS, THE MATORAN CALLED DALU RUNS FOR HER LIFE.
RUNNING IS NOT NATURAL TO HER. SHE IS A FIGHTER.
BUT SHE HAS SEEN HER ISLAND INVADED... MOST OF HER FRIENDS ENSLAVED... HER HOPE AND HER HEROES CRUSHED.
SO DALU CAN BE FORGIVEN IF SHE WISHES SHE WERE SOMEWHERE ELSE RIGHT NOW...
ANYWHERE ELSE.
WELL, WELL, WELL...

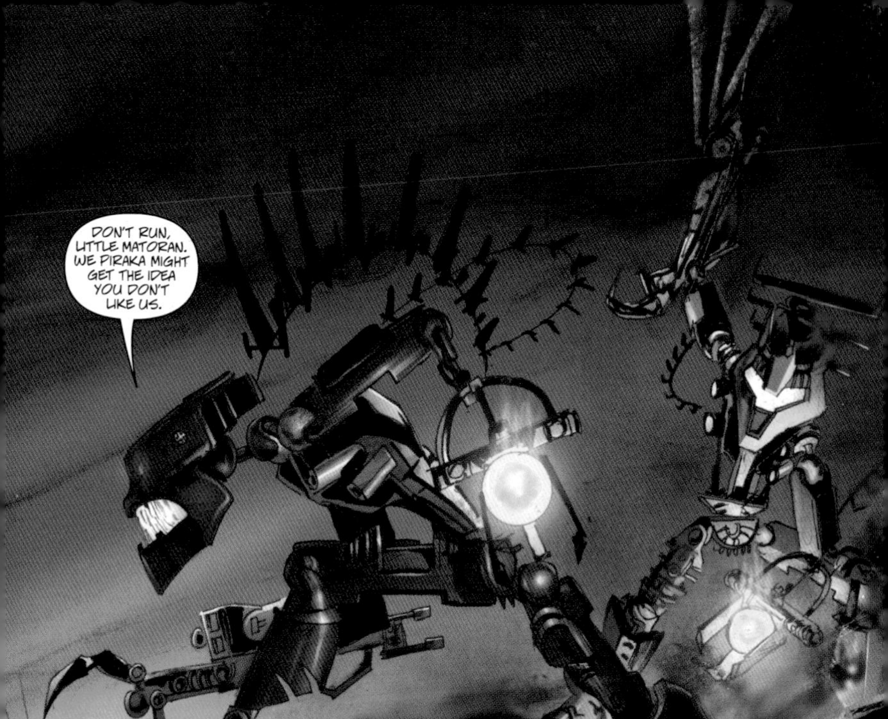
DON'T RUN, LITTLE MATORAN. WE PIRAKA MIGHT GET THE IDEA YOU DON'T LIKE US.
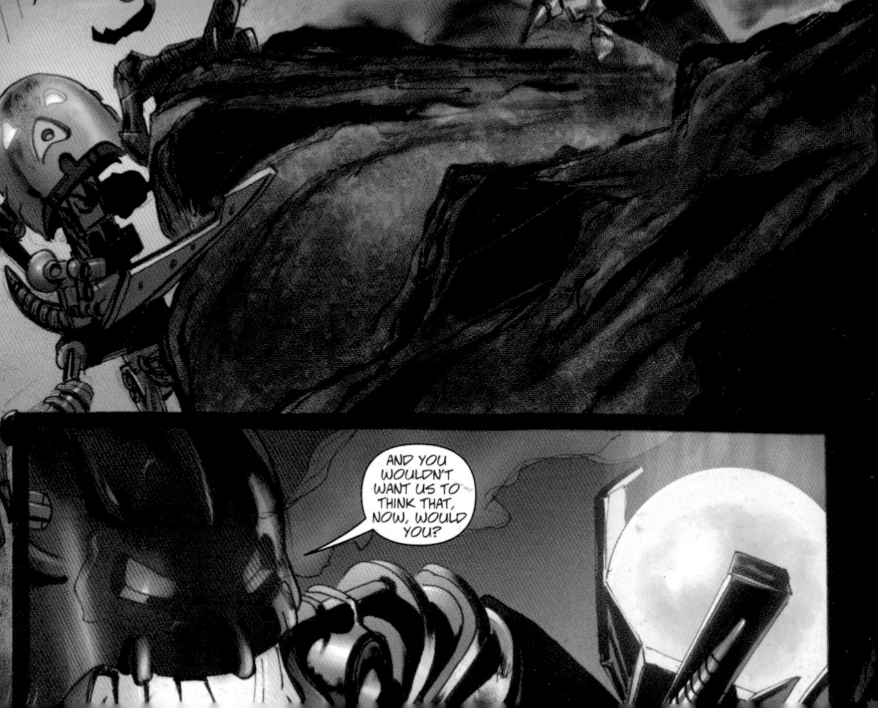
AND YOU WOULDN'T WANT US TO THINK THAT, NOW, WOULD YOU?

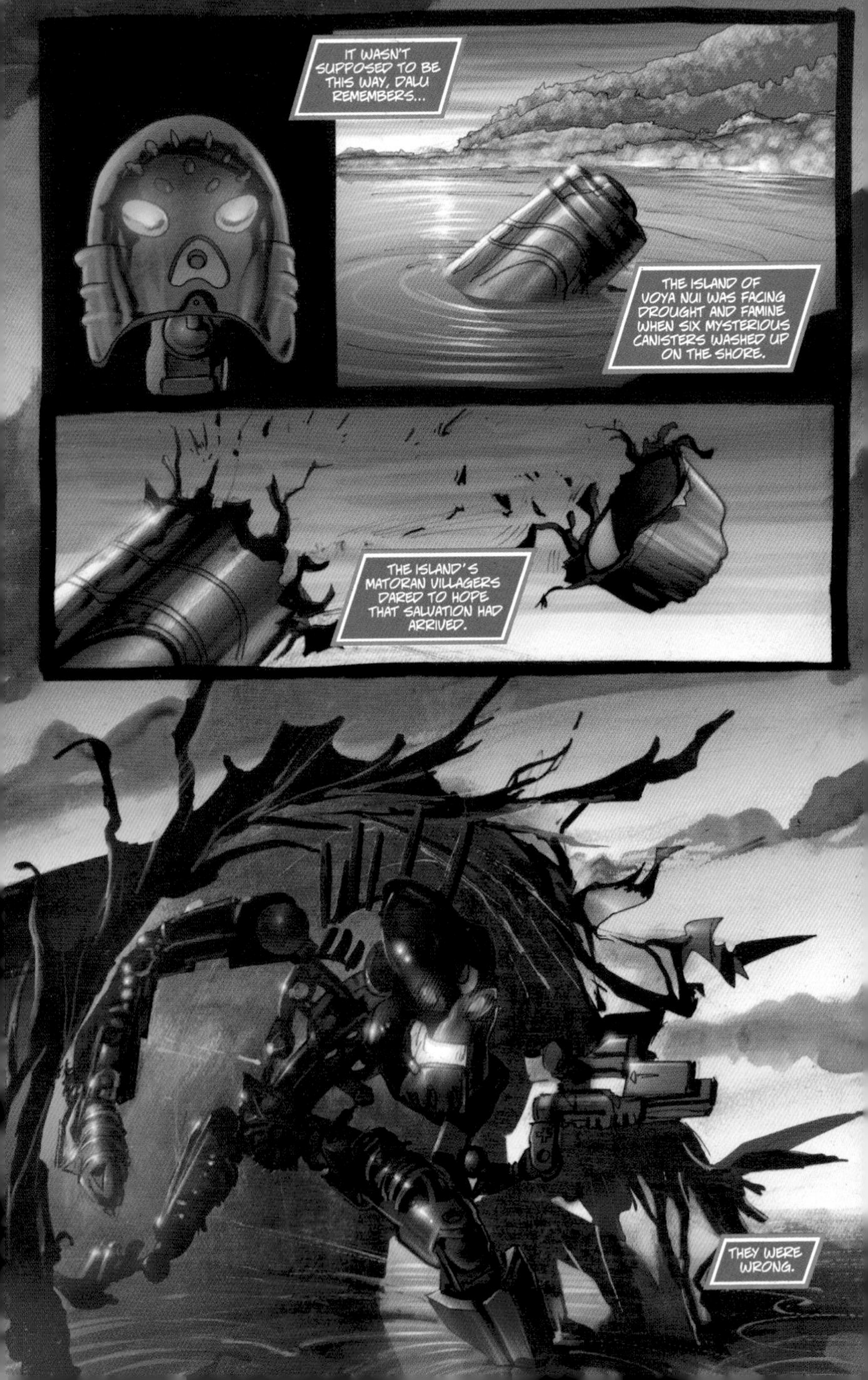
IT WASN'T SUPPOSED TO BE THIS WAY, DALU REMEMBERS...
THE ISLAND OF VOYA NUI WAS FACING DROUGHT AND FAMINE WHEN SIX MYSTERIOUS CANISTERS WASHED UP ON THE SHORE.
THE ISLAND'S MATORAN VILLAGERS DARED TO HOPE THAT SALVATION HAD ARRIVED.
THEY WERE WRONG.

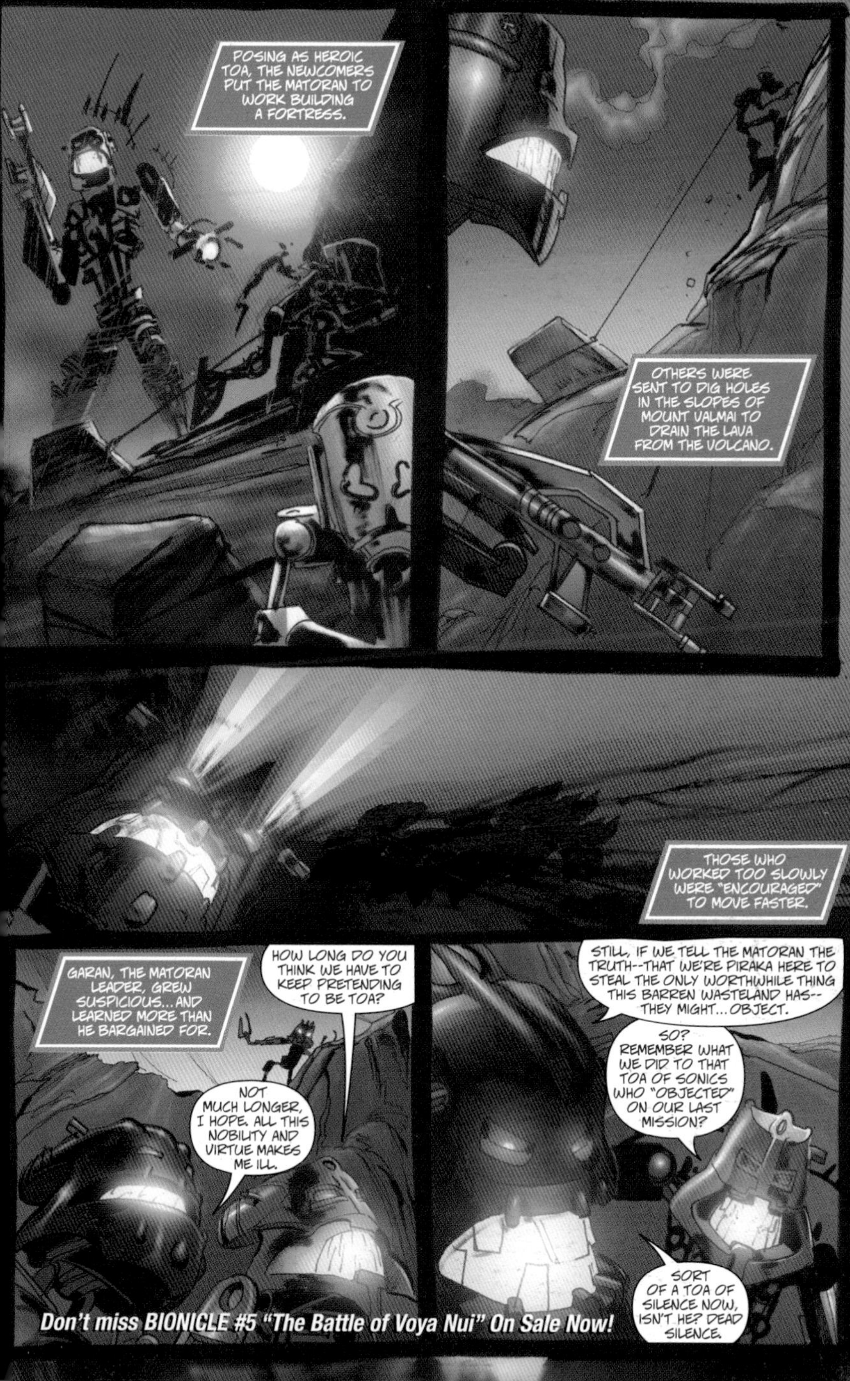
POSING AS HEROIC TOA, THE NEWCOMERS PUT THE MATORAN TO WORK BUILDING A FORTRESS.
OTHERS WERE SENT TO DIG HOLES IN THE SLOPES OF MOUNT VALMAI TO DRAIN THE LAVA FROM THE VOLCANO.
THOSE WHO WORKED TOO SLOWLY WERE "ENCOURAGED" TO MOVE FASTER.
GARAN, THE MATORAN LEADER, GREW SUSPICIOUS...AND LEARNED MORE THAN HE BARGAINED FOR.
HOW LONG DO YOU THINK WE HAVE TO KEEP PRETENDING TO BE TOA?
NOT MUCH LONGER, I HOPE. ALL THIS NOBILITY AND VIRTUE MAKES ME ILL.
STILL, IF WE TELL THE MATORAN THE TRUTH--THAT WE'RE PIRAKA HERE TO STEAL THE ONLY WORTHWHILE THING THIS BARREN WASTELAND HAS--THEY MIGHT...OBJECT.
SO? REMEMBER WHAT WE DID TO THAT TOA OF SONICS WHO "OBJECTED" ON OUR LAST MISSION?
SORT OF A TOA OF SILENCE NOW, ISN'T HE? DEAD SILENCE.
Don't miss BIONICLE #5 "The Battle of Voya Nui" On Sale Now!

Here's a sneak preview of "Murder M.A.I.D" by Greg Farstey and Mr. Exes from TALES FROM THE CRYPT # 6 "You Toomb"...

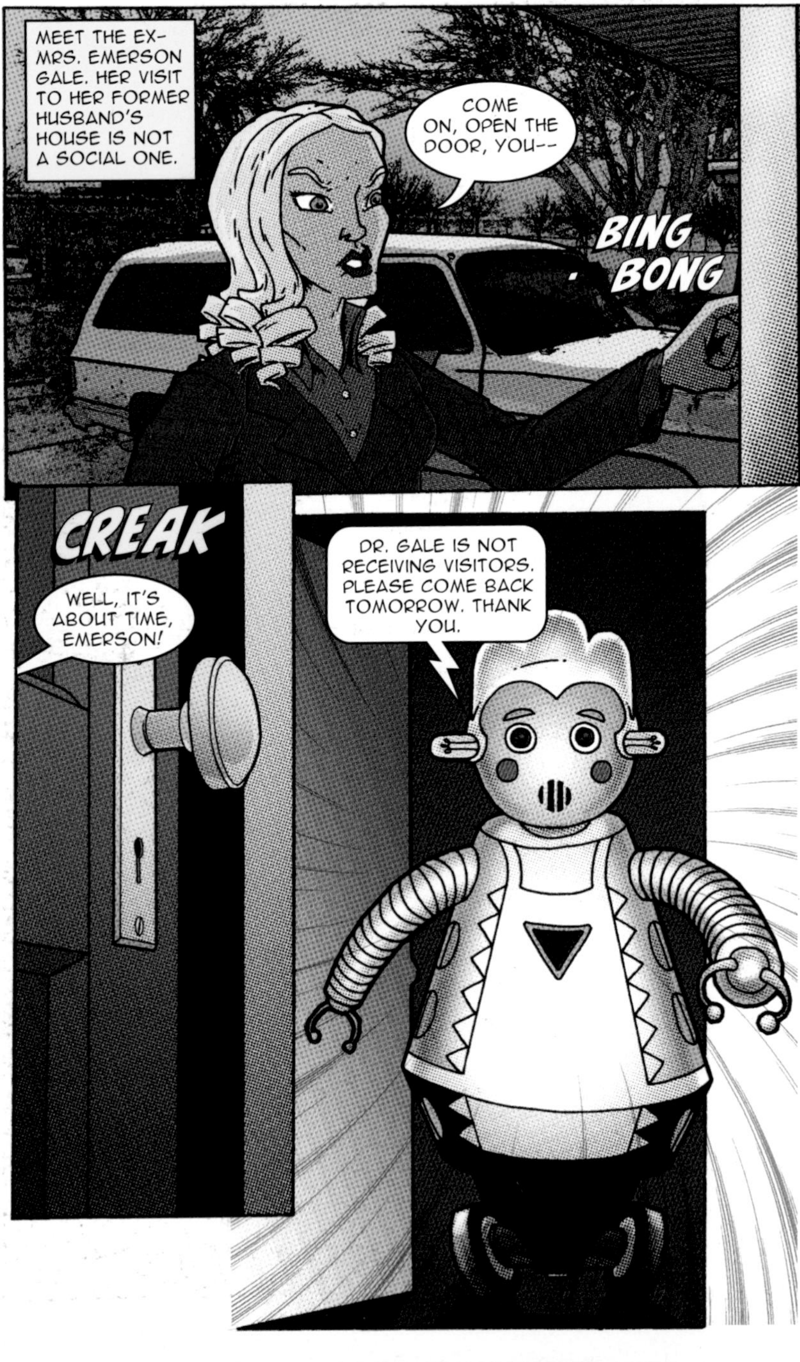
MEET THE EX-MRS. EMERSON GALE. HER VISIT TO HER FORMER HUSBAND'S HOUSE IS NOT A SOCIAL ONE.
COME ON, OPEN THE DOOR, YOU--
BING BONG
CREAK
WELL, IT'S ABOUT TIME, EMERSON!
DR. GALE IS NOT RECEIVING VISITORS. PLEASE COME BACK TOMORROW. THANK YOU.

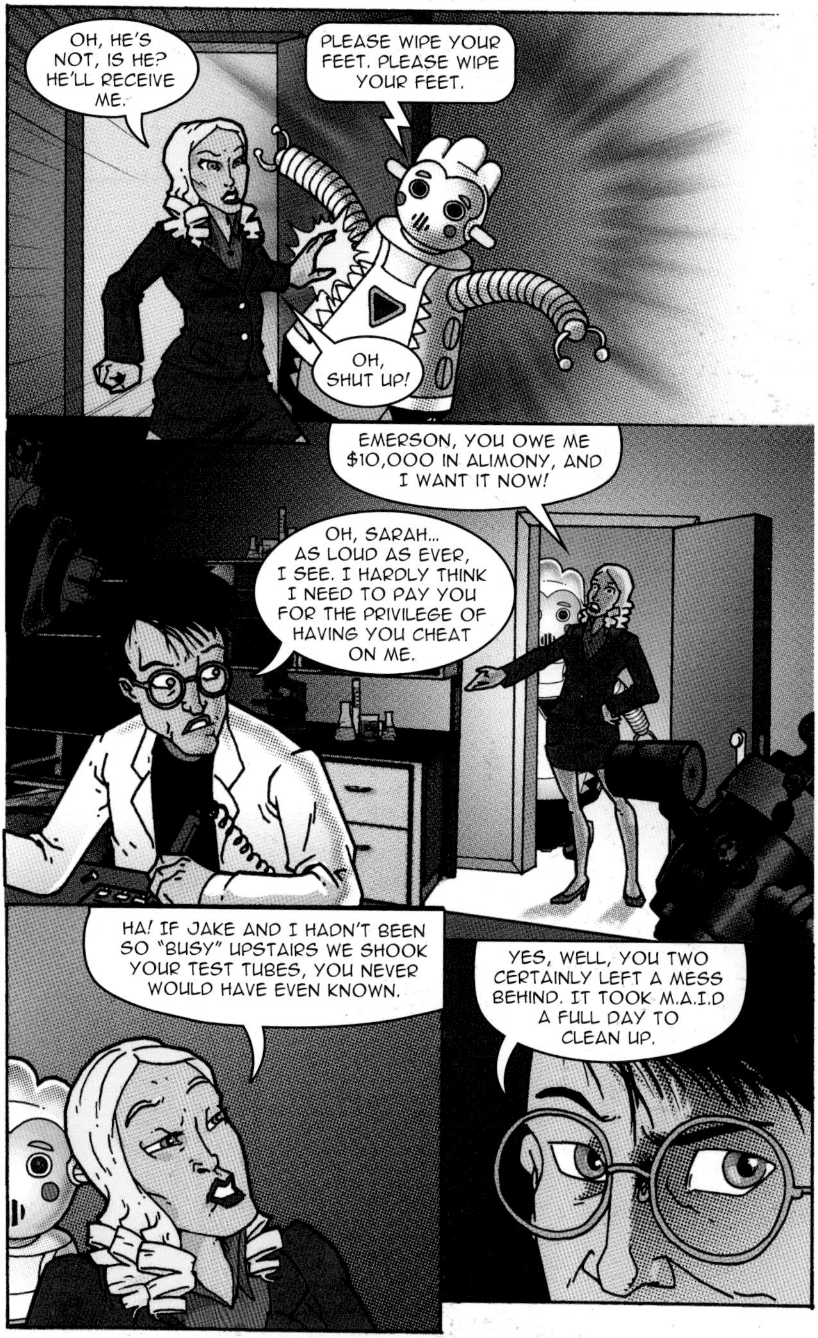
OH, HE'S NOT, IS HE? HE'LL RECEIVE ME.
PLEASE WIPE YOUR FEET. PLEASE WIPE YOUR FEET.
OH, SHUT UP!
EMERSON, YOU OWE ME $10,000 IN ALIMONY, AND I WANT IT NOW!
OH, SARAH... AS LOUD AS EVER, I SEE. I HARDLY THINK I NEED TO PAY YOU FOR THE PRIVILEGE OF HAVING YOU CHEAT ON ME.
HA! IF JAKE AND I HADN'T BEEN SO "BUSY" UPSTAIRS WE SHOOK YOUR TEST TUBES, YOU NEVER WOULD HAVE EVEN KNOWN.
YES, WELL, YOU TWO CERTAINLY LEFT A MESS BEHIND. IT TOOK M.A.I.D A FULL DAY TO CLEAN UP.

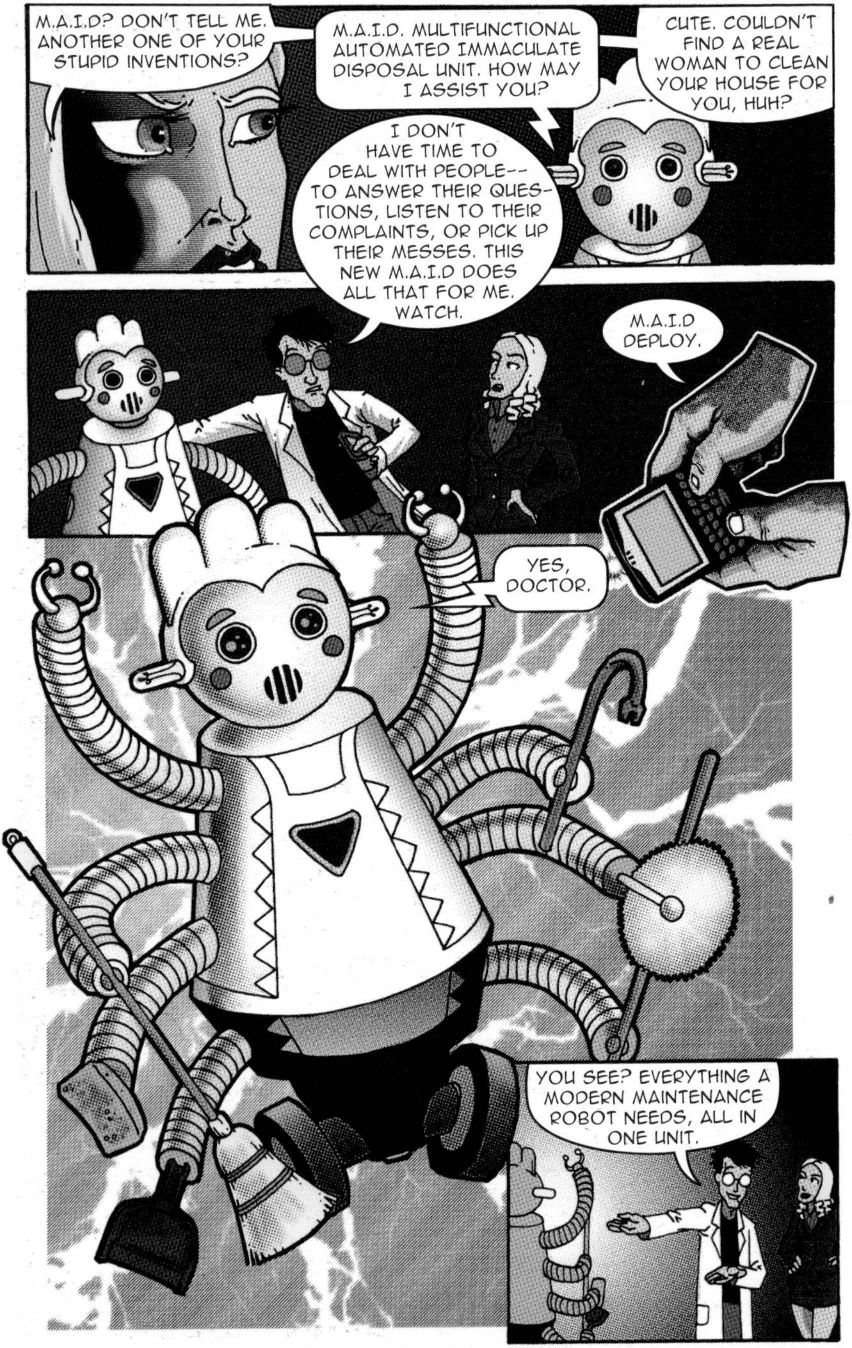
M.A.I.D? DON'T TELL ME. ANOTHER ONE OF YOUR STUPID INVENTIONS?
M.A.I.D. MULTIFUNCTIONAL AUTOMATED IMMACULATE DISPOSAL UNIT. HOW MAY I ASSIST YOU?
CUTE. COULDN'T FIND A REAL WOMAN TO CLEAN YOUR HOUSE FOR YOU, HUH?
I DON'T HAVE TIME TO DEAL WITH PEOPLE-- TO ANSWER THEIR QUESTIONS, LISTEN TO THEIR COMPLAINTS, OR PICK UP THEIR MESSES. THIS NEW M.A.I.D DOES ALL THAT FOR ME. WATCH.
M.A.I.D DEPLOY.
YES, DOCTOR.
YOU SEE? EVERYTHING A MODERN MAINTENANCE ROBOT NEEDS, ALL IN ONE UNIT.

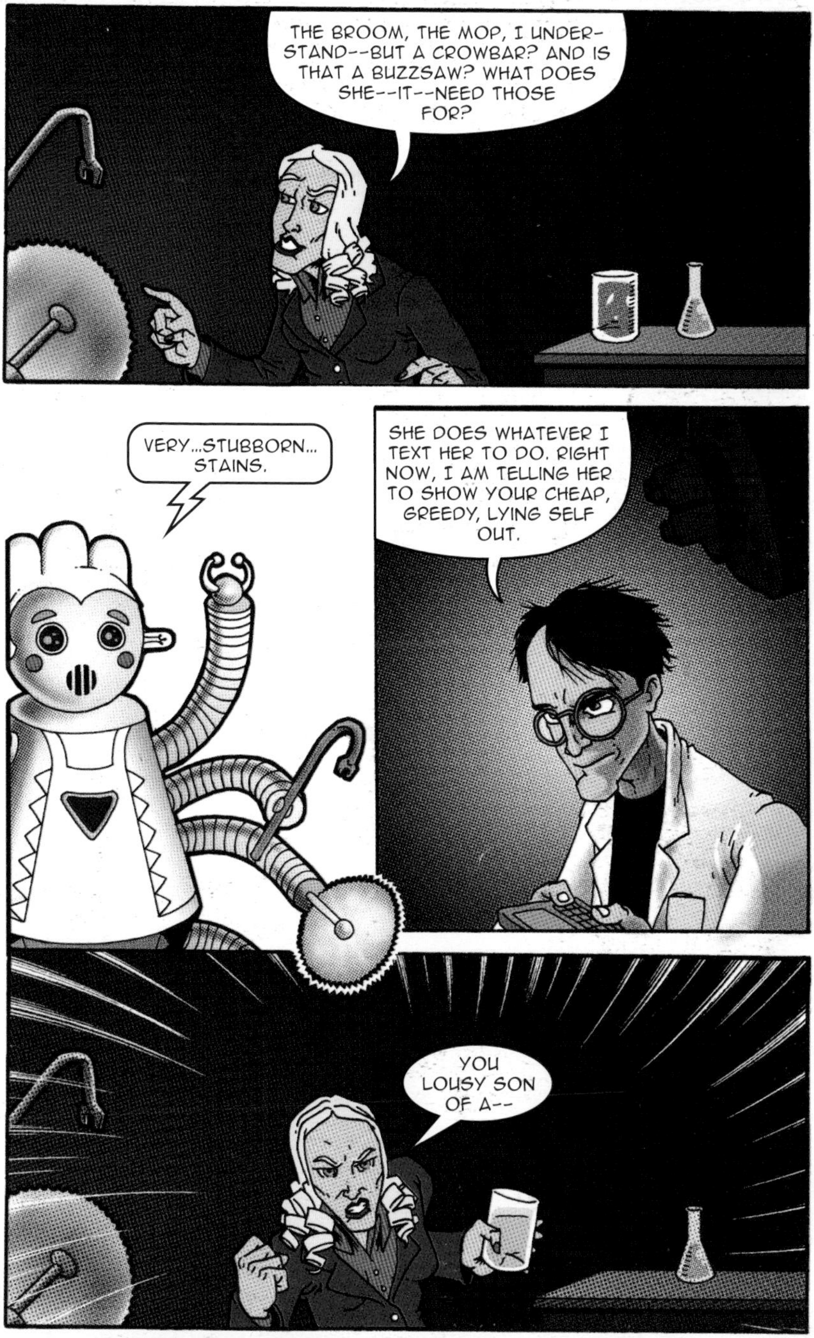
THE BROOM, THE MOP, I UNDERSTAND--BUT A CROWBAR? AND IS THAT A BUZZSAW? WHAT DOES SHE--IT--NEED THOSE FOR?
VERY...STUBBORN... STAINS.
SHE DOES WHATEVER I TEXT HER TO DO. RIGHT NOW, I AM TELLING HER TO SHOW YOUR CHEAP, GREEDY, LYING SELF OUT.
YOU LOUSY SON OF A--

"Don't Miss TALES FROM THE CRYPT #6 "YouToomb" for much, much more!"

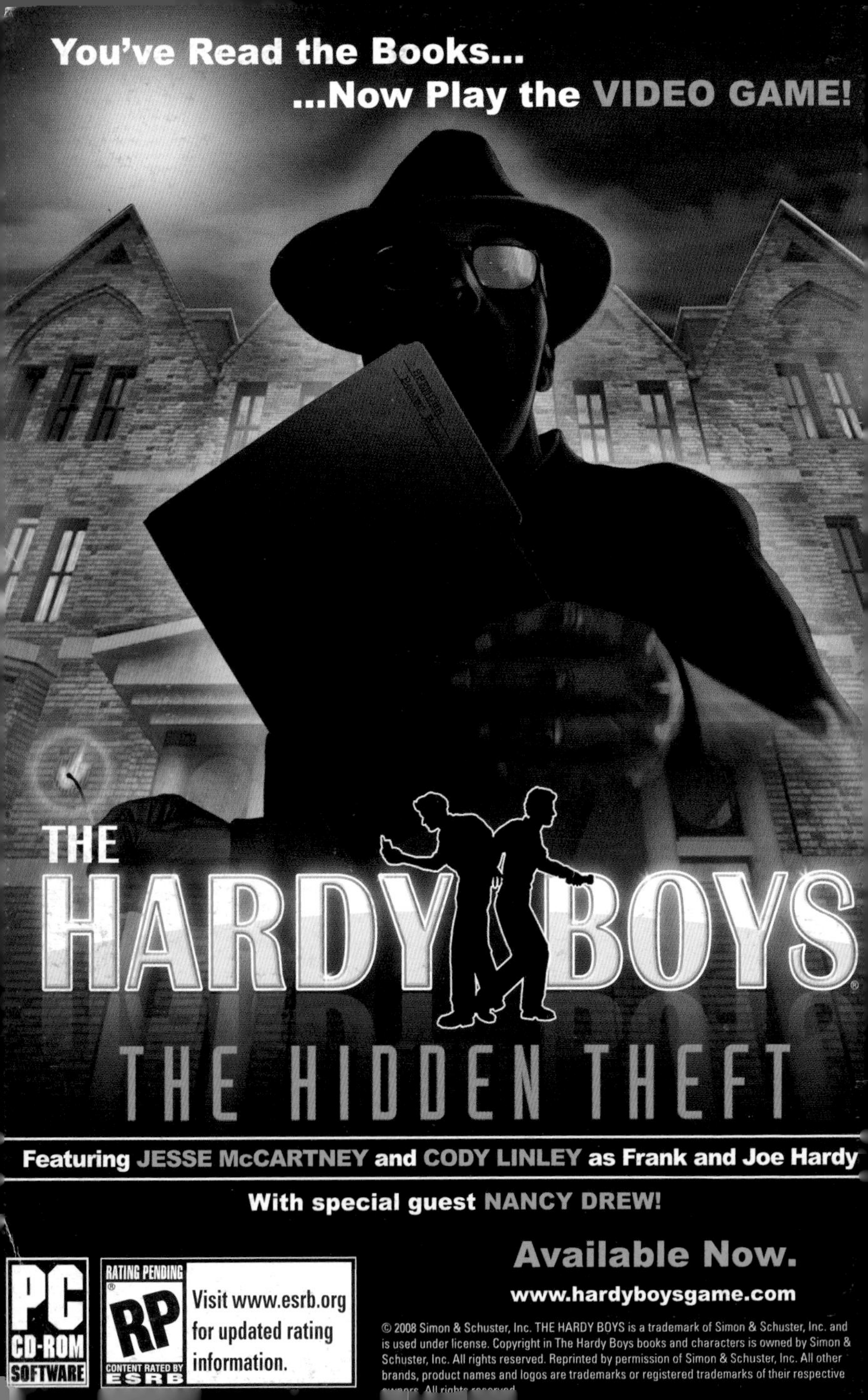

You've Read the Books...
...Now Play the VIDEO GAME!
THE
HARDY BOYS
THE HIDDEN THEFT
Featuring JESSE McCARTNEY and CODY LINLEY as Frank and Joe Hardy
With special guest NANCY DREW!
Available Now.
www.hardyboysgame.com
PC
CD-ROM
SOFTWARE
RATING PENDING
RP
CONTENT RATED BY
ESRB
Visit www.esrb.org for updated rating information.
© 2008 Simon & Schuster, Inc. THE HARDY BOYS is a trademark of Simon & Schuster, Inc. and is used under license. Copyright in The Hardy Boys books and characters is owned by Simon & Schuster, Inc. All rights reserved. Reprinted by permission of Simon & Schuster, Inc. All other brands, product names and logos are trademarks or registered trademarks of their respective

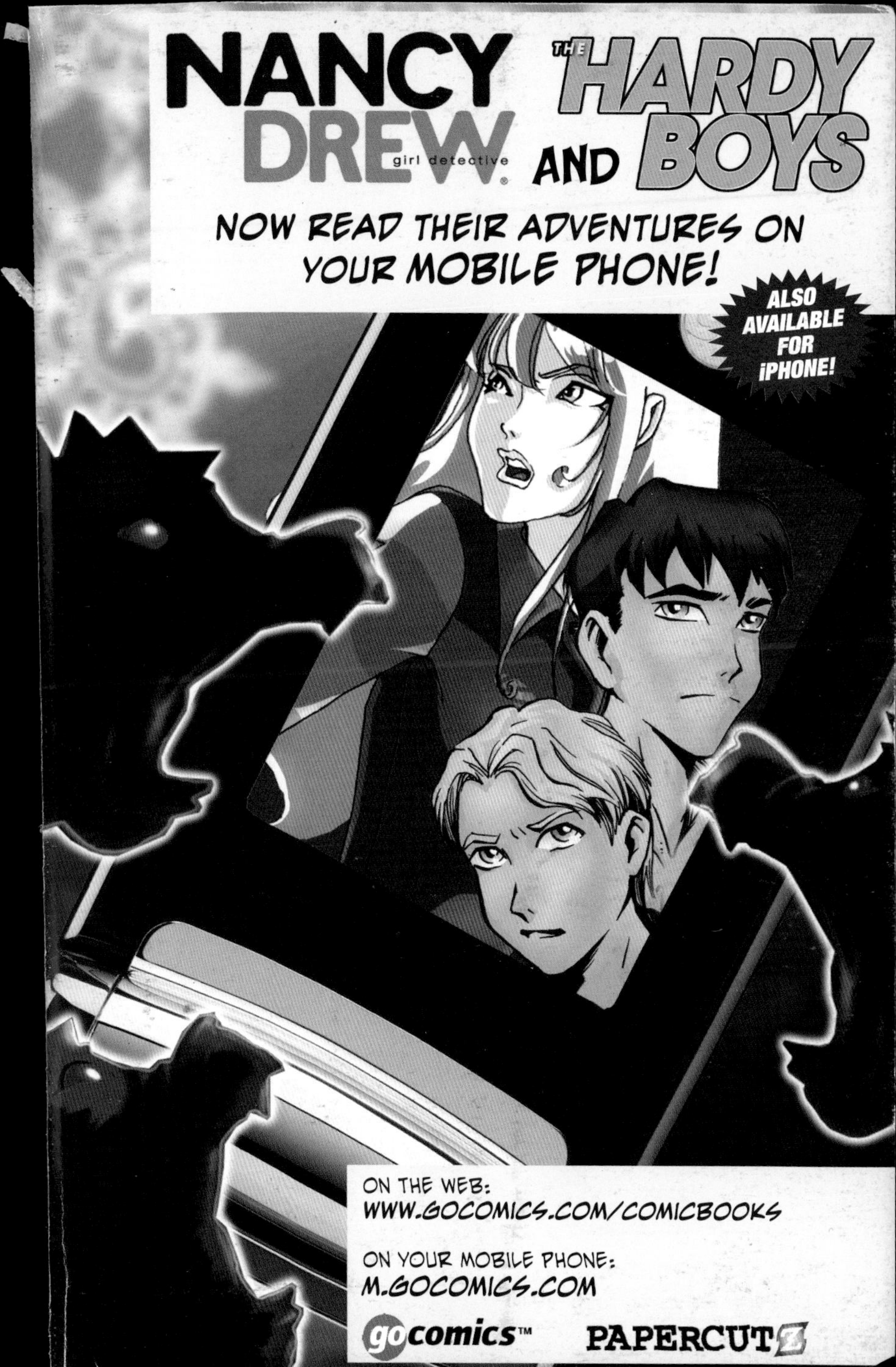
NANCY DREW girl detective
THE HARDY BOYS
AND
NOW READ THEIR ADVENTURES ON YOUR MOBILE PHONE!
ALSO AVAILABLE FOR iPHONE!
ON THE WEB:
WWW.GOCOMICS.COM/COMICBOOKS
ON YOUR MOBILE PHONE:
M.GOCOMICS.COM
gocomics™
PAPERCUTZ

THE HARDY BOYS

Undercover Brothers®

New reality show Deprivation House is supposed to show how long contestants can survive without modern luxuries.

Trouble is, some of the contestants aren't surviving at all.

Catch undercover agents Frank and Joe Hardy in the new Murder House trilogy!

BOOK ONE IN THE MURDER HOUSE TRILOGY
HARDY
BOYS
Deprivation House
FRANKLIN W. DIXON

Deprivation House

BOOK TWO IN THE MURDER HOUSE TRILOGY
HARDY
BOYS
House Arrest
FRANKLIN W. DIXON

House Arrest

BOOK THREE IN THE MURDER HOUSE TRILOGY
THE
HARDY
BOYS
Murder House
FRANKLIN W. DIXON

Murder House

Available wherever books are sold

ALADDIN • SIMON & SCHUSTER CHILDREN'S PUBLISHING • SIMONSAYSKIDS.COM

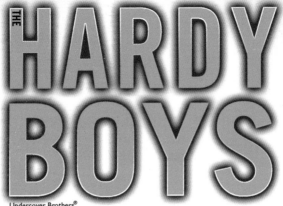

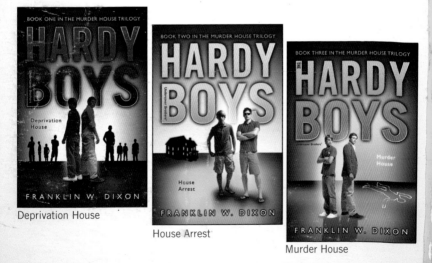